The [illegible]

Library

Of

Tayos

C J Bessell

Books by the Author

Pioneers of Burra
For the Love of Family

Margaret
Burnt Bridge

ISBN: 978-0-6459265-2-1

There are many ancient mysteries yet to be discovered.

Chapter 1

Monastery of Santa Maria de Huerta
Spain 1596

Alonso had been waiting in the wide corridor leading to the Abbot's office for twenty minutes. He had many things on his mind, and uppermost were the strange dreams he'd been having ever since Brother Miguel's pages had arrived from New Spain.

For months now, he'd been charged with transcribing the pages. He couldn't understand the language used by Brother Miguel, and so his vow of silence on the matter hadn't been difficult. But now, the strange words and images had invaded his mind and he wasn't sure if it was God who spoke to him in his dreams. He feared it was not.

The longer he sat waiting to see the head of his order, the faster his heart was racing. It was not an easy subject to raise with Padre, and Alonso wasn't sure he'd understand his fears. He glanced nervously at the large panelled door in front of him. There was still no sign of the Prior and he breathed heavily.

Patience was a virtue he understood well and was generally able to practise the habit without undue anxiety, but not today. His right leg was bouncing up and down of its own accord and his furtive glances revealed the extent of his nervousness.

Finally, the door opened and Brother Benito, the Prior of the monastery, stepped out into the corridor. His arms were wrapped in his drab robes and a slight incline of his head was the only indication he gave. Alonso sighed as he rose to his feet and entered Padre's office.

The Abbot smiled and waved his hand towards a hard wooden seat. Alonso bowed his head before perching himself on the edge of it. He swallowed and breathed heavily as he tried to calm his nerves.

"Brother Alonso, this is unexpected," said the Abbot raising his grey bushy brows.

"I'm sorry to disturb you," said Alonso shifting his position. "I wouldn't trouble you with this matter, except that I'm worried for Brother Miguel."

"Go on."

"Well, I've been having strange dreams, which have grown more concerning since the last despatch arrived, and I think it has to do with Brother Miguel's strange writings."

"You're sworn to silence on this matter," said the Abbot with a note of finality to his voice.

"I do not wish to discuss the actual writings," Alonso quickly added. "But rather, the odd dreams and the voice I hear. I fear it isn't God who speaks to me, Padre. I fear Brother Miguel may be in some danger."

The Abbot's expression softened and his shoulders relaxed. "Fear not, Brother Alonso. I can assure you that Brother Miguel is in no danger. Dreams rarely hold any meaning. I'm sure you know this."

"I do, but this is different," said Alonso drawing a breath. "The strange writing speaks to me in a language I am beginning to understand. It is not of this world, Padre, and I fear there is some evil at work."

"Perhaps a day of prayer would ease your mind," said the Abbot. "I agree that these writings are very odd indeed, and there is much about the new world we are yet to understand, but they are just words, Brother Alonso." He leaned on the desk in front of him and pressed his fingertips together. "Seek God's guidance in this matter, and speak of it to no one."

"Yes, Padre."

Alonso left the Abbot's office with the weight of his strange dreams squarely on his shoulders. He blamed himself. He hadn't been able to make Padre understand that the dreams were more than just dreams. There was a presence and its intent was unclear. His worry for Brother Miguel was undiminished.

He walked slowly with his head bowed as he ambled towards the chapel. Perhaps a day of prayer would help to ease his mind, although he doubted it. The dreams had become so real, so real he thought he could reach out and touch the parchment. The strange images of plants he didn't recognise almost leapt from the page and the words swam up towards him. But that was not the most disconcerting thing. It was the voice that spoke in a strange tongue that disturbed him the most. That, and the smooth rock caverns.

He was drawn back to the cold corridor by someone calling his name. "Brother Alonso." He stopped and smiled when he spied Brother Diego hurrying towards him.

Diego was panting slightly when he reached his side. "What did Padre say?"

Alonso glanced down the corridor. Several of his Brothers were walking along the wide hall. "Walk with me," he whispered.

The two walked side by side as they continued towards the chapel. "He said Brother Miguel is quite safe, although I do not know how he knows such a thing," said Alonso in a low voice. "He's forbidden me to speak of it and suggests a day of prayer may help to ease my mind."

Diego raised his dark eyebrows and his brown eyes bore into Alonso. "But what about the strange dreams you've been having? What did he say about those?"

Alonso groaned. "He said they're just dreams and hold no meaning." He drew back his shoulders and glanced sideways at Diego. "I couldn't make him understand. I just pray that he's right about Brother Miguel."

"As do I," Diego said resting his hand briefly on Alonso's shoulder. "I pray you're only having these dreams because you spend all day transcribing those pages."

"Hmm," said Alonso with a nod, "I pray you're right." He stopped and stared intently at his friend. "Do not speak of this to anyone. Padre would be more than displeased if he knew I'd confided in you."

"I understand, Alonso," he said with a solemn nod. "You can trust me, I'll not mention it to anyone."

"Thank you…well, I'll see you at supper tonight no doubt."

"May your prayers be answered," said Diego straightening. Wrapping his hands in the sleeves of his robes he continued walking down the hall, leaving Alonso to make his way to the chapel.

The chapel was deserted and Alonso was grateful it was so. He was in no mood for company and sighed as he knelt and bowed his head. He began by reciting his favourite psalm which had the effect of soothing his mind almost immediately. The words slipped from his tongue with familiarity and he found comfort in their meaning. After several psalms, he fell silent and closed his eyes. Reaching out to God in his mind he sought reassurance that all would be well, that Brother Miguel would be safe and if God could do anything to stop the dreams, he'd be most grateful. He called upon the Saints and the Holy Mother to watch over Brother Miguel.

His Brothers came to pray throughout the day, but Alonso paid them no heed as he continued to seek reassurance and ease his concerns. He had to admit that a day spent with God had helped more than he imagined it would. It was nearly dusk when he finally rose to his feet and rubbed his aching knees. A small weight had been lifted although a crease still marred his forehead. *What would tonight bring?*

***

Alonso yawned and stretched and a wide smile spread across his face. He hadn't slept so well in months and the strange dreams which had plagued him had been absent last night. God had answered him and he planned on spending morning prayers thanking the Lord for his mercy. There was an extra spring in his step as he made his way to the chapel. He wasn't even dreading the day that lay ahead of him in the scriptorium.

After morning prayers, he let himself into his tiny compartment which contained a chair and desk, with shelves for holding blank parchment and his writing implements. Miguel's pages were stored away in a locked drawer at Padre's insistence. The room was small, airless and cramped, but his work required absolute privacy and he enjoyed the solitude. A shaft of light hit the floor near his chair illuminating the blank parchment on his desk.

After retrieving a small key from his pocket, he unlocked the drawer and drew out the top page. The writing was just as strange as all the others but this one also had a drawing of sixteen naked women surrounded by a green haze. Why on earth Miguel had drawn naked women was beyond him. Written beside the drawing was the Latin word *dabas*. He squinted at it to be sure. It was definitely Latin – *you gave*. He had no idea what that was supposed to mean and it was the first time Miguel had used Latin. It was a curious thing.

Alonso spent the day bent over his work and was pleased with the result. He'd had trouble getting just the right shade of green but hoped it would be close enough. He packed away his completed page and stretched his aching back before locking the parchment away in the drawer. His stomach rumbled as he left the scriptorium and made his way to the dining hall for supper.

He retired early with every intention of doing his daily Bible reading. He felt closer to God than he had done in a while and was confident in the protection he offered. He settled back against the bedhead with his Bible in hand. A lamp flickered on the small table beside his bed offering just enough light for him to read. He turned to Psalms and ran his fingers down the fine parchment.

Alonso woke with a start. The lamp had burned low and his Bible lay open on his lap. The image of a smooth rock tunnel lined with carved animals was still vivid in his mind. The rock looked like polished stone the colour of brandy, guarded by tall animals the likes of which he'd never seen. The tunnel was illuminated, but by what he couldn't see. At the end of it was a large double door – the vision was foggy and unclear and he closed his eyes as he tried to recapture the image of the door. It was important, he was sure of it.

In his dream, he'd reached out to open it, but as soon as his fingers touched the cold metal handle a voice had erupted from the other side of it. *Do not come here*. Alonso rubbed his hands down his face and swallowed. It was the first time he'd understood the voice and it scared him to his core. He was sure it wasn't him in the dream, but Miguel. *Miguel*. He was in some sort of danger – he knew it.

It was still the middle of the night and the Abbot would be most displeased if he disturbed his rest. He closed the Bible and leapt from his bed, slipping it back into the drawer. He poured water from the ewer into the bowl and splashed his face. The cool water helped somewhat to calm his panic, but he knew sleep would evade him. He dried his face and drew in several deep breaths.

Taking up his lamp, he stepped out into the dark hallway. The dormitories lay to the east and the smaller cells, where he slept, were towards the west. He padded barefoot down the hall, his lamp illuminating the dark shadows as he went. He had no real idea of where he was going, he just needed to walk and to try and push the dream from his mind.

He was sure Miguel was in some sort of danger, but had no idea why he thought so. The voice had been loud and definite but he didn't think it had sounded threatening, and yet, it had scared him. *What strange place was it*? He stopped walking as he recalled the image of the tunnel to his mind. It had not seemed frightening, just strange and unworldly. He wished he understood it. When he'd been charged with transcribing the pages sent from Miguel in the new world, Padre had simply told him to not speak of it. He continued walking – the cool stone slabs beneath his feet anchoring him to the present as he once again pushed the dream from his mind.

Chapter 2

Manchester 1968

Lana stepped from the bus as soon as the door opened. She hurried down the street towards her grandmother's house as fast as she could. Her heeled boots clicked loudly on the footpath and her mini skirt rode up around her thighs. She tugged it down with one hand as she turned left down Montague Street.

The phone call she'd received from her father kept replaying over and over in her head. *'Your grandmother will likely not last the day. Get there as fast as you can, I'll see you there.'*

She blinked back the tears that stung her eyes and swallowed the ache across her throat. Her Nan hadn't been well for some months but she hadn't considered that she might die. She wasn't that old – mid-sixties maybe. She wasn't sure, but it made little difference now. Lana clicked open the gate to the single-fronted Georgian house and almost skipped up the path to the front door. She knocked and then, without waiting, pushed it open and went inside.

Stepping into her Nan's house was a bit like stepping back into the past. It hadn't changed in living memory, and the thirties-style wallpaper and busy hall rug immediately brought back childhood memories.

"You made it," said her father appearing at the end of the hall.

"Oh, Dad, I just can't believe it," she said throwing herself into his arms. She clung to him briefly before pulling from his embrace. "Is she really going to die?"

He nodded. "I'm sorry, Kitten," he said patting her arm. "Doctor Murphy says there's nothing more he can do." He looked solemn as he guided her to the foot of the stairs. "She wants to see you."

Lana nodded as she blinked back her tears. "What about Uncle Rob and Aunt Rose? Are they here too?"

"Not yet, but they're on their way," he said with a nod. "Your cousins too. You should go up and see her before they get here."

She put her hand on the worn timber handrail as she slowly climbed the stairs. She paused on the landing as memories of losing her mother flooded her mind. She swallowed. She'd only been little when that had happened and Nan had always been there, filling the hole left behind with love and encouragement. Nan always said that she wished it was her who had been killed that day, but Lana would be forever grateful that Nan was there. And now she was going to die too. A soft sob escaped her lips and she covered her mouth with the back of her hand. *Life was so unfair!*

The door to her grandmother's bedroom stood ajar. Lana gathered herself together and took a deep breath before entering. The curtains were drawn almost closed, leaving the room dim and gloomy. She could see her Nan's slight form beneath the coverlet and her laboured breathing filled the air. Lana placed her bag softly on the dressing table as she passed and then approached the bed.

"Nan…are you awake?" she whispered as she lowered herself into a chair which had been placed beside the bed. "It's me, Lana."

Her Nan's pale blue eyes fluttered open and a weak smile tugged at the corner of her mouth. "You came."

Her voice was barely above a whisper, and Lana reached out and took her gnarled hand in hers. "Yes, Nan, of course I came," she said swallowing the tears that pricked her eyes. She looked so thin and frail. "Perhaps you should be in hospital, Nan."

"Nonsense. I wasn't born in a hospital and I'll be damned if I'll die in one. Here," she said struggling to sit up. "Be a dear, and put those pillows behind my back."

Lana stood and grabbed one of the spare pillows. "Perhaps you should stay lying down."

"Nonsense," she scoffed. "I might be on my deathbed, but I'll be damned if I won't sit up to speak with you."

Lana hid her smile as she stuffed two pillows behind her Nan's back and she lay back against them. "Ah…that's much better. Now sit, I've got something important to discuss with you."

Lana did as she was bid. It was so good to hear her Nan hadn't lost her spirit. She'd always been a woman in complete control, and it seemed like dying would be no different to the way she'd lived her life.

"Now, in the bottom of my wardrobe … left-hand side from memory," she began and then paused as she sucked in a great lungful of air. "God, I get so breathless at the least little thing."

"Can I get you anything? A glass of water perhaps?"

"No, no my dear," she said with a wave of her gnarled hand. "There's a box, a wooden box. In the bottom of the wardrobe."

Lana obediently got to her feet and made her way across the room to the large ornate wardrobe. She opened the door and peered in. It was stuffed, to breaking point, with clothes, and the bottom of it was a higgledy-piggledy pile of shoe boxes and handbags.

"Right at the back," called her Nan.

"I'm looking," called Lana as she lifted several boxes aside to get to the back corner. She was then faced with a pile of old clothes that had been tossed any old how into the corner. She dragged them out and finally spied a large flat wooden box, which she retrieved, before stuffing everything back in the wardrobe. She shut the door and prayed it wouldn't spring open on her.

"Good, good. Bring it over here."

She walked back to the bed and placed the box on it. It was a rather battered old box, with a rusty-looking lock but was otherwise quite plain.

"Now, on my dressing table," said Nan gasping in another lungful of air. "Open up my jewellery box and in the little tuck spot you'll find a key for this thing. It's got a bauble hanging off it, you can't miss it."

Lana did as she was ordered and returned a minute later with a small key in hand. She went to hand it to her Nan, but she brushed her aside.

"No, no, you keep it…and the box."

Lana sat down and smiled. "What's in the box, Nan? Old love letters?"

"Hmph, no." She closed her eyes and lay there breathing heavily.

Lana waited, almost holding her breath. *Was she alright? Should she call her father?* Just when she was thinking of doing that, Nan's eyes fluttered open again.

"Sorry, my dear…now, where to begin." She patted the old box with her hand several times. "I had hoped to have more time…to explain, but God appears to have other ideas," she began and then paused as she looked intently at Lana. "Our family has protected this box for generations. Don't ask me how many, I have no idea. I only know it's passed from one generation to the next for centuries. And now, I pass it to you."

This was not what Lana had expected and a slight frown creased her brow as she stared at the box. "What's in it?"

"Ah…well, that's a good question," Nan said with a nod. "I suppose the best description would be a key, but not just any key you understand."

"A locked box for a key?" Lana was puzzled by the explanation and really thought her Nan had lost her mind. She wasn't making any sense whatsoever.

"To be honest with you, I haven't opened it in many a year. But, it holds several very old parchments with odd writing and such." She drew in another lungful of air and closed her eyes. "I'm so tired."

"I'll go and let you rest, Nan," said Lana getting to her feet.

"No." Her eyes flew open and she gestured to her to sit down. "I have to tell you about this, it's very important that you understand, Lana."

"Alright," she said slowly as she resumed her seat.

"Now, you must promise me not to tell your father about this. Make up some story or other, but you cannot tell him what's really in the box. You understand?"

For the life of her, she didn't understand, but it seemed very important to Nan that she did. Lana nodded. "I promise."

"Good, good. Now, the key part from what I remember is that the writing on the parchment holds the key to understanding some manuscript or something. I don't really remember exactly. I only know that it must be kept safe and away from prying eyes." She paused and reaching out squeezed Lana's hand. "Promise me you'll keep it safe, and then one day you'll hand it on. You understand?"

"I understand, Nan. I promise to keep it safe…at the back of my wardrobe perhaps?" she said with a grin.

"Perfect."

Voices wafted into the room from the landing and Lana's eyes went to the open door. It sounded like Uncle Rob and Aunt Rose had arrived. She gathered the box under her arm and stuffed the small key in her pocket.

"It sounds like you have more visitors," she said getting to her feet. "I'll pop back in later to see you." She leaned forward and kissed her Nan's cheek. "I'll just be downstairs, alright?"

"Alright, my dear," she said and then reached out and grabbed Lana's arm in a vice-like grip. "Keep it safe."

"I promise I will," said Lana with a nod.

Nan lay back against the pillows and closed her eyes with a sigh. Lana grabbed her bag and quietly left the bedroom with her mind whirring about the box under her arm. What an unexpected and odd thing to be given. She planned on opening it as soon as she got home, whenever that would be. She almost ran into Uncle Rob on the landing and grabbed the railing to steady herself.

"Oh, sorry," she stammered.

"Lana, how nice to see you," said Uncle Rob wrapping her in a warm hug. He quickly let her go and looked intently down at her. "How is she?"

"Really tired."

"Well, we won't keep her too long," he replied with a grim smile.

"How nice to see you," said Aunt Rose before following Uncle Rob into the room.

"Likewise," said Lana to her retreating back. She shrugged as she went back downstairs. "Are you there, Dad?"

"In the kitchen, Kitten," came his muffled reply.

The kitchen was at the end of the hallway and she quickly made her way there. She pushed open the half-closed door and stopped. She had spent so many hours in this kitchen with her Nan, most recently they'd had dinner here together. She grimaced and swallowed. Now Nan was upstairs, frail and weak and likely to die tonight. It was all too much and a loud sob escaped her lips. She dumped her bag and the box onto the kitchen table before throwing herself into her father's arms.

He wrapped her in his arms and held her tight. "I know…we're never ready to lose the ones we love."

"It's so unfair," she managed to say in between sobs. "I'm not ready to lose her."

"I know," he crooned, rubbing her back. "But, we were lucky to have her for so long."

He released her and Lana wiped her hand across her face. "You're right. I have to hang onto that."

A weak smile spread across his face. "I've just made a pot of tea, would like a cup?"

She shook her head. "Coffee?"

"There must be some here somewhere."

Lana spun around at the knock on the door, which quickly opened and her cousins appeared in the hall. "Morris, Pat," she called as she made her way towards them. "How nice to see you both."

"Hey Lana," said Morris giving her a peck on her cheek. "Are Mum and Dad here yet?"

"Yes, they're upstairs with Nan," she replied as she greeted Pat.

"We'll go straight up and see her," said Pat with a grim look. "Is she really going to die?"

Lana compressed her lips and nodded as tears welled in her eyes. "I'm afraid so."

"Come on, Pat. You can catch up with Lana later," said Morris as he started for the stairs.

Lana watched them go before returning to the kitchen.

"Here you go, Kitten. I found some coffee," said her father plonking a steaming mug on the table. His eyes rested on the box sitting on the table beside her bag. He looked at Lana with a quizzical expression. "Where did the box come from?"

Lana stared at the box in alarm. She should've dropped it on the hall table or something. She shrugged and did her best to look disinterested. "It's just some old box that Nan wanted me to have."

He shrugged his shoulders. "Have Morris and Pat gone up to see her?"

"Yes," said Lana flopping down on the kitchen chair. "I should give them some time with her before I join them."

"Good idea," he said sitting opposite her. He reached across the table and squeezed her hand. "We'll get through this."

Chapter 3

Monastery of Santa Maria de Huerta
Spain 1596

Alonso had spent the night walking the dark halls of the monastery, and he knew he should've been exhausted, but he wasn't. The images from his dream were going around and around in his head and he could think of nothing else. Miguel was in some sort of danger, and Padre had to listen to him.

As soon as morning prayers were dispensed with, he sought out Brother Benito and an audience with the Abbot..

"I'm afraid that's impossible Brother Alonso, he's not here," said Brother Benito with a look of calm disinterest.

"Not here? Where is he?"

Benito cleared his throat and stared down his long nose at Alonso.

"My apologies, that is none of my business," said Alonso.

"Indeed, it is not."

Alonso sucked in a deep breath and blinked several times. "May I ask when he will return?" He could feel his heart pounding in his chest and panic squirming in his belly like a viper.

"He will be gone at least two weeks, maybe three," Benito replied. "Perhaps I can assist you in the meantime?"

"No, I'm afraid not," said Alonso with a shake of his head. "Only Padre can assist me."

"Then I suggest you seek an audience when he returns."

"Thank you, Brother Benito. I will do just that."

He left the Prior's office with a heavy heart and a gripping sense of doom. Walking the halls last night had done nothing to ease his mind, and so he hoped another day spent with God would bring him some comfort.

***

Over the next week or so, his dreams became more frequent and his fear for Miguel grew. God had deserted him and he had no one to turn to. It would still be at least a week before the Abbot returned, and by then he feared it would be too late. He lay back on his narrow cot and sighed. He dreaded falling asleep, but he was exhausted and in desperate need of rest.

He awoke with a start – his heart was pounding and he was sweating profusely. *Miguel was dead.* How, he wasn't sure. He rubbed his hands down his face as he recalled his dream. He was sure he'd been Miguel in the dream and the booming voice, *do not come here*, had rung out, but Miguel had ignored it.

He slowly pushed the heavy door open and stepped into a large cavern lined with shelves and glinting with gold. His eyes swept the room, stopping to stare at the metal tablets crammed onto every shelf. They looked like they were engraved with the same strange writing. In the centre of the room was a pedestal with a glowing orb sitting on top of it. It seemed to be emitting an odd humming sound. Miguel approached the orb and then everything went black.

Alonso leapt from his cot and fumbled on his nightstand for the tinderbox. He lit it and then lighting a splint, his lamp finally illuminated his small cell. He sucked in several deep breaths before splashing his face with cold water. *Miguel.* His heart was pounding and he was gasping for air as the dream replayed in his mind. *What had just happened?* He couldn't make any sense of it, only this overwhelming knowledge that Miguel was dead. He had no idea how or why, but he was sure. There was some evil at work and he was shaken to his core.

He should destroy the pages Miguel had sent; he should destroy them all. Padre would be angrier possibly than he'd ever seen him, but he was sure they were evil, they had to be destroyed. He'd pay the penance later; he might even be expelled from the monastery. He paused with his hand on the door handle to his cell. *What would he do if he was expelled? He knew no other life than this…no, he would pay the price, whatever it was.*

He raced down the dark hall, his lamp causing shadows to dance on the walls as he went. He had to do it before he changed his mind. He unlocked the door to his scriptorium and entered. Placing the lamp on his desk he retrieved the small key from his pocket. He held it flat in the palm of his hand and stared at it for several minutes.

Steeling himself, he unlocked the drawer and reached into the back, pulling out the pages he'd already transcribed. He placed them on his desk and then retrieved the dozen or so pages that he was yet to work on. He slumped into his chair and flipped through the pages in his hand. His heart was pounding, not from his dream, but from what he was about to do. He'd be expelled from the order for sure. He knew it. Padre was generally a kind and forgiving man, but he knew in his heart that he wouldn't forgive this.

He stopped flipping the pages as some words jumped out at him. They weren't in the strange writing. He set the rest of the pages aside and stared at the page in his hand. The first paragraph was in the odd writing that Miguel always wrote in. Then there were two other passages, one in Latin and the other he thought was possibly Greek. He placed it on the desk in front of him and sucked in a deep breath before reading the passage in Latin.

Brother Alonso, this is for you. It is the key to you understanding the strange writing. I have wrestled with myself for many months over this, but I want you to understand what this all means. Do not ask how I have deciphered the writing, because I cannot answer you. It is a mystery to me. There is some unknown force at work here, it is ancient and all-knowing. What I have discovered here is some sort of scriptorium, but unlike any I have ever seen. Use my words written in both

> *Latin and Greek to decipher the strange language. You will learn much and understand less, but I feel this is of great importance to Spain. I have written several pages in all three languages for you to use as your guide. Use this information wisely my Brother.*

Alonso sat back in his chair and stared at the wall. His mind was racing and his breathing shallow. Miguel's words were mysterious and frightening. *What had he discovered? Ancient and all-knowing...what could that mean?* His gaze rested on the pages on his desk for several minutes, before he started searching through them for the other pages Miguel had mentioned. It didn't take him long to find three more pages written in all three languages. He set them aside with the first page and ran his hands down his face.

If Miguel was right, and these writings were important to Spain, then he couldn't destroy them. He gathered the first pile of copied pages and slipped them back into the drawer. He then put the rest of them away and locked the drawer before dropping the key back into his pocket.

What of the strange dreams? They had to have something to do with this. But what? He had no idea how Miguel had spoken to him in his dreams, but Alonso was sure he had. And he was also sure Miguel was now dead. He sucked in several large breaths as he tried to calm himself. He wished he understood, but he couldn't fathom how these things were connected. He still wasn't sure if he should destroy the pages or not.

He groaned as he got to his feet and picked up his lamp. He would decide what to do in the morning.

Chapter 4

Manchester 1968

Lana felt drained of all emotion. She doubted she'd ever cry again; she'd used up all her tears last night. It was still early in the morning when she arrived at the semi-detached house she shared. The house was owned by Diane and Toby's parents, who'd moved to London for their father's work. She'd been friends with Di since before they went to school, and Toby was just like the brother she never had.

She drew in a deep breath as she opened the door and stepped inside. Her boots clunked loudly on the bare floorboards and Di immediately stepped from the lounge and stared at her.

"Lana, are you okay?" Without waiting for a reply Di wrapped her arms around Lana and squeezed. Letting her go she took a step back and compressed her lips. "She's gone, isn't she?"

Lana nodded. "I just want to take a bath and go to bed."

"Of course you do," she said with a solemn expression. "I'm so sorry."

"Thanks."

Lana climbed the narrow stairs to the second floor and went into her bedroom. It was so strange really. Her room had no right to look exactly like it had yesterday, with clothes hanging off every available space and shoes strewn across the floor. The world had changed forever last night, and yet… She tossed her shoulder bag onto the tall boy which was already strewn with a range of makeup, perfume bottles and general debris. She looked at the box in her hands and tears threatened again. She blinked them back as she opened the wardrobe.

Lana couldn't help the wry smile that tugged at the corner of her mouth. The bottom of her wardrobe looked a lot like Nan's. Shoe boxes, bags and a pile of scarves all tossed in any old how. She made room for the box at the back of the wardrobe and tossed the pile of scarves on top of it. No one would ever notice it.

She sat on the bed, unzipped her boots and tossed them aside, before rummaging among the bedding for her pyjamas. She found the top but had to search further for the bottoms, which she retrieved from under the bed before heading for the bathroom.

***

Lana had no idea what time it was when she awoke. Rain was pattering against her window and the afternoon gloom told her it was late. She rolled over and stared at her clock – three thirty. She couldn't believe she'd slept so long. Stretching, she climbed out of bed and wrapped her dressing gown around herself. She wasn't really in the mood for company, but she needed a coffee and she hoped Di wouldn't be too chatty.

She padded downstairs and into the kitchen at the back of the house. She found Di relaxing with a magazine in her hand by the fire, smiling as Lana entered.

"Feeling better?"

"Yes, thanks," she replied with a nod. "Coffee?"

"Please," said Di setting her magazine aside. "Do you want to talk?"

"Not really," said Lana turning on the kettle and retrieving two mugs from the cupboard. "I just never expected her to die." She turned to face Di with the jar of coffee in hand. "I feel kind of numb."

"Yeah, I know what you mean. When my Pa died it took ages for it to sink in. I still miss him so much."

"I think I feel the same," said Lana spooning coffee into the mugs. "It's sort of not real. And yet…" She poured the hot water into the mugs and breathed in the delicious aroma. "She gave me a box of things before she died…it was really weird."

"Weird how?"

Lana wasn't sure how to answer that, or even if she should. She already regretted saying anything. She shrugged as she added milk and sugar to the coffee and handed one to Di.

"I don't know," she said easing herself into the other chair set by the fire. She sipped her coffee and closed her eyes briefly as she felt the hot liquid slip down her throat. The warmth from the fire was the perfect accompaniment.

Lana opened her eyes and stared at her coffee. "She gave me this old battered box and said that it had been handed down through our family for generations. How weird is that?"

"Pretty weird," said Di before sipping her coffee. "What's in it?"

"I haven't opened it yet," she replied with a shake of her head. "Some old papers that are the key to something." She shook her head again and pulled a face. "It was really strange. She told me to keep it safe in the bottom of my wardrobe, and the weirdest thing was, she told me not to show my Dad, or even to tell him about it."

"Oh, Lana, you've got to open it." Di sat straight up in her chair with an expectant look on her face. "It's so mysterious. Maybe there's lots of money in there or jewellery." She slumped back in her chair with a disgruntled look. "No one's ever left me anything, let alone a mysterious box."

Lana grinned. She'd been wrong about not wanting company, this was exactly what she needed. "Money would be nice, but I don't think so. I think it's just some old papers." She was silent for several minutes as she sipped her coffee. "Perhaps we should wait until Toby gets home. Where is he anyway?"

"God, he's such a dork. He's gone to some university thing. On a Saturday! He loves the place."

Lana hid her grin behind her mug. She didn't really understand the brother-sister thing between Di and Toby. Not having any siblings had not prepared her for the love-hate relationship between them. "I think he's just conscientious."

Di rolled her eyes. "He ought to get on with life instead of spending all his time pouring over his books and stuff. I mean, how long does it take to become a history teacher or whatever he's going to be." She gulped down her coffee and shook her head. "Admit it, Lana, he's just plain boring."

Lana didn't find him at all boring. He always had such interesting things to talk about. Yes, they always had something to do with history, but they were still interesting. "He's just not like us."

"No, he's stuffy and boring."

Lana had no intention of arguing with Di about her brother, it was a no-win argument. She stood up and put her mug on the mantle. "Shall I go get the box then?"

"Ooh, yes."

Lana smiled as she left the kitchen and headed upstairs. She was pretty sure Di was going to be very disappointed with the contents of the box. According to her Nan, they were just old papers. Why they were so important made no sense. She retrieved the box and rummaged through her bag for the key before rejoining Di in the kitchen.

Di frowned as she looked at the box sitting on the kitchen table. "It's not what I expected," she said glancing at Lana. "I thought it'd be more fancy than that."

Lana smiled. "I know, it's just a plain old box, and I don't think what's inside will be any better."

Di sighed as she sat back down. "Well, it's still mysterious." She sat forward in her chair with an expectant look on her face as Lana put the key in the lock. "Wait…what if it's stuff about your Dad? Maybe that's why she didn't want you to tell him about it."

Lana paused. "I don't think so. You're forgetting it's been handed down for generations."

"Oh yeah," said Di with a sheepish grin. "Alright, open it."

Chapter 5

Manchester 1968

Lana drew in a breath and tried to turn the key – it wouldn't move at all. She frowned as she wiggled it and tried again. The lock was rusted on the outside, and she was now beginning to realise that it was possibly rusted beyond use on the inside as well.

"It won't turn," she said with a grunt as she tried again.

"What?" said Di leaping to her feet. "Come on, we have to know what's in there."

"I know, but I think it's rusted beyond use," said Lana as she wiggled the key and tried again. "My Nan said she hadn't opened it in years." She pulled the key out and peered at the lock.

"Here, let me try," said Di holding out her hand.

"Alright."

Lana handed her the key and stood back, waiting and hoping that Di would be able to open it. "Well?"

Di shook her head, “I can’t get it to budge at all. Damn,” she said trying harder to make the key turn.

“Don’t break it,” said Lana in alarm. She reached out and grabbed Di’s hand. “Don’t force it.”

“Well, what are we going to do?” Di’s eyebrows raised quizzically as she stared at Lana.

Lana shook her head and stared at the old box. “I know!” she exclaimed. “Soap. What if we rub soap on the key, that might lubricate the lock.”

“Great idea,” said Di returning the key to Lana. Racing across the kitchen she opened the cupboard under the sink and retrieved the soap shaker. Opening it, she grabbed the cake of yellow soap and grinned as she handed it to Lana. “Try this.”

“Good old velvet soap,” said Lana rubbing it all over the shaft of the key. “Let’s hope this works.” She handed the soap back to Di and then slipped the key into the lock. She wiggled it in and out a few times before turning to Di. “Here goes.”

Lana held her breath as she tried turning the key again. There was some resistance, but with a little more force it turned and she heard the lock click. “It worked,” she said with a grin.

“Oh, God, this is so exciting,” said Di almost jumping up and down. “I can’t wait to see what’s inside.”

Lana drew in a breath and lifted the lid. Lying in the bottom of the shallow box were what looked to be old written pages.

“Oh,” said Di slumping her shoulders. “I felt sure there’d be something good in there, but it’s just old papers.” She plonked down on the nearest chair and grimaced. “Oh well, I guess it’s still a neat present from your Nan.”

“It is,” said Lana with a smile. Reaching in, she lifted the top page out of the box. It had strange writing on it that she didn’t understand, and the pages underneath appeared to be just like the first. “Somehow, these are important.” She ran her thumb down the smooth parchment. “And I think they’re really old. Look at the writing, Di, I think it’s written in different languages.”

Di glanced at the page and shrugged. “Maybe.”

Lana put the page aside and pulled the others out of the box. There were nineteen in total, all written in languages she couldn’t read. “I guess I was hoping that I’d understand what the key was,” said Lana putting the pages back in the box. "But I've got no idea what this is all about."

Di's eyes widened and she stared at Lana. "Ask Toby. He's such a history freak, I bet he'd know what they're about."

"Probably," she said slowly shutting the lid. "But I don't know if I should."

"Why not?" said Di rolling her eyes.

Lana picked up her coffee and eased herself into the other chair. She took a sip; it had gone cold and she put it back down. "Nan said to keep it safe from prying eyes."

Di rolled her eyes again and leaned forward in her chair. "Toby's not prying eyes. He'll absolutely love it."

He would, thought Lana. He was studying history at university and she knew he'd love to see her box of papers, but should she show him? She couldn't really think of a reason not to, it was only that she felt the weight of responsibility. *What if something happened to the box after all these years?* Right at this moment, she wished she knew nothing about it.

"Show him," said Di getting to her feet. "He might be able to help you work out what they mean." She walked to the sink and dropped the soap on the bench before rinsing her mug. "I'm sorry to leave you, but I've got a date with Russell tonight and I need to get ready."

"Ooh," said Lana pulling a face. "Another date with Russell. It's getting serious."

"I don't know," said Di with a shake of her head. "I really like him, but I wouldn't say it's serious. At least, not yet."

"Ah, so you haven't slept with him." Lana giggled at the outraged look on her friend's face. "I'm teasing."

Di reddened and smiled. "I didn't say that."

She marched from the kitchen leaving Lana with a wide grin on her face. So, she had slept with him. Well, good on her. She hadn't had any luck with boyfriends in the past, and Lana hoped this one would work out. She liked Russell too. He was reliable and decent, unlike some of the other guys Di had dated.

She heard the front door open and reached out and grabbed the box. She got to her feet and was in the doorway when she spied Toby hanging his overcoat on the hook by the door. She breathed a sigh of relief. It wasn't her father.

"Hi," he said noticing her. He walked towards her with a solemn look on his face. "How's your Nan?"

"Gone," she replied compressing her lips and blinking back the sudden tears that pricked her eyes.

"I'm so sorry, Lana," he said reaching for her. He wrapped his arms around her briefly and pecked her on the cheek. "I know how close you were."

"Yeah, thanks."

"Is there anything I can do?"

"Not really," she said shaking her head.

"Well, if you'd like to go down the pub for a pint, I'd happily join you."

"Thanks, but I'm not really in the mood."

"Fair enough." He peered behind her and then looked back at her. "Where's Di?"

"Upstairs getting ready, she's got a date with Russell tonight," said Lana pulling her dressing gown closer around herself. All of a sudden she felt rather self-conscious.

"So, it's just you and me then." He ran his fingers through his unruly mop of hair and grinned. "How about we send out for pizza and sink a few beers?"

Lana smiled. "That sounds perfect." She noticed his eyes were resting on the box under her arm. "Um…it was a gift from my Nan."

"It looks old," he said returning his gaze to her.

She drew in a breath while she considered whether to tell him about it or not. She was curious to know what the pages were and he'd probably be able to tell her. But her Nan's words rang in her ears – *keep it safe and away from prying eyes*.

"I need a coffee, do you want one?" he said heading into the kitchen.

Lana followed him and put the box on the table. "Yeah, I've got a mug around here somewhere," she said running her fingers over the smooth wood. She pulled herself away from the box and retrieving her mug, she tipped out the cold coffee.

"Sit down, Lana, I'll make the coffee," he said taking the mug from her.

"Thanks." She sat down at the table and wrestled with whether to tell him or not. She could trust Toby and her curiosity was outweighing any warnings. "My Nan told me a really weird story when she gave me the box."

"Really?" said Toby glancing over his shoulder. "What did she say?"

Lana told him the whole story of the box and its contents. "Di and I have no idea what they are or what's written on them. It appears to be in several languages."

"Well, now I'm really intrigued," said Toby putting a mug of steaming coffee in front of her. He sat down opposite and ran his fingers over the box. "It's really old, Lana. Like I'd say several hundred years old. Can I open it?"

"Yes…oh wait." She put her hand on top of the box to stop him. "I forgot to tell you. You can't mention this to my father. For some odd reason, Nan told me not to tell him about it or show it to him or anything. You have to promise."

"I promise," he said with a nod.

Lana removed her hand and took a large mouthful of coffee. Her heart was beating faster than it should have and she watched Toby in anticipation as he lifted the lid.

"Wow."

"What?" said Lana leaning forward in her chair.

"These look like pages from a manuscript…like medieval."

"My Nan said something about them being a key to understanding a manuscript. Do you think they're real?"

"Well, I'm no expert on old manuscripts, but yes, I think they are." He peered at the pages in the box for several minutes. "It looks to me like they're written in

Latin and Greek and some other language. I have no idea what."

"Can you read them?"

"Ah, no, sorry I can't. My Latin isn't that good," he said shaking his head. "But, I'll be able to translate them for you." He looked up at her and smiled. "I'll bring my books home from uni on Monday and start work. Do you know how many pages there are?"

"There's nineteen," she said sipping her coffee. "Di and I took them out earlier and counted them."

"Don't do that," he said with an alarmed expression on his face. "You shouldn't touch these without gloves on."

"Okay, I won't do that again then." Lana was surprised at his fervour.

"Ah, sorry," he said with a sheepish grin. "It's just that you'll leave oil from your fingers on the vellum which will discolour it over time."

"Oh, well, I wouldn't want to damage them."

"No. God, Lana this is so exciting. Do you know how rare these things are?"

"No, but I'm starting to get the feeling that my Nan was telling me the truth. I thought she'd gone a bit loopy," she said with a grin. "I can't wait to find out what they say."

"Me either."

Chapter 6

Monastery of Santa Maria de Huerta
Spain 1597

Alonso had spent the last few days avoiding his scriptorium at all costs. He'd spent much of that time in prayer and just wandering the corridors. After sleepless nights and wrestling with his own conscience, he'd finally reached a decision. He finished his morning prayers and made his way to his scriptorium. He was now standing at the door and his heart was pounding in his chest. He was afraid but resolute in his decision.

Sucking in a deep breath, he unlocked the door and went inside. He closed it behind him and eased himself into his chair. Without another thought, he pulled the key from his pocket and unlocked the drawer. He pulled out the four pages he'd left on top of the pile and placed them on his desk and stared at them.

An hour later he was still sitting there staring at them. He finally reached for the first page and read Miguel's words again. He hoped he'd be able to translate the strange writing using Latin as his guide. But he had no idea how the writing was structured and he groaned as he stared at the page. Nothing made any sense.

He turned the page over and was encouraged to see Miguel had broken the writing down into a single sentence. He read the Latin several times before comparing it to the strange writing above it.

> *The writing is opposite to Latin and you must start at the beginning. I will try and create a list of meanings for you.*

It didn't take him long to realise this was going to be much harder than Miguel had imagined. *If only he knew the order of the words* – Miguel had said they were opposite, but opposite how? He groaned as he reread the sentence, with no clearer understanding of the words. *Had Miguel had time to write a list for him before he died?* He thought not.

He leaned back in his chair and mulled over the words in his mind. If Miguel was talking about it being opposite to Latin, then the verb would be at the beginning. *Is that what he meant?* He stared at the page again and noticed the same sentence was repeated below the Latin in Greek. He hadn't studied Greek and had no idea if that would be easier to translate.

He ran his hands down his face before shoving the pages back in the drawer and locking it. He hurried from the scriptorium and made his way outside and along the covered walkway towards the carpenter's workshop. He slowed as he reached the small stone building and walked inside at a sedate pace.

Several Brothers looked up from their work but paid him no heed. He smiled and nodded in their direction as he made his way over to Brother Diego. He was working on a piece of timber, which was already smooth and lustrous.

"Brother Alonso," said Diego looking up from his work. He stared at him for a moment before reaching out and touching his arm. "Are you alright?"

"Can we speak?"

"Of course," he said nodding. "Come, out into the garden where we won't be overheard."

The two made their way out of the workshop and into the garden. Alonso glanced around and headed for an arbour overhanging with vines. He stopped and drew in a deep breath.

"I need your help, Brother Diego," he said without preamble. "If I remember correctly you studied Greek?"

"I did," he replied slowly. "Is this about Brother Miguel and his strange writing?"

"Yes, and you must swear to tell no one."

Diego nodded. "I swear it."

"Good." Alonso slowly let out his breath and smiled weakly. "Brother Miguel has sent me some pages to translate. He's written them in the strange writing as well as Latin and Greek. I've spent all morning trying to make sense of it, and I can't."

"So, you want me to see if I can translate them?"

Alonso nodded.

Diego shook his head. "You are far better at this than me, Alonso. I doubt I'll be any help, but I'm happy to try." He paused and closed his eyes briefly before staring at Alonso. "I can't leave the workshop right now."

"Of course not. I thought we might try after supper if you're willing."

"We may have to wait until later. If I'm seen near the scriptorium it may raise questions that we don't want to answer."

Alonso saw the wisdom in his words. If anyone suspected that he'd broken his vow of silence he'd be severely reprimanded, maybe even expelled, but he thought it was worth the risk. "Come to my room when the others have gone to bed."

"Alright. Now I must go."

He turned to leave and Alonso grabbed him by the arm. "Wait, there's just one more thing you should know." He swallowed and compressed his lips. "Brother Miguel is dead, and you may well be risking your life by helping me."

"Brother Miguel dead? How?"

"I don't know," said Alonso with a strained expression. *How could he explain this?* "I dreamt of Brother Miguel a few nights ago, and I know he's dead. There's some evil at work, Diego." He let go of his arm and sighed. "If you want to change your mind, I'll understand."

"No, my friend," said Diego with a grin. "I'm curious to see these strange writings, even if it does come with great risk."

Alonso watched Diego as he turned and walked back across the garden to the workshop. He waited in the arbour for several minutes before returning to his scriptorium. He was grateful Diego had agreed to help him, but regardless, he spent the afternoon hunched over his desk trying to make sense of Miguel's words.

***

Alonso paced his small cell. It was well past suppertime, and he hoped Diego would come soon. He opened his door and peered down the dark hall, hoping to catch sight of his friend. It was deserted, and the monastery was quiet. Now would be the perfect time. He swallowed as he closed the door and slumped down on his cot. *Come on, Diego.*

Ten minutes later, there was a soft knock on his door and he dived from his cot and wrenched it open. Diego's grinning face peered at him. "Sorry, I ran into Brother Benito."

"Does he suspect?"

"No," said Diego with a shake of his head. "Come on, the halls are empty."

Alonso snuffed out his lamp and grabbed it before heading out the door. They made their way to the scriptorium in darkness, keeping close to the shadows in case they should see anyone. Thankfully, Diego had waited until their Brothers were in bed, and they saw no one. Alonso's heart was racing as he pulled the key from his pocket and fumbled to get it into the lock.

"Here, give me the lamp," said Diego taking it from him. "Did you bring a tinderbox?"

"In my pocket." He retrieved it and handed it to Diego, before trying once again to slip the key into the lock. He couldn't see a thing and he slammed his fist against the door.

A moment later the lamp sputtered to life and Diego illuminated the lock. Alonso sighed and let his frustrations go as he unlocked the door and went inside. Diego placed the lamp on the desk and blew out his breath.

"We made it."

"Yes, well done. It was a good idea to wait until everyone was in bed." Alonso retrieved the small key from his pocket and unlocked the drawer. He placed Miguel's four pages on the desk and nodded. "Sit down, Diego. See if you can make any sense of these."

Diego sat and picked up the top page and peered at it. Alonso watched and waited, almost holding his breath. If Diego couldn't help, then he didn't know what he was going to do. *Perhaps he should've destroyed them?* He ran his hands down his face and paced the small scriptorium mumbling a quick prayer under his breath.

"This shouldn't be too difficult," said Diego glancing up. "According to Brother Miguel, the strange writing is similar in arrangement to Greek."

"It's not opposite?" said Alonso coming to stand beside Diego. He stared down at the pages and then at his friend with his brows raised.

"Opposite? I don't know what you mean," said Diego with a shake of his head.

"The Latin phrase says it's opposite."

"Ah…well I wouldn't know about that," he said with a shrug. "I never learned Latin. But, it should be nearly word for word in Greek."

A wide grin spread across Alonso's face. "So, you think you can translate it?"

"I didn't say that. But I might be able to tell you what each word means in Greek, and then you can translate that to Latin I suppose."

Alonso pulled a fresh sheet of parchment from the stack sitting on the shelf and prepared a fresh quill. Retrieving a bottle of ink, he looked expectantly at Diego. "Alright, let's start with this simple sentence and see if we can make any sense of it."

Diego drew in a breath. “Well, this word here is writing.”

Alonso copied it down onto his parchment and then wrote it in Latin beside it. “So, if this is written word for word, or nearly, that word there should mean writing?” He pointed to the strange writing above the Latin translation and looked at Diego.

Diego nodded. “It should be.”

Alonso scratched his chin. “How can we be sure?”

Diego shrugged. “We can’t…unless Brother Miguel has used the same word somewhere else.”

“He did,” said Alonso with excitement. “Here, let me look.”

Diego slid the pages towards Alonso and he flipped through them, scanning each one. “I spent all day pouring over these, and I’m sure he mentioned writing several times.”

After a couple of minutes, he pointed to the word written in Latin. “Here,” he said pushing the page back towards Diego. He waited impatiently while Diego read.

“Well, if we’re right, it should be the fifth word in the strange writing.” Diego ran his finger along the parchment to the fifth word. “Does that look the same?”

Alonso peered at the writing and then back at the page he'd written it on. "I don't think so."

"Quiet," said Diego grabbing Alonso's arm. "I hear footsteps. Douse the lamp."

Alonso paused and listened. Sure enough, he could hear footsteps slowly coming down the hall. His heart was pounding as he first locked the door and then extinguished the lamp. He stood in the darkness with his breathing shallow and his mind racing. *Who would be coming down here this late at night? And why?* He was sure no one had seen the two of them come down here.

The footsteps grew louder and then stopped outside the scriptorium. Alonso almost held his breath while he waited for whoever it was to move on. Time seemed to stand still and the silence was deafening. He prayed whoever it was would keep walking, but they didn't. A moment later the door handle creaked, as whoever it was, tried to open it. He stood stock still, fearful to even breathe. The seconds ticked by before finally, the sound of footsteps started again.

Alonso didn't move until the sound of the footsteps had completely faded. He exhaled as he relit the lamp. "That was close."

"Who was that?" said Diego pulling down his dark eyebrows. "No one saw us come down here, I'm sure of it."

"So am I," said Alonso with a nod. "And I have no idea who it was, but one thing is clear. We need to be careful."

"Shall we call it a night?"

"Yes, I don't think we're going to get any more done tonight." He gathered the pages together and slipped them back into the drawer before locking it. "Will you come again tomorrow night? I won't blame you if you want nothing more to do with this."

"Yes, my friend," said Diego with a grin. "But tomorrow night I'll meet you here. The less chance of us being seen together, the better."

"Good idea."

Chapter 7

Manchester 1968

Lana rang work early Monday morning to let them know her Nan had died and she wouldn't be in. She thought she could've gone to work, but not at the risk of breaking down in the office. That would be too embarrassing. Her boss was really understanding, but said she expected her at work tomorrow. Mrs Clausen wasn't known for her generosity.

Toby and Di had both left by the time she made her way downstairs. She pulled her dressing gown around herself as she settled down in the kitchen with a mug of coffee in hand. The last couple of days were a bit of a blur and the realisation that her Nan was gone was yet to sink in. She sighed as she sipped her coffee. *What would life be like without her?*

The phone rang and she stared at it for several moments before getting to her feet. "Hello," she said picking up the receiver. "It's Lana."

"Hi Kitten," came her father's voice down the line. "Oh, good you're home."

"Yeah, I didn't feel up to going into work."

"That's understandable," he said with a note of sadness. "If you're up for it, would you like to join Uncle Rob and me for lunch? Down at the Arms?"

She considered his invitation for a mere split second. "I'd love to."

"Great, we'll meet you there at twelve."

"Thanks, Dad," she said before hanging up the phone.

She sank back into her chair and picked up her coffee. It would be good to see her father, and maybe get an understanding of what would happen next. Of course, there was a funeral to arrange and then whatever was going to happen to her Nan's house. She presumed that would go to her father and Uncle Rob. Thankfully, she wouldn't have to worry about any of it.

She drank down the last of her coffee and rinsed her mug. Tears unexpectedly pricked her eyes and she swallowed the ache that now stretched across her throat. Her Nan would no doubt be buried with Pop, and that thought brought a fresh wave of grief. *Oh, God*, she didn't want to think about that. She wiped the back of her hand across her face and did her best to push all thoughts of deep dark holes in the ground aside. She couldn't bear to think about it.

***

She spied her father and Uncle Rob as soon as she entered the pub. They were sitting at a table in the front corner, each had a pint sitting in front of them. She smiled and waved before ordering a pint for herself at the bar.

She headed for their table and slung her bag over the chair before leaning forward to kiss her father. "Hi, Dad."

"Hey, Kitten."

She put her beer down and greeted Uncle Rob.

"Nice to see you again, Lana," said Uncle Rob with a nod.

"Thanks for inviting me," she said sitting down. "It's just what I needed."

"Yeah, it's been a tough couple of days," said her father. "But, let's not dwell on the sad bits, but rather how lucky we were to have had her."

"Hear, hear," said Rob raising his glass. "To a wonderful woman."

They clinked glasses, and Lana felt herself relax somewhat. "So, do you need a hand with anything?" She felt like she should offer, but was also hoping the answer would be no.

"No," said her father reaching out and squeezing her hand. "Rob and I have it under control…I think."

"Yeah," said Rob with a laugh. "Actually, Mum already made most of the funeral arrangements herself. You know her, she didn't like to leave anything to chance."

"We're meeting with the funeral people this afternoon," said her father slurping his beer. "We're hoping to arrange things for Thursday. That'll give us time to put the notice in the paper and such."

Lana nodded. She didn't want to think about it

"And we're seeing her lawyer on Friday," said Rob with a grimace. "I just hope to God her Will is in order."

"Relax, Rob, it'll be fine," said her father with a reassuring smile. "She won't have left that to chance either."

"Well, let's hope not," he grumbled. "Rose is expecting the crystal collection to go her way, and I think Morris will be pretty disappointed if he doesn't get the car."

"Good Lord," said her father looking incredulous. "She hasn't driven the car in years. I doubt it'd even start."

Lana shifted uncomfortably in her chair. Talk of dividing up her Nan's things was making her feel very uncomfortable. It wasn't something she wanted to even think about, let alone talk about.

"How about I go and order lunch," said her father emptying his glass. "What do you two want?"

"Pie and chips," said Rob, "and another pint."

"I'll have the same," said Lana as she put her hand over her glass. "No more beer for me."

He smiled and nodded before walking across to the counter. Lana smiled at Uncle Rob sitting across from her. "I hope everyone's well," she said. It was lame, but she didn't know what to say to him.

"Yes, everyone's fine," he replied leaning forward on his elbows. "And you?"

"I'm good, thanks."

He glanced across at her father, who was still standing at the bar. "Your father tells me Mum gave you a box before she died."

Well, she hadn't expected that. She sipped her beer and nodded. "Yeah. It's just an old box." She hoped she sounded bored and disinterested in the subject.

"Right. So, what was in it?"

She swallowed and shook her head. “Nothing.”

He frowned and scratched his ear. “Odd that she’d give you an empty box.”

“Yeah,” she nodded and smiled. “She was a funny old thing sometimes.”

Her father arrived back at the table with two more pints and plonked them down. “What are you two talking about?”

Rob reached for his beer. “I was just asking Lana about the old box Mum gave her.”

“Yes, that’s intriguing,” said her father taking his seat. “Did you open it?”

Hell, what was she going say now? She’d just lied to Uncle Rob but it was a lot harder lying to her father. “Yeah…the lock was rusted but I managed to open it.” Well, that wasn’t a lie. “It was empty,” she said before burying her face in her pint.

“Well, that’s really strange,” said her father with a frown. “Why would she give you an empty box?”

“That’s what I said,” said Rob.

She did her best to keep her face passive as she shrugged her shoulders. She was a dreadful liar. “What will happen to Nan’s things?”

“We won’t know until we meet with her lawyer and see what her Will says,” said her father slurping his beer. “But, I expect you, Morris and Pat will be able to take a few mementoes. Was there anything you particularly wanted?”

“No,” said Lana with a shake of her head. “Just a little something to remember her by would be nice.”

“Well, I’m sure we can do that.”

Her father and Rob chatted over lunch about the funeral arrangements and other things. Lana did her best not to listen – she didn’t want to know about it. She’d only agreed to lunch because she wanted to get out of the house and not think about her Nan. Now, she couldn’t wait for lunch to end and to get out of there. It was all too raw and talking about it wasn’t helping one bit.

She kissed her father goodbye as soon as they stepped out of the pub. “Thanks for lunch.”

“You’re welcome. Call me if you want to talk,” said her father pecking her cheek. “I’ll call you later and let you know about the funeral.”

“Okay, thanks,” she said nodding. “Gotta go, bye Uncle Rob.” She gave him a wave and started walking down the street towards home as fast as she could. At least she'd managed to not tell her father anything about the box, and she was glad to have that conversation over and done with. All she had to do now was get through to the end of the week. Saying her final farewell to Nan was going to be awful and she'd be glad to put it behind her.

Lana was surprised to find the front door to the house unlocked. "Hello," she called as she entered.

Toby immediately popped into the hall from the lounge. "Hey." He gestured to her with half a sandwich. "Want one?"

"No, I've just eaten. What are you doing home?"

"Oh…honestly…I can't stop thinking about your box of manuscripts," he said grinning. "I left early and I was kinda hoping you'd be home."

She grimaced. "I wish I could say the same. I've just been to lunch with my Dad and Uncle Rob and all they can talk about is funerals and Wills."

"Ah…I'm sorry, Lana. We don't have to do this now, we can leave it 'til you're ready."

"No, no, I'm ready. I'm kind of curious to find out what they say," she said shaking her head. “Give me five. I’ll go change and grab the box.”

“Brilliant!”

Chapter 8

Manchester 1968

Lana and Toby settled at the kitchen table with the box between them. She was intrigued to find out what the pages would reveal, and if Toby could indeed translate them. Toby pulled on a pair of cotton gloves and grinned at her.

"Alright, I'm ready, let's open it."

"I'm so excited to see if you can read these," she said as she unlocked the box and lifted the lid.

He reached in and pulled out all the manuscript pages. "I thought we'd see what's in here before we begin," he said as he began sifting through them, placing each page carefully to one side as he scanned them. He stopped and stared at the page in front of him before looking up at her and grinning. "This is brilliant. Look, this is like a vocabulary list. It's going to make it possible to decipher the unknown writing…whoever wrote these, knew we'd need this."

"That's incredible," said Lana leaning forward and peering at the page. It made absolutely no sense to her, but if Toby said it was brilliant, then it must be. She sat back and stared at him. “Is that the key? You know, my Nan said this was some sort of key.”

“Exactly,” he said drawing in a breath. “I think I’ll start with this page here and see if I can translate it for you.” He reached for his books and pen and paper. “Although, it might be better to translate the vocabulary first…I don’t know.”

Lana fiddled with the key in her hand, running the smooth crystal around between her fingers. It was a pretty thing and colours glinted off it in every direction as she twirled it around. “No, let’s find out what some of it says first. It might not be worth translating.”

Toby paused with his pen poised and glanced up at her. “Alright, but I’m hoping it’s something interesting. Why else would they’ve kept them?”

Lana shrugged. “I hope you’re right. Coffee?”

“No…I’d hate to spill any on these,” he said before returning his attention to the page in front of him.

Lana made coffee for herself and sat quietly watching Toby work. She tried to read what he was writing, but she couldn’t work it out reading it upside down, so she gave up. She sat back in her chair, waiting with anticipation, wondering that if this was the key to a manuscript, where was it? *Would there be any clues in the writing?* She had no idea where you'd even start to look for an old manuscript. *A museum perhaps?* It seemed unlikely that they'd ever be able to find it. Perhaps this was all just a waste of time.

An hour or so later the phone rang and she sprang to her feet. "Hello, it's Lana" she said putting the receiver to her ear.

"Hi, Kitten," came her father's voice. "I've just got home from the funeral directors."

"Did everything go okay?"

"Yes, the funeral's arranged for ten o'clock Thursday. I just thought I'd let you know."

"Thanks, Dad. At St Mary's?"

"Yes. It'll be a graveside service and we'll go back to her place afterwards. Aunt Rose is arranging morning tea."

"Is there anything I can do?"

"No, no, and I'll understand if you don't want to come to the graveside."

Lana didn't want to even think about her Nan going into that dark hole let alone be there. She swallowed and steeled herself. "No, I'll be there. I want to say goodbye."

"Well, if you're sure, I'll see you there on Thursday. Call me if you need anything."

"I will. Thanks, Dad," she said before putting down the receiver. She stood there staring into space for several moments. It was all so final.

"Is everything okay?" asked Toby.

"Yeah," she said turning around. She sighed as she sat back down. "My Nan's funeral will be on Thursday morning. I'm just not sure I'm ready for it."

He grimaced and nodded. "It's never easy, Lana, and you were close. What time?"

"Ten o'clock at St Mary's. Are you going to come?"

"I'd like to," he said with a nod. "It just depends." He smiled before turning his attention back to his notebook. "I'm nearly done with this paragraph and it's amazing."

"Really?" said Lana sitting up straight and peering at his writing. "What does it say?"

"Just give me a few more minutes," he said grinning.

Lana swivelled around as the front door opened and Di came stomping down the hallway. She dumped her bag on the sideboard and came into the kitchen looking like a thundercloud.

"What's wrong?" said Lana with concern etched on her face.

"You won't believe it," said Di as she lifted the kettle and then turned it on. "My hours have been cut." She groaned as she pulled a mug from the cupboard. "They've cut me to three days a week. God…I needed that money."

"You'll be right," said Toby glancing at her. "You know Mum and Dad'll cover you."

"That's not the point," she said glaring at him. "I'm trying to save for a car, and I can't do that on three days a week."

"Maybe you could pick up something else," said Lana getting to her feet. She wrapped her arm around Di's shoulders and squeezed. "It's not that bad."

Di smiled weakly. "Yeah, maybe. But it's just so unfair. I thought I was doing really well. In fact, I've been expecting to get a promotion. Mr Porter's been praising my work and says I'm a natural seamstress."

"Here, let me make the coffee," said Lana gently pushing her aside. "Want one, Toby?"

"Yeah."

Di slumped down at the table. "Maybe I should move down to London with Mum and Dad. I'm sure things are better down there."

"What, and leave us?" said Lana with feigned hurt. "And what about Russell?"

Di grinned. "He is kinda cute."

"And put up with Mum?" said Toby pulling a face. "You'd hate it down there with Mum asking you a thousand questions every time you left the house."

Di groaned and put her head in her hands. "Yeah, that's not the answer."

"So, how's the translation going? Have you done it?" asked Lana as she put two mugs of steaming coffee on the table. "Toby's been translating some of the writing."

"Ooh," said Di brightening up immediately. "What does it say?"

"Well, it's rather intriguing," said Toby carefully putting the manuscript page back in the box. He closed it and pushed it to the end of the table before picking up his notebook. "Shall I read it to you?"

"Yes, please," said Lana sitting down with her coffee in hand. "This is so exciting."

"Alright, here goes. Bear in mind that I may not have it completely right." He drew in a breath. "One cavern holds an orb. I am yet to transcribe the tablets in this room, but I believe they hold the key to understanding their powers."

"Who do you think wrote this?" Di interrupted.

"No idea," said Toby shaking his head before he continued reading. "The orb emits a strange humming sound and I am fearful of getting too close. From what I have read, the library holds the history of these people. They settled here a millennium ago and flourished for centuries before a calamity befell them." Toby paused and frowned at the page. "That may not be right…it might not be calamity, but something like that."

"A library…far out," said Lana before taking a sip of her coffee. "I honestly didn't think these would be that interesting."

"I know," said Toby grinning. "I thought they'd be about medicinal plants or something."

"What sort of library has tablets?" said Di with an unimpressed look.

"An old one," said Toby. "Like the Egyptians, they wrote on stone tablets."

"Do you think it could be Egyptian?" Lana's eyes widened as she glanced from Di to Toby.

"No, this isn't in hieroglyphs, so they're not Egyptian. Anyway, there's more," said Toby returning to his notes.

"They simply vanished. I know this sounds unbelievable, that an entire civilisation could disappear. Before then, they built this monument to themselves, underground. It is carved, smooth to the touch, out of the very bedrock. How they were able to do this is beyond my understanding."

Toby put down his notebook and grinned. "This is so cool. And there must be some reason these were handed down through your family, Lana. This isn't just a key to a manuscript."

"An underground library without any books sounds kind of boring to me," said Di with a groan. "Sometimes you're such a nerd, Toby."

"Sticks and stones, Di."

"Well, I for one think this is really cool. Imagine an underground library carved by an ancient civilisation. It's fascinating," said Lana.

"Well, I'm glad you two think it's a gas," said Di getting to her feet. "I'm going to run a bath."

"Ignore her," said Toby after Di had departed. "She's just bummed because of her job."

"Yeah, I know. So, what do we do next? Ooh, wouldn't it be cool if this tells us where the library is?"

"Yeah, but I wouldn't get your hopes up," said Toby scratching his chin. "I get the feeling that would be well hidden, even if it still exists." He grinned as he put his notebook on top of the box. "I'll do some more tomorrow if you like."

"Oh, yes, please. I want to know what they all say"

"So do I."

***

Thursday dawned bright and sunny and Lana thought the day had a cheek being so happy. A grey gloomy day would've matched her mood so much better. Her dream from the night before was still vivid in her mind. It was unusual because she rarely remembered her dreams, but this one was different. She replayed it over in her mind as she readied herself. She thought she'd been in her Nan's house but she wasn't sure. It was dark, with the only illumination coming from a flickering candle. She paused as she tried to grab hold of it before it evaporated. She'd been rummaging through cupboards and drawers looking for something. *But what?* The more she tried to remember, the more the dream was fading. Finally, she shrugged and gave up.

St Mary's was only a short distance from home and she hoped the walk might improve her spirits. It didn't. She walked up the path towards the church and immediately spied a group of people in the churchyard beyond the yew trees. She paused and drew in a breath before making her way between the headstones.

Before she reached them, she saw her Nan's coffin, draped in a red cloth with a spray of flowers covering the top of it. Tears came unbidden. *God this was going to be awful*. She pulled her handkerchief from her pocket and dabbed at her eyes. She shouldn't have worn mascara, she was going to look like a panda before the day was done. Slowly, she approached the small group.

"Kitten," called her father when he saw her. He walked over and wrapped his arms around her, pecking the top of her head.

She clung to him as tears welled in her eyes. "Hey, Dad."

"It'll be alright," he crooned.

Keeping his arm around her he guided her over to the graveside. "Uncle Rob, Aunt

Rose and Pat are here already. Morris should be along soon."

She briefly hugged her aunt and uncle and murmured hello to Pat. There were a few more people here than Lana had expected. Some old friends of her Nan's, who she knew by sight and a smattering of others who she had no idea who they were. There was no sign of Toby. She'd hoped he'd come but understood he might not have been able to get away. Di had made it clear she wasn't coming. She couldn't afford to take any time off work.

Lana positioned herself towards the back of the group while they waited for Father O'Malley, who was yet to arrive.

"Are you coming back to the house afterwards?" asked her father sidling up beside her.

"No. I only got the morning off." She had no idea how she was going to get through the afternoon in the typing pool.

"That's a shame."

The silence stretched between them and Lana was glad her father had nothing more to say. She didn't want to talk about this or even think about it. She pulled her coat more firmly about herself as the breeze tugged at her hair. She just wanted it to be over.

"Hey, Lana."

She looked up and smiled as she saw Toby approaching. She was so relieved to see him. “Hi Toby, thanks for coming.”

He gave her cheek a peck and smiled. “I wanted to come.” He turned to her father with a sober expression. “Hello, Mr Fuller. I’m sorry for your loss.”

“Thank you, Toby.”

Finally, Lana spotted Father O’Malley coming towards them in his flowing robes. He greeted the mourners before taking up his position at the head of the grave. He folded his hands in front of him and smiled benignly. “Let us pray.”

Lana bowed her head and let the words wash over her. She wasn’t particularly religious, in fact, she couldn’t remember the last time she went to church, but there was some comfort in the rhythm of Father’s voice.

She couldn’t hold back her tears as Father O’Malley began the eulogy. She dabbed at her eyes with her handkerchief but it was rather ineffectual. His voice droned on and Lana got lost in her own thoughts. She wasn’t ready for any of this.

She raised her tear-stained face as Toby nudged her in the ribs. “There’s someone hiding behind those bushes. Do you know who it is?” he whispered.

She glanced towards the small clump of bushes and noticed that a man was half-concealed behind them. “No,” she said shaking her head. “Probably the gravedigger.” Her voice caught in her throat at the words.

“Hmm, maybe.”

“Let us pray,” said Father O’Malley and lowering his head, he began to recite the Lord's Prayer.

Lana turned her attention back to the gathering, putting all thoughts of the gravedigger out of her mind. “Amen,” she murmured when Father was finished.

Her father kissed her cheek. “I’m sorry you’re not coming back to the house, but I understand.”

“Thanks, Dad,” she said wiping her eyes once again.

“I’ll call you tonight.”

“Alright.”

“Come on, Lana I’ll walk with you,” said Toby looping his arm in hers.

“Thanks. Bye, Dad.”

Well, that was that she thought as she walked arm-in-arm with Toby through the graveyard. She couldn’t wait to get out of there.

Chapter 9

Monastery of Santa Maria de Huerta
Spain 1597

Alonso was leaving the chapel following morning prayers when Brother Benito approached him.

"Good morning, Brother Alonso," he said with a smile. "Padre has returned and I told him you wanted an audience."

"Thank you, Brother Benito." He no longer needed an audience with Padre having decided what to do, but he had no intention of sharing that information with Benito.

Benito took a couple of steps away from him before turning back. "He's waiting for you now."

"Then I shall not keep him."

What reason was he going to give Padre for wanting an audience? He had no idea but prayed he'd come up with one before he reached his office. He'd been in a state the night he'd dreamed of Miguel's death and had been desperate to tell Padre, but now…everything had changed. Not that he was confident Diego and he would unravel the writing, but he was going to put in every effort to do so. And until he knew what this was about, he wasn't going to tell Padre or anyone else what he was doing.

His pace slowed as he neared the Abbot's office and he tried to think of a good enough reason. He stopped at the Abbot's door and drew in a breath before knocking. He could tell him about the dreams, perhaps that would be enough not to raise too many questions.

"Come," came a muffled voice.

He swallowed as he opened the door and stepped into Padre's office.

"Good morning, Brother Alonso, won't you sit down?" said Padre sweeping his hand towards a hard wooden chair.

"Thank you for seeing me, Padre," said Alonso as he seated himself.

"Brother Benito seemed to think you needed to speak to me about a matter of some urgency," he said with a frown. "I went looking for you late last night when I returned, but I couldn't find you. I thought you might've been working late in your scriptorium."

Alonso did his best to keep his face passive. So that's who had tried the door last night. "I'm sorry you went to so much trouble,

Padre. I was walking the corridors trying to clear my mind."

"The dreams persist then?"

"Yes," he lied. He hadn't had a single dream since Miguel's death and he didn't expect to have any more. But he couldn't think of any other reason that would require an urgent audience. He drew in a breath and slowly let it out. "I have not been able to put them out of my mind."

"Perhaps another day in prayer would help," said Padre leaning back in his chair. "They are just dreams, Brother Alonso. You must remind yourself of this – they hold no meaning."

"I'll try, Padre."

"Good. Now how goes your work? Have you completed transcribing Brother Miguel's writing?"

"Not quite, but I will have them done before his next despatch arrives."

"Excellent news. I expect his next despatch will arrive in the next week or two. The sooner you finish the sooner we can have the codex bound and you can put this matter behind you." He pinned Alonso with his gaze. "I'm concerned these writings are having an adverse effect on you, but I cannot give the work to another. I'm sorry."

"I understand," said Alonso with a nod. "I will spend the day in prayer and do my utmost to complete the work."

"Thank you, Brother Alonso. Please seek me out if you require further guidance."

"I will," he said getting to his feet. "Thank you, Padre."

He left the Abbot's office with a sinking feeling in the pit of his stomach. He'd just lied to Padre and it didn't sit well with him. A day in prayer asking forgiveness may not be enough to rid him of the guilt.

***

Over the next two weeks, Diego and Alonso poured over Miguel's writing, deciphering and translating. Progress was slow and Alonso wasn't even sure if what they'd translated was correct. He had covered one whole page in deciphered words, but he had no confidence in their accuracy. He feared they'd never get to a point of being able to translate even one page.

"This is odd," said Diego raising his brows.

Alonso peered over his shoulder. "What?"

"This word isn't in the strange language, but I don't know what it is."

"It's Hebrew," Alonso said slowly. "That is odd."

"What does it say?"

"Ancient."

"Ah, well, that's what I would've expected," said Diego with a grin. "So that's good. Maybe there isn't a word for ancient in whatever language this is."

"Maybe," said Alonso scratching his quill across the parchment. "So, we have, 'the smooth caverns were carved from rock by ancient'. I think we're getting somewhere. What's the next word, Diego."

"Hmm, I'd expect it to be people. Have we deciphered that?"

"Yes," said Alonso scanning his page of deciphered words until he found it. "Here, does this look the same?"

Diego shook his head. "No."

Alonso rubbed his hands down his face. "I think we've done enough for tonight. I can't think straight anymore."

Diego exhaled. "I agree."

He sounded frustrated and Alonso put his hand on his shoulder. "I couldn't do this without you, Diego. I know it's harder than you thought it would be."

"After weeks of doing this, all we have is a few fragmented paragraphs," he said with a groan. "I really thought we'd have some idea what this was about by now."

"I think Brother Miguel put too much faith in me," said Alonso as he put the parchments in the drawer and locked it. "Come on, let's call it a night. I can barely keep my eyes open."

The two made their way back to the dormitories, keeping to the shadows. Alonso shared Diego's frustrations. Miguel clearly thought he'd given them enough to decipher the writing, but Alonso doubted it. Diego was right. Nearly three weeks and all they had were a couple of fragmented paragraphs that made no sense.

Alonso climbed into his cot and spent the rest of the night tossing and turning. He must've fallen asleep at some point because he awoke with a start. The gloomy grey of dawn filled his small cell, and he groaned as he swung his legs over the side of his cot. He rubbed his hands down his face - he wished the dreams would return. He was sure the answers were in that large cavern filled with metal tablets.

Pushing aside his frustrations, he readied himself and made his way to the chapel for morning prayers. He spent longer than usual at prayer. It eased his mind and he could feel the tension leaving his body. By the time he got off his knees, the chapel was empty and he headed for his scriptorium feeling lighter and more optimistic.

He had one more page left to transcribe, and so he set to work. The words made no more sense to him now than they had a year ago when he'd started transcribing Miguel's writing. A few of them were now familiar, but without his list, he had no idea what they meant.

A soft knock on his door startled him. "One moment," he called as he quickly put his work in the drawer. "Come in."

"Good morning, Brother Alonso," said Pedro as he entered the small room.

"Brother Pedro."

"A delivery has arrived for you," he said putting a large leather satchel on his desk.

"Thank you," said Alonso running his fingers over the soft leather. He prayed Miguel had sent him some further clues, but he didn't hold much hope.

Pedro glanced around the small room before settling his gaze on Alonso. "If you ever need assistance, I'd be happy to offer some."

Alonso shook his head. “That is most kind, but I’m sworn to silence on this matter. You know that.”

“Of course,” he said and with a slight bow he left, closing the door behind him.

Alonso didn’t entirely trust Pedro. He’d never done anything to make him feel that way, it was just a feeling he had. Of course, he was the eyes and ears of Brother Benito and reported everything to him. That was enough for him to distrust Pedro.

He unstrapped the satchel and pulled out a small pile of pages. They were wrapped in parchment with a wax seal that didn’t look like it had been tampered with. He broke the seal and pulled off the wrapping revealing Miguel’s pages. They didn’t look any different to the others – strange writing and drawings. He put them on his desk and began sorting through them until he found what he was looking for.

A wide grin spread across his face as he pulled aside four pages. Miguel had written him lists of words in Latin, Greek and the strange writing. The sort of vocabulary that he and Diego had been trying to create. He could hardly wait to get started deciphering, and to show them to Diego. He knew his friend would be as delighted as he was.

He opened the drawer and lifted out the pages they'd been trying to decipher before putting the new pages safely away. He prepared a quill and placed his pot of ink on his desk before reaching for the vocabulary list.

The paragraph that he and Diego had partly deciphered was the first one he started work on. They had the first few words, and he prayed that with the new vocabulary, he'd be able to decipher the rest.

He spent the entire day meticulously translating the paragraph until he was satisfied that he had it right. At least it made sense, and he could hardly wait to share it with Diego. He left the scriptorium with a light heart and full of optimism. He also understood now why Miguel had told him that these writings were of the utmost importance to Spain. He could never have imagined such a possibility.

Chapter 10

Manchester 1968

Lana had just settled herself in front of the TV when there was a knock on the door. She frowned as she got to her feet and made her way into the hall. "Who is it?"

"Me," came her father's muffled voice.

She unlocked the door and opened it. "I thought you were just going to call me," she said kissing his cheek. "You didn't need to come around, I'm fine."

"I had to come and check on you," he said stepping over the threshold. "Are Toby and Di home?"

"No," she said closing the door. "Toby's down the pub and Di's out with Russell. Why? Is everything okay?"

"No, not really. Your Nan's house has been broken into," he said following her into the lounge.

"What? When?" She flicked off the TV and stared at him.

"We don't know. No one's been there for a few days, but when we all went back there after the funeral it was clear someone had broken in. They've ransacked the place. Drawers and cupboards have been gone through…there's stuff everywhere."

"Oh my God. What did they take?" Her dream from the night before came rushing back and she gasped. It was exactly what she'd dreamed of, *but how could that be?*

"I have no idea," he said with a shrug. "The police are looking into it, but we have no way of knowing what they took. Her jewellery box was still there, and there's nothing obvious missing." Her father stopped and stared at her. "Are you alright, Kitten?"

"Ah…yeah, no," she said grappling with indecision. "It's probably nothing."

"What?"

"Well, I had this really weird dream. I thought I was at Nan's house and I was searching for something. I rummaged through her cupboards and drawers. It's just like what you described, Dad. How can that be?" She stared at him with her brows raised. "I swear it was just a dream."

"I don't think it was just a dream, Kitten." He stared at her for several long seconds. "Have you had dreams like that before?"

Lana shook her head. “Ones that came true…no, but I’ve had a few odd dreams since Nan died. They’re too fuzzy to explain.” She didn’t know how to describe the odd sensation, that felt like she had some sort of connection to something, or someone.

The box. She knew her Nan didn’t want her to tell him, but there seemed to be no good reason not to, and maybe that’s what the burglar was looking for. The idea scared her. “You know the box Nan gave me?”

“Yes,” he said slowly as his eyes watched her face intently.

“It wasn’t empty.”

His eyes widened. “Alright. Do you think that’s got something to do with this?”

“I don’t know, Dad, but it seems odd that a burglar would break in and not take Nan’s jewellery box.”

“True,” he said with a nod. “So, what was in it?”

“It’ll be easier to show you,” she said with a smile. “Wait here and I’ll go get it.”

She hurried upstairs and grabbed the box and the gloves sitting on her dressing table. She paused in her bedroom doorway and drew in a breath. *Well, it was too late now, she’d told him. She trusted him, he was her father for God’s sake.* She convinced herself that Nan’s reason for not telling him wasn't important. She went back down to the lounge and placed the box on the coffee table. She unlocked it and slipped the key into her pocket.

"You can't touch what's inside without gloves on, or Toby will kill you," she said handing him a pair of white cotton gloves.

"Well, alright, I wouldn't want to upset Toby." He grinned as he slipped on the gloves before opening the box. "Oh…what are these?"

"They're old manuscript pages," said Lana sitting down on the couch. "Toby's translated one of them, and it's so incredible. There's some library, somewhere underground, made by these ancient people."

Her father carefully lifted the pages from the box one by one. "These are very old, and probably worth a lot of money. I mean, a lot of money."

"Yeah, Toby thought so too. I don't know about a lot of money though, Dad."

"Oh, trust me, Kitten, these are incredibly rare." He put them back in the box before joining her on the couch. "I can have these translated for you in a matter of a day or two."

"Really?"

"Yes, I have contacts with a lot of dealers of antiques and such."

"I don't know. Toby's kind of enjoying it I think."

"Well, I for one would like to know more about this library you mentioned. That sounds incredible."

"Yeah, it does. Nan told me these pages were some kind of key. I thought they might be the key to reading the whole manuscript if we knew where it was."

"Well, I think you may be right about our burglar. I bet they were looking for this, and I don't mean to scare you, but they might come here next."

"You think so?" she said in an alarmed voice.

He wrapped his arm around her shoulders and squeezed. "I hope not…but they were looking for something, and I think that something was this."

Lana had to agree with her father's assessment. "Maybe I should put it in a safety deposit box or something."

"Good idea," he said getting to his feet. "But let me get these translated first."

"Alright," she said slowly nodding.

"How about a coffee?" said her father. "I'll wait with you 'til Toby gets home."

“Thanks, Dad, that would make me feel better.” She got to her feet and hugged him. “I love you.”

“I love you too, Kitten.”

***

Lana got to work early the next morning. Thank God it was Friday. It had been an awful week and she was looking forward to the weekend. She put her bag in the bottom drawer of her desk and removed the cover from her typewriter. She was carefully folding it when Mrs Clausen approached her with a pile of letters. She dropped them in her tray and smiled.

“How are you, Lana?”

“I’m fine, thank you, Mrs Clausen,” she replied with a smile.

“Good…you’ve had a trying week I’m sure, but you’ve got a lot of work to catch up on,” she said with a stern look. “The other girls have done some for you…you should thank them later.”

“I will.”

Mrs Clausen moved off and Lana slumped down in her chair. She’d never get through that pile of typing today. Blowing out her breath she put the cover in the drawer and loaded her typewriter with fresh paper. Best to get on with it.

It was mid-morning when Mrs Clausen came by her desk again with a deep frown on her face. “There’s a phone call for you, in my office,” she said with a forbidding stare. “As you well know, staff are not permitted phone calls. It’s only at your father’s insistence that I’m permitting it. Make sure it doesn’t happen again.”

“Yes, Mrs Clausen,” said Lana getting to her feet. “I’m really sorry.”

“Hmph,” she said. “Don’t tarry.”

Lana hurried between the desks of the typing pool and into Mrs Clausen’s office. She picked up the receiver. “Hi, Dad. Please don’t call me at work.”

“Sorry, Kitten. I wouldn’t have if it wasn’t important. Can you meet Uncle Rob and me at the lawyer's office in your lunch hour?”

“I don’t know, Dad, I’ve got a load of work to do.”

“Please…we can’t get the Will read without you, and we need to get things sorted.”

Why did they need her? “Alright, but I can’t be late back. Where?” she said with a groan.

“Robinson and Sons on Church Street. I’ll meet you there at twelve-thirty.”

"Okay, bye."

She put down the phone and hurried back to her desk. The only reason she could think of why they would need her was if Nan had left her something. That seemed rather odd. If she'd wanted her to have anything else she would've given it to her with the box, surely? She did her best to put thoughts of her Nan's Will out of her mind as she got back to work - not with a lot of success.

***

She didn't get away from the office until nearly twelve-thirty, and she hurried as fast as she could in her heels down the street to Church Street. By the time she arrived outside Robinson and Son's office, she was panting and had a stitch in her side.

"Hey, thanks for coming," said her father as soon as he spied her.

"That's okay," she said gasping for air. "Mrs Clausen's on the warpath and I can't be late back."

"This won't take long," he assured her as they went inside. "But, Mr Robinson wouldn't discuss the Will with us without you."

"That's odd," she said shaking her head.

"What do you know about this?" said Rob turning on her as soon as they entered.

He sounded angry and Lana was taken aback by his tone. "Nothing. I'm just as surprised as you."

"Please tell Mr Robinson we're here to see him," said her father to the blonde receptionist. "Leave off, Rob," he said turning his attention back to them. "I don't think Lana knows anything about this."

"No, I don't."

"Forgive me if I don't believe that." His angry tone hadn't abated and he glared at her. "It seems to me that you've wheedled your way into my mother's affairs."

Lana was shocked by his words and stood gaping at him.

"Lana has done no such thing. You know very well..."

"Mr Robinson will see you now," interrupted the receptionist. "Second room down the hall."

Rob turned on his heel and marched down the hall leaving Lana and her father to follow in his wake.

"Ignore him," whispered her father. "He's not himself."

Lana had to agree. She'd never seen him act like this before and she was rather disconcerted. She followed her father into the office and took a seat. The small office was lined with bookshelves, crammed with legal books and papers. She'd never been into a lawyer's office before and was intrigued by all the volumes.

A few moments later, a short squat man with a thatch of greying hair came bustling in. "Good afternoon, gentlemen. I presume this is Miss Fuller? I'm Alan Robinson, your grandmother's lawyer, I'm so glad you could come in at such short notice." He didn't seem to need a reply, as he sat down and grabbed a file from the pile on his desk. Putting on his glasses he opened it and retrieved what Lana presumed to be her Nan's Will. "Now, that you're all here I can inform you of her wishes."

He glanced up at them and smiled. "Bear in mind that, until the death certificate is in hand, we can't begin to deal with the estate."

"We understand," said her father.

"Good. Well, Mrs Fuller has requested that her estate be divided into three parts. The first part pertains to the disposal of her house on Montague Street. She's bequeathed the property to Lana, Robert and Ian Fuller, with Lana receiving a forty percent share, and Robert and Ian a thirty percent share each."

"What?" said Rob glaring at Mr Robinson and then at Lana. "You little witch." His tone was angry and full of malice.

Her father grabbed Lana's hand and squeezed and she smiled weakly at him. She had never heard Uncle Rob raise his voice before, let alone be so angry – and never directed at her. A part of her didn't blame him. She certainly hadn't expected to get a share of her Nan's house, and she was quite sure her father and Uncle Rob hadn't expected it either. She wasn't sure how she felt about it at all.

"Mr Fuller, such outbursts are quite unnecessary," said Mr Robinson frowning. "I can assure you, your mother wasn't influenced in any way and was of quite a sound mind when she gave us her final instructions."

"I don't believe it," said Uncle Rob getting to his feet. "And I'll be damned if I'll sit here any longer and listen to this drivel."

Mr Robinson rose to his feet, looking quite undaunted by Rob's behaviour. "It makes little difference to me, Mr Fuller. I have fulfilled my legal obligations by inviting you all here today. Your leaving will change nothing."

"We'll see about that," said Uncle Rob before storming out the door.

Mr Robinson sighed as he sat back down.

"I'm sorry about my brother."

"It's not your fault, Mr Fuller, but he's clearly quite unhappy with your mother's wishes. I expect he'll lodge a challenge."

"Yes, I think you're right."

"Now, onto the second part. She has bequeathed her 1961 Mini Cooper to her granddaughter, Lana. The remainder of her estate, which consists of investments and cash in the bank is to be divided equally between, Lana, Robert and Ian." Mr Robinson passed a copy of the Will to each of them. "This is an uncertified copy, and is purely for your reference."

"Thank you," said Lana's father. "What happens next?"

"As soon as I receive a copy of the death certificate, I will commence fulfilling your mother's instructions, and pay any and all debts relating to her estate," said Mr Robinson closing the file in front of him. "Call me if you have any questions."

"Thank you, we will." Ian got to his feet and ushered Lana from the office.

As soon as they stepped out onto the footpath he gathered her in his arms and hugged her tight. “Ignore, Rob, he’s just hurt. He’ll get over it.”

“I swear I knew nothing about this,” said Lana shaking her head. “I can’t believe it.”

“I know, I believe you, Kitten,” he said letting her go. “I know you’ve got to get back to work. We’ll talk about this later.”

“Okay, Dad,” she said nodding.

Chapter 11

Monastery of Santa Maria de Huerta
Spain 1597

No sooner had Alonso and Diego settled themselves in the scriptorium than Alonso placed his deciphered page on the desk in front of his friend.

"I'll read it to you," said Alonso with a note of excitement. "With Brother Miguel's lists, I'm sure we'll be able to decipher all the writing."

"Well, get on with it then," said Diego with a grin. "I want to know what it says."

"Right, well, we got the beginning right," said Alonso picking up the parchment. "It says 'the smooth caverns were carved from rock by ancient people.'"

"I can't believe we got that right," interjected Diego, his face alight with excitement. "Sorry, read on."

"'They have left a library of their civilisation in the form of metal tablets. The pages I have sent you are of tablets I have copied so far. They tell of an ancient civilisation of people far more advanced than us'." Alonso paused and drew in a deep breath. "I'm sure I saw this in my dreams."

Diego reached up and squeezed his arm. "I'm sorry Brother Miguel gave his life for this."

"So am I," said Alonso with a nod. Breathing in, he continued reading. "'They had the power to heal people of the most deadly diseases. I have some idea how they did this. There are some strange crystals and artefacts here that I believe they used to heal.' Well, that's it. What do you think?"

"It's so intriguing. Imagine being able to heal people like that," said Diego with a look of amazement. "Let's get to work and decipher the next paragraph. I hope Brother Miguel worked out how they did that."

"So do I," said Alonso pulling up a chair beside Diego. "Right, here's the lists." He pulled them from the drawer and placed them on the desk between them. "You read the Greek and tell me what it is and I'll find the translation."

"Right," said Diego.

They worked on the translation for several hours, before Alonso called a halt. He could barely keep his eyes open or think straight. "We'll finish this tomorrow night."

"Good idea," said Diego with a yawn. "I won't be able to get up in the morning if we work any longer."

Alonso put away the pages before the two of them headed for their respective beds. He was fascinated by what the writing had revealed. An ancient civilisation able to heal any disease. It was astounding.

***

Alonso was impatient for morning prayers to be done so he could begin work. He and Diego had partially deciphered another passage last night, which had something to do with how they healed people. He prayed Miguel had worked out how they were able to do that. He couldn't imagine what a difference that would make to the war with the Dutch Republic. If they could heal their soldiers, Spain would be invincible.

He spent the rest of the morning bent over his desk deciphering the next paragraph. The writing looked rushed and Miguel had only written it in Greek and the strange language. He was frustrated at his slow progress. Without the Latin translation, he had no idea what it said. He leaned back in his chair and stretched. It would take years to translate all of the writing, and he didn't have that much time. No doubt, as soon he'd transcribed the last lot of pages, Padre would order him to bind them and they'd be sent to the monastery library, and he'd never see them again. He knew there would be no more despatches from Miguel.

There was a knock on his door followed by the muffled voice of Brother Pedro. "Brother Alonso, may I come in?"

"One moment." He put the pages in the drawer and locked it before slipping the key into his pocket. "Come."

The door opened and Brother Pedro smiled and nodded. "The Abbot has requested your presence."

"Of course," said Alonso getting to his feet. "I'll attend to him at once."

He left the scriptorium and hurried along the corridor to Padre's office. Alonso had no idea why he wanted to see him. Surely, he had assuaged his concerns at their last meeting. His heart began to race as it dawned on him that Padre might know about his and Diego's clandestine meetings. Maybe they'd been seen. *How would he explain that*? He couldn't.

He knocked on the Abbot's door and waited until he heard Padre call out, "Come."

"You wanted to see me, Padre?"

"Yes, Brother Alonso. Please, won't you sit down?"

The Abbot was wearing a rather serious frown and Alonso's stomach did a somersault. His mind was racing as he tried to think of some plausible reason for his midnight meetings. Perhaps he could say he was teaching Diego to read Latin, although for what possible reason he couldn't think.

"I'm afraid I have some very bad news," said Padre shaking his head.

Alonso relaxed a little – perhaps this had nothing to do with Diego. "What news, Padre?"

"I received word from Father Acevedo…Brother Miguel has apparently been killed. He didn't have any other information than that."

"Killed?" said Alonso with feigned surprise. "Poor Brother Miguel to come to such an end."

"Indeed, it's a tragedy, not just for Brother Miguel, but for all of Spain. He has done much to send us words from the new world." He paused. "I know you have been concerned for his welfare for some time, but I assure you, his death has nothing to do with the work you're doing."

"Thank you, Padre. That gives me some comfort."

"I understand you will need some time to grieve our Brother, but I cannot give you more than two weeks. You will replace Brother Miguel in New Spain. Brother Pedro will take over your work."

It took a moment for the Abbot's words to sink in. "You're sending me to New Spain?"

"Yes. You leave for Valencia in two weeks. Brother Benito is making the arrangements and he will accompany you as far as the port."

Alonso's heart was pounding. He never imagined he'd be sent to take Miguel's place, and he was scared of what he'd find when he got there. "You do me a great honour, Padre." His words belied the thoughts whirling around in his mind.

"Ready yourself, Brother Alonso, and we'll talk again soon. I will prepare letters for you and provide full instructions soon."

"Thank you, Padre." Alonso got to his feet and bowed. "May I speak of Brother Miguel to others?"

"Not yet," he said with a shake of his head. "I will formally announce the news before evening prayers."

Alonso bowed again and left the Abbot's office. His mind was racing with a million thoughts all at once. *What was he going to do?* He couldn't allow the deciphered pages to end up in Brother Pedro's possession. He couldn't trust Brother Pedro. He might be able to take some of them with him, but not all. Perhaps he could hide them until he returned, *but where?*

He settled back down at his desk, determined to decipher whatever he could in the time he had left. He was distracted and had difficulty concentrating, but by supper time he had nearly translated another paragraph. He sat back in his chair and read over the words with a feeling of rising excitement.

> *One of the tablets speaks of their healers and the tools and crystals they use to heal their people. I have found one such apparatus that they speak of, but it is beyond my understanding. I have sent it to the Abbot of our order in the hopes that our healers can find some understanding. The page that describes its use is in this despatch.*

There was more to the paragraph and, ignoring his grumbling stomach, he bent back over his desk. So, Miguel had made some progress in determining how these ancient people had the power to heal. An hour later he had translated the rest of it, and immediately began sorting through the latest lot of pages. According to Miguel, he'd translated a page into Latin and wanted him to give it to Padre. It had drawings of six people lying prone, surrounded by what he thought was light.

It didn't take him long to find it, buried at the bottom of the pile. He was surprised he hadn't noticed it earlier, but he hadn't looked further once he found Miguel's vocabulary. As he read it, he wondered why Miguel hadn't sent it directly to Padre? *Did he want him to know what it said?* He had no idea. The reason for all of this was no clearer than it had been a year ago. He reread the note:

> *The Azu are masters at aligning the body and healing all ills. With the aid of the ashipu, all diseases can be treated and eliminated. Care must be taken when preparing a body for healing. They must be cleansed in both body and spirit before healing can commence. The blessing of God (this is the best translation, although it may not be God) should be sought before*

seeking the Azu. More than one treatment may be needed to fully heal one from the disease. In such cases, the Azu will determine how often the body will need to be treated.

I have not found any detailed instructions on how the apparatus was used, or what aligning the body might involve. I pray our healers may be able to find some understanding.

Alonso packed the pages back in the drawer and locked it. He would share what he'd learned with Diego later tonight, but now, he needed to get supper, if there was any still to be had.

***

Alonso paced the small scriptorium while he waited for Diego. He'd formed a bit of a plan and prayed Diego would oblige in helping him. He had no intention of leaving anything for Brother Pedro to use. He would leave him pages to transcribe, but nothing more. He thought he might only be sent to New Spain for a year or two. He stopped pacing – he wasn't sure he wanted to go at all. He knew Miguel hadn't been killed by the natives, those caverns were dangerous, and what if it killed him too? He ran his hands down his face and then jumped at the sound of Diego tapping on the door.

He let him in and immediately showed him what he'd translated and the note for Padre. "Padre's sending me to New Spain…I leave in two weeks."

"What?" said Diego looking up from the page in his hand. "Is this because Brother Miguel is dead?"

"Yes…but Diego, I cannot leave all of this. Brother Pedro will be taking my place and I don't trust him," he said with a strained expression. "We must hide these until I return."

"I agree," said Diego nodding. "But where? I can't take them, if I get caught with these, Alonso, I'll be expelled."

"I know, and I wouldn't ask you to risk that." He put his hand on Diego's shoulder. "Could you make a small box to hold these papers?"

"Of course."

"Something plain that no one would pay any attention to," said Alonso as he searched for the courage to ask his friend the next question on his mind. "I wondered if you might ask your sister to hide it for us."

"Maria?" said Diego frowning.

"Yes. Doesn't she live in the village?"

"She does," he said slowly nodding.

Alonso waited patiently. He could see Diego was struggling with an answer and he prayed he'd agree. If he didn't, then he had no idea where they might conceal it where it wouldn't be discovered.

Diego put the pages on the desk and turned to face Alonso. "I can't think of a better idea, but I'd have to ask her first. If it was discovered somehow, I don't know what they'd do to her."

Alonso smiled inwardly. "There's no reason anyone would suspect we were hiding anything, let alone that your sister was. Please ask her, Diego."

Diego smiled. "I will." He picked up the pages again and reread them. "What do you think this apparatus is that Brother Miguel speaks of? And crystals? To think they could have such power."

"I have no idea," said Alonso shaking his head before his face lit up with excitement. "I just remembered. Brother Miguel sent me a crystal. I have no idea if it's like the one he's sent to Padre." He went over to the shelf and reached into the jar that held his quills and retrieved a small multi-coloured crystal. "I can’t believe I forgot about this,” he said handing it to Diego.

Diego turned it over in the palm of his hand and as it caught the lamp light, a rainbow of colours emanated from it. “I’ve never seen anything like it.”

“Neither have I,” said Alonso with a look of awe as he watched the crystal. The colours appeared to be moving and changing inside it. “We can’t leave that for Brother Pedro either.”

“No, we can’t.” He handed it back to Alonso. “I’ll get the box made before the end of the week. We can put everything we want to hide, including that, in it.”

“Thank you, Diego. I would be lost without you.” He put the crystal back in the jar and groaned. If only he had more time to translate the strange writing and understand it.

Chapter 12

Manchester 1968

Ian Fuller prided himself on being able to sniff out antiquities both above and below the counter. How his mother had managed to hide the box of manuscript pages from him, right under his nose, was unbelievable to him. He knew this was big, possibly the biggest breakthrough of his life.

He rented office space in a shabby building not far from the river Irwell and his mind was racing as he slipped the key into the lock. First, he had to get the pages translated and copied. He'd promised Lana he could do it in a day or two. He put the box on his desk and slumped down into his well-worn chair. Several people came to mind who could achieve that for him, but if this was as big as he imagined, he had to be careful who he brought in on the deal.

He flipped open his teledex to D and dialled Dave's number. "Come on," he muttered under his breath as the familiar burr of a phone ringing sounded in his ear. "Hi

Peggy, can I speak with Dave?" he said as soon as it was answered. "It's Ian Fuller."

"Morning, Ian," came Dave's voice down the receiver.

"Dave? Sorry, I expected Peggy to answer."

"She's just popped out. What have you got?"

"A library of metal tablets and an old manuscript."

"You have my undivided attention," he said with a chuckle. "Are you serious?"

"Very. But first, I need a few pages translated from Latin into English. It needs to be done in a day or two. Can you do it?"

"Jesus, Ian…a day or two? Give me 'til the end of the week and I'll get it done for you. Now tell me about the manuscript and the library thing."

Ian grinned. He knew Dave wouldn't be able to resist, and more importantly, he could be trusted. "The pages are the key to an old manuscript which is about some library of metal tablets. I'm hoping the pages I've got will tell us where that is. This is big, Dave."

"Wow…drop them off at my office and I'll get right onto it. Do you have any idea where this library is?"

"None at this point, but I'm sure we'll work it out," said Ian tapping his fingers on the lid of the box. "Expect me in ten minutes."

"Okay."

He hung up the phone and reached into the top drawer for a pair of cotton gloves which he slipped on. Lifting the lid of the box he carefully pulled out each page. He counted them and laid them on his desk. He trusted Dave, but still, he needed to make sure he got back exactly what he was giving him. There were nineteen, plus a page translated by Toby. He left that to one side as he began putting them back in the box. He paused and stared at the one in his hand – it looked like something was written in the margin. It was faint and he squinted as he tried to make it out. *Santa Maria de Huerta.*

Grabbing a scrap of paper and a pen he wrote it down. *What or where was that?* It was Spanish without a doubt and he suspected it was a big clue. He finished packing the box and tucked it under his arm as he headed out the door. He was sure this was just the big break he'd been needing.

Dave's office was just a few blocks down and around the corner, a brisk ten-minute walk. Ian had a slight niggling feeling of guilt in the back of his mind as he hurried down the street. He wasn't really doing anything wrong.

He was sure Lana was just as interested in what the manuscript pages said and had no intention of doing anything with them. She probably had no idea how to go about such a thing anyway. He had every intention of returning the box to her, and she needn't know what his intentions were. He pushed all thoughts of Lana aside as he went inside Dave's office building. It was far more upmarket than his own with gleaming glass and a tiled foyer. Dave's office was on the second floor, and he took the stairs, not wanting to wait for the lift.

Dave's receptionist, Peggy greeted him as soon as he entered. "Mornin', Dave's in his office."

"Thanks," he said with a smile as he pushed open the door and went inside. He closed it behind him before turning his attention to Dave.

"I must say you've got me excited," said Dave rubbing his hands together. "Tell me everything."

"Well, I don't know much more than what I told you over the phone," said Ian placing the box on the desk between them. "Take a gander at these."

Dave wasted no time in lifting the lid.

"Gloves," said Ian with a smile.

Dave nodded as he retrieved a pair of gloves and put them on before he started pulling the pages from the box. He whistled as he lay them on the desk. “These are worth a bomb.”

“I know, but we can’t sell them,” said Ian pulling up a chair. “They belong to Lana.”

“Bugger. So, you want me to get these translated? What else?”

“Yeah, and make copies if you can,” said Ian sitting back in his chair. “I noticed some faint writing in one of the margins. It said Santa Maria de Huerta. That’s obviously Spanish, but where and what I don’t know. I think it could be a clue to either the library or the manuscript’s whereabouts.”

“I’ll see what I can find out,” said Dave as he began putting the pages back in the box. “So, you think the rest of the manuscript will lead us to the library?” He looked up at Ian and his blue eyes searched his face. “This could be huge.”

“Yeah. According to Lana, these pages are the key to understanding the original manuscript. I just don’t know where it is. But, if we can find it maybe we can find this library – that’s the real prize.”

“Agreed,” said Dave grinning from ear to ear. “Leave it with me. I’ll get them back to you as soon as I can, and I’ll see what I can find out about this Santa Maria.”

"It's a deal," said Ian getting to his feet. "I'll see what else Lana knows. Keep it quiet, Dave. We don't want anyone else getting wind of this."

"You know me. The master of discretion."

Ian left Dave's office feeling rather pleased with himself. Dave was a true professional when it came to antiquities, and he was sure with his help they'd be rich men.

Chapter 13

Monastery of Santa Maria de Huerta
Spain 1597

Brother Benito opened the door to the Abbot's office and gestured to Alonso. "Padre will see you now."

"Thank you, Brother Benito," said Alonso said with a slight bow.

"Leave us, Brother Benito," called Padre through the open door.

Brother Benito inclined his head before walking slowly down the hall. Alonso watched him for a moment before entering the Abbot's office and closing the door behind him.

"Good afternoon, Brother Alonso."

"Good afternoon, Padre," said Alonso putting the page on the desk. "This note from Miguel is for you, Padre. I don't know why he sent it with my despatch."

"Oh?" he said with a frown.

He reached for the note and Alonso watched him as he read it; his face not giving away any of his thoughts. Alonso hoped he might shed some light on the crystal Miguel had sent him. *Did the apparatus also have a crystal?* He wished he had more time to unravel it all.

"Well, that is curious," said Padre sliding the drawer in his desk open.

He pulled out a circular device made of gold that fitted in the palm of his hand. It appeared to have several concentric wheels engraved with strange symbols. In the very centre was a hollow that seemed to Alonso as if something fitted in there. *Maybe a crystal?*

"To think that this magnificent apparatus has such power. Thank you for bringing this to me, Brother Alonso. I pray our healers can make some sense of it."

"As do I, Padre. It's inconceivable that such power could exist."

Padre smiled as he slipped the device back into the drawer. "Speak of this to no one, Brother Alonso. We must be vigilant against our enemies."

"Of course," he said and with a bow, he turned to leave.

"I trust you've been readying yourself to depart?"

"Yes, Padre," he said turning to face him. "I'll be ready."

"Excellent."

Alonso left the Abbot's office and made his way to the scriptorium. He still had nearly two weeks before departing for the new world, which was plenty of time. Before then, he hoped to translate more of the strange writing and leave Brother Pedro with nothing except a few pages to transcribe.

The vision of the gold apparatus kept going around in his mind. *Did his crystal fit into the device?* Surely Miguel would've said if he thought so. He could only hope that somewhere amongst the writing the multi-coloured crystal would be mentioned.

He spent the next hour sorting through Miguel's latest despatch in case he'd missed something else important. One page stood out from the others. It was written entirely in the strange language, but in Latin, written at the very top, was the word *importans* – important. He set to work with his lists by his elbow.

It was painstaking, translating one word at a time, and after working all afternoon he'd only managed to write one sentence. He was frustrated with his progress and the realisation that he didn't have enough time left to make sense of any of it.

***

A week later, Diego arrived at his scriptorium late at night with a plain wooden box under his arm. He presented it to Alonso with a serious look on his face. “I hope this is what you wanted.”

It was perfectly plain, without embellishments of any kind, with a small bronze lock.

“It’s just as I imagined.”

Diego dropped a small key into Alonso’s hand. “To keep it secure.”

“Thank you, Diego. You have done well to get this done. I hope no one questioned you?” He raised his brows as he looked intently into his friend's face.

“No, I was very discreet,” he said shaking his head.

Alonso placed the box on his desk and opened the lid. He picked up a page and slid it into the bottom of the box; it fitted perfectly. “It’s perfect. Have you spoken with your sister yet?”

“I have. Didn’t you get my note?” said Diego with a nod. “I slipped it under your door.”

“No. I’ll check when I return to my room,” said Alonso.

"It took some convincing…she's more than a little afraid of our Abbot. But, she's agreed to hide it and keep it safe for you."

"God bless her," he said gripping Diego's arm. "Thank you, my friend."

Diego brushed Alonso's gratitude aside with a shrug. "I'm only sorry you're leaving."

"Ah…well, there's nothing I can do about that." He sat down and slid a page across the desk towards Diego. "I finished deciphering this. There's more on this page that I think may explain what happened to the ancient people. Although, I don't fully understand its meaning."

"I wish we had more time," said Diego slumping into the spare chair. "I'm sure Brother Miguel has discovered something significant."

"I agree, but we're running out of time. I'm worried the Abbot may send me away any day now. I can't risk any of this falling into Brother Pedro's hands."

"Let me read, Alonso," said Diego holding up his hand.

Alonso smiled to himself but immediately went quiet. He understood and shared Diego's frustrations, but he was also fearful. This would be their last night trying to understand the pages, he couldn't risk it anymore. The sooner the box was safely secreted, the better.

"What do you think this means?" said Diego with a frown. "How can they depart this time? And the crystals they speak of…?"

"I don't know." Alonso shook his head and leaned forward to read the passage again. Diego was right, it didn't make sense. "I may have deciphered it wrong, but I checked several times, and I couldn't find any other word for it. As for the crystals…I don't know."

Alonso picked up the page and sighed. "We have to pack the box tonight, Diego, and I'm sure Brother Miguel marked this page as important for a reason. I'm not leaving it for Brother Pedro."

He nodded. "And the vocabulary list. You can't leave that either."

"Agreed. Or the ones written in Latin."

They spent the next hour sorting through pages and deciding what should go into the box, and what could stay. They ended up with nineteen pages packed into the box. Alonso retrieved the coloured crystal from his jar of quills and placed it inside with the pages. He was satisfied - he'd left nothing for Brother Pedro except a few pages to transcribe.

"Well, that's it then." He closed the lid and locked the box.

"I'm going to miss our clandestine meetings," said Diego getting to his feet. "Thank you for bringing me into your confidence, Alonso. I've enjoyed it immensely."

Alonso smiled and slapped him on the back. "I couldn't have done any of it without you." He picked up the box and held it out to Diego. "Take it to your sister, tomorrow if you can."

"I will." He tucked the box under his arm and held out his hand for the key. Alonso dropped it into the palm of his hand. "I should attach this to the box somehow so it doesn't get lost."

"Good idea," said Alonso opening the door to the scriptorium. He peered down the dark hall – there was no sign of anyone. "It's all clear."

***

Alonso rose from his knees after saying a final amen. He stretched and rubbed his hands down his face before turning to leave the chapel.

"Brother Alonso, a moment."

He looked sharply towards Brother Benito's voice and nodded. "How can I help you, Brother Benito?"

"Two things. Padre requests an audience. And there's a small sea chest waiting for you in your room. We leave tomorrow after morning prayers."

"Thank you. I shall attend to Padre at once."

So, the time had come. He left the chapel and made his way towards the Abbot's office with his mind in a whirl. He hadn't given much thought to the sea voyage. All he'd been thinking about was the caverns and what he'd find when he got there. His stomach squirmed at the thought of weeks, or maybe even months at sea.

He knocked on the Abbot's door and waited to be invited inside. "Come."

"Good morning, Padre."

The Abbot was busy writing and waved his other hand in his direction. Taking his cue, Alonso perched on the edge of the hard seat and waited. He'd have to get packing if he was going to be ready to leave in the morning. Luckily, he didn't have much. Parchment, quills and ink would be the most important items.

"Good morning," said Padre finally pushing his parchment aside and smiling. "You'll be departing for the coast in the morning. I trust you're prepared?"

"Yes, Padre. It won't take long to pack the few things I'll need."

"Good." He slid a creamy folded and sealed parchment across the desk towards him. "This is for Father Acevedo. I've written to him advising of your imminent arrival, so this letter is just to be sure he extends you every assistance."

"Thank you, Padre."

"To reach your final destination, you will need to travel inland some two hundred miles. An arduous journey, but I'm confident arrangements can be made for you." He sat back in his chair and smiled. "I've requested that Father Acevedo meet you and accompany you from Guayaquil. He knows the terrain better than anyone."

Alonso nodded. His stomach was squirming as he imagined the hardships he'd face. He was not a particularly brave man, or one of adventurous spirit, and the thought of trudging across unknown terrain was a frightening thought.

"I cannot stress enough, Brother Alonso, that you keep your destination an absolute secret from everyone, except Father Acevedo of course. If anyone was to learn of our mission, all would be lost."

"I understand."

"I'm not sure that you do." The Abbot leaned forward in his chair and pinned Alonso with a serious stare. "All will be destroyed if we are discovered."

"No one will learn it from me, Padre. I'll be careful."

"Take extra care, Brother Alonso." He smiled and clasped his hands together. "Now, if you can, send your pages to Father Acevedo every few weeks. He'll see that they're sent onto me."

"Yes, Padre."

"Well, I wish you a safe journey, and I pray you'll be able to continue Brother Miguel's work without too much difficulty."

"I'll do my best."

"I know you will. Now, go and pack and ready yourself."

"Thank you, Padre."

Alonso left the Abbot's office with a heavy heart. He wasn't sure what he'd imagined when he was told he would replace Miguel, but the reality of it was frightening.

Chapter 14

Manchester 1968

Ian grabbed the receiver and put it to his ear as soon as the phone rang. “Ian Fuller.”

“Ian,” came Dave’s voice. “I’ve got news.”

“Excellent,” said Ian with a rising sense of excitement. “What have you got for me?”

“Santa Maria is a monastery in the province of Soria in Spain.”

“Hang on while I write that down.” Ian pulled his notepad and pen closer and scribbled down the details. “Is it still a monastery then?”

“Yes, but it was closed down for a number of years and only started up again in the thirties. It’s likely that any manuscripts they had were moved.”

“Any idea where?” asked Ian.

“No. I reckon a trip to Santa Maria is in order. They do tours for tourists a couple of times a week. Maybe you can ask them what happened to their manuscripts.”

A number of things ran through Ian’s mind all at once but settled on a trip to Spain. It was too early to call in favours until he knew where the manuscript was. "That sounds like a plan. Can you get Peggy to book me a flight and a couple of nights in a cheap joint?"

"Sure, leave it with me," said Dave with a chuckle. "You sure you want a cheap joint?"

"Yeah, it'll only be for a couple of nights." He had no intention of blowing a whole lot of cash on a reconnaissance mission. "Tell her to get me a flight for Sunday if she can."

"Consider it done."

"Thanks. How's the translation going?"

"Great. It should be done by Saturday. I'll drop them around."

"Thanks, Dave. See you then."

Ian hung up the phone and sat back in his chair. He let his mind wander as he imagined what the manuscript would tell them about the library. It was so frustrating to have such a big prize waiting for them, but no way of getting to it. He hoped that would change – and soon.

His office door clicked open, which was quickly followed by Rob's head. "Good, you're here," he said coming into the office and closing the door.

"Rob, nice to see you." He smiled and gestured to a shabby chair. "What's up?"

"Well, I wanted to tell you in person," he said easing himself into the chair. He had a grim expression on his face and his eyes didn't quite meet Ian's. "I've spoken with a lawyer, and I'm contesting Mum's Will."

"Rob." Ian exhaled and sat back. "Why? You know Lana and Mum were close, it's understandable that she'd want to look after her."

"I know you believe that, but, no, she's manipulated her, I know it. She'd have left something for Pat and Morris otherwise." He compressed his lips and nodded. "Anyway, I just wanted to let you know. My lawyer says I've got a good chance of overturning it."

Ian blew out his breath and nodded. There was no changing Rob's mind once it was made up so he wasn't going to bother trying. This was going to hold up the estate, probably for months though, and he needed the money. "What if I talk to Lana about it? I'm sure she didn't expect this, and I bet she'd agree to give you a larger share. Let me talk to her."

"No," Rob said flatly shaking his head. "She doesn't deserve any of it, and I won't accept crumbs." He stood up and ran his hands down his trousers. "I'm sure Robinson will be in contact with you. This isn't personal, Ian, and I hope it doesn't come between us." His eyes finally met Ian's with an imploring look.

"It won't," Ian said with a shake of his head. "I understand, Rob. I just wish you'd let me talk to Lana about it first."

"It's done." He walked to the door and held it open as he looked at Ian over his shoulder. "Thanks." He left and shut the door behind him.

Ian stared at the closed door for several minutes. *Shit!* This was the last thing he needed right now.

***

Ian had been pacing up and down his small flat for the past half an hour. Dave should've been here by now with Lana's box and his plane ticket. He was excited to find out what information the pages contained. Maybe they'd mention the location of the library and his trip to Spain wouldn't be necessary. Either way, he just hoped they'd find out. This was going to be life-changing, he just knew it.

The doorbell rang and he raced to wrench open the door. He grinned as he stepped back to allow Dave to enter. "It's all done then?" He closed the door and with his heart beating hard in his chest he joined Dave, who'd dumped the box on the coffee table.

"Yeah, all done," said Dave handing him a manilla folder. "This is for you. I got

Peggy to type up a copy for you and me. There's a folder with the translated copy for Lana as well of course."

"Have you read them?" asked Ian sitting on the edge of the couch and flipping open the folder.

"I have," said Dave joining him. "I've put the page that I want you read on top, and marked it. Go ahead, you won't bloody believe it."

Ian began reading the paragraph that Dave had marked.

> *We have now been down in the caverns for many weeks and our supplies are dwindling. We must depart soon or perish. Attawal has sent scouting parties through time to find a safe place and we await their return. What is left of our food has been packed and will be carried by the women when we leave. Our supply of water is adequate, but Attawal and his advisors are anxious for our departure.*

Ian slumped back and stared at Dave. "It's a hoax…"

"No," said Dave shaking his head. "I know it sounds unbelievable, but it's not a hoax." He pulled the next page from the folder and shoved it under Ian's nose. "Read that bit there. It's part of a letter and it asks whoever the receiver was to give it to the Abbot. That can only mean one thing."

Ian read the bit Dave had pointed to and nodded. "That must be the Abbot of Santa Maria."

"Exactly. So, it's not a hoax my friend." Dave grinned and sat back on the couch. "Where did Lana get this stuff?"

Ian grimaced. "You won't believe where she got it. Shit, I don't believe where she got it." He put the pages back in the folder and closed it. "My mother."

"Your mother?" Dave's eyebrows raised almost to his hairline. "You've got to be kidding me. Where did she get them?"

"Apparently, they've been handed down through our family for generations. She gave them to Lana right before she died."

"Maybe she's got some more of it hidden away. Shit, Ian, she might even have the damned manuscript."

"No," said Ian shaking his head. "I searched the house…there's nothing more."

"Alright, well it's Spain for you then." He reached into his breast pocket and pulled out a plane ticket and handed it to Ian. "You fly out tomorrow afternoon, and Peggy's booked you into the Sundos Feria. I reckon it sounds better than it is."

"I'll write you a cheque. How much do I owe you?" said Ian getting to his feet.

"I don't bloody know. We'll sort it out later."

"Alright. Thanks, Dave. I just hope I can find out where this manuscript is."

Dave got to his feet and stretched. "So do I. I'm sure it holds the key to all of this. Anyway, good luck. Call me when you get back."

"Will do."

Dave left, and Ian immediately called Lana to let her know he had her box back. Ten minutes later he headed out the door with the box and folder for her tucked under his arm. He was sure she'd never know what he intended, and it wouldn't matter. He convinced himself that she was never going to do anything with it anyway.

Chapter 15

Monastery of Santa Maria de Huerta
Spain 1968

Ian arrived in Valencia late Sunday afternoon and checked into his hotel. It was perhaps a bit shabbier than he'd imagined, and not entirely clean, but as long as there weren't any bed bugs, he didn't care. Next time he'd ask Peggy not to book the cheapest she could find.

He set off before dawn the next morning on the long drive to Santa Maria. He couldn't stop himself from imagining what he might find out. He agreed with Dave, it was unlikely the manuscript was still held at the monastery. *But, would anyone know where it was?* That question dogged him the whole way.

He arrived at the impressive walled monastery about fifteen minutes before the tour was to commence. He parked the car and walked through the wrought iron gates. The monastery was an imposing red brick building with eight towers. Above the doorway was an image of the Virgin Mary, and Ian almost crossed himself as he entered. It opened into a large atrium where there were already half a dozen people milling about.

"Good morning," said a well-dressed blonde woman with a clipboard in hand. "I'm Anna, and I'll be your guide today." She handed him a brochure. "What's your name?"

"Ian. Ian Fuller," he replied taking the brochure and glancing briefly at it.

"Ah, yes," she said marking off his name. "We're just waiting on one other before we get started. Please, have a look around the courtyard while we wait."

"Thanks."

He wandered around the atrium for a few minutes. He was beginning to think this was a waste of time. He wasn't remotely interested in the architecture or the history of the place and was anxious to get on with it.

Five minutes later Anna called them all to attention. "Welcome, ladies and gentlemen, to the Monasterio de Santa Maria de Huerta. This morning we'll be touring the chapel, workshops, kitchen and gardens. If you have any questions, please feel free to ask. Please follow me."

Ian positioned himself at the back of the group as they headed off through the courtyard and into the Hall of the Conversi as Anna called it. He was rather bored with the whole affair and anxious to ask Anna about the scriptoria.

She hadn't mentioned that it was included in the tour. Half an hour into the tour he found himself at the front of the group as they turned around and headed outside into the garden.

"Excuse me," he said. "Is there any chance of seeing the scriptoria?"

"No, it's off-limits. It's used as a storeroom these days," she said with a smile. "I'd be happy to answer any questions you may have about it after the tour though."

"Thanks."

Well, that answered his main question. Obviously, the manuscripts were no longer stored here. He wondered how much Anna might know about them – probably not much. He wasn't holding out much hope of finding out where it was now.

After the tour, he waited until the other tourists had departed before approaching Anna with his questions. "So, do you know what happened to the manuscripts that were here originally?"

"Many of them were transferred to a museum in Barcelona, and I believe a few were sent to the Vatican Library. Before the monastery was closed in the late nineteenth century, they had a magnificent collection."

"Interesting," said Ian nodding. "I heard they originally had a manuscript here that no one could read. It was written in an unknown language." Ian groaned inwardly at her blank expression. He'd hoped she might know something about it, but obviously not. "Did they keep a manifest of where each one was sent? Do you know?"

"They did," she replied slowly. "I can see you have a real interest in old manuscripts. So do I." She smiled and glanced towards the hall. "Tourists aren't normally allowed in the office, but I can show you if you like."

"Really? That's most kind of you."

She took a key from her pocket and unlocked a door on the left side of the atrium. "Come."

Ian could hardly believe his luck as he followed her into the office. A large desk took up most of the room and it was piled high with papers and paraphernalia. Anna scooped some papers off a chair and gestured to him to sit down. One wall was lined with large timber bookcases, and Anna lifted a well worn leather volume down and with a sweep of her arm made room on the desk for it.

"I don't know if there's any way to identify the manuscript you want to know about," she said opening the ledger. "Honestly, I haven't looked at this in ages."

Ian joined her at the desk and peered at the small scrawling writing on the page. There were lists of manuscripts by number. A few had notes beside them, and in the next column they were marked either BM or VL.

"Unfortunately, if it was sent to the museum in Barcelona it probably hasn't survived," she said turning the page. "A fire destroyed much of their collection."

It was a bit like looking for a needle in a haystack and Ian didn't hold out much hope of identifying the one he was looking for. Nothing was jumping out at him. Anna turned the page again and he scanned down the lists, looking for anything that might indicate it was an unreadable manuscript. He noticed several had the word 'destroyed' written beside them and his heart sank. If it had been destroyed then there was no way they could find the library.

"They had a lot of manuscripts," he said as Anna turned the page again.

"Yes, they had several hundred at one time," she said glancing at him. "It would've been wonderful to see them all."

"It would've," he said with a nod. "They must've had a large scriptoria."

"It wasn't so large, but it dates back to the twelfth century." She turned the page again. "I'm sorry, but it doesn't look like we're going to find your manuscript."

"No, it doesn't," he said scanning the page. "I thought they might've listed them by description rather than numbers."

"Hmm, it probably didn't matter to them," she replied. "Hang on…look at this one. Number 213."

His heart jumped as he squinted at the page. "And 214."

Noted under each of them in tiny writing was the word 'unknown'. It wasn't much of a clue, but it was something. W*ere there two copies or two manuscripts*? He had no idea.

"Number 213 was destroyed," said Anna in dismay, "but it looks like 214 was sent to the Vatican Library. Do you think this is the manuscript you're looking for?"

"I think it might be," he said as he peered closer. "Can you read what that says in the next column?" The writing was so small and illegible, but he thought it said 'sold 1912' with a name beside it.

Anna leaned closer and shook her head. "The first word's sold, but the name is…it looks like Hans or Haas, but I can't make out the surname."

Ian wasn't about to give up now. He was sure this was it. None of the others had any kind of notation like it. He was mystified about there being two, and he hoped it meant two copies rather than two manuscripts.

"I don't suppose you've got a magnifying glass do you?" he said glancing at Anna.

"No…but if you make a fist and peer through it." She curled her index finger inward and wrapped her thumb around it before holding it up to eye. "It can make things appear bigger."

Ian watched and waited while Anna moved her head and hand closer and then further away from the page. "It's definitely Haas…and the surname looks like…Kraus." She continued to adjust her distance from the page. "That's the best I can do I'm afraid." She stopped and smiled at him. "You have a go."

Ian did as Anna had done and peered through the small gap made by his finger. He was amazed that it did appear to make the writing bigger. "Yes, it's Haas," he said as he tried to make out the surname. It certainly looked like Kraus or something like it. He straightened and grinned. "I think you're right."

"Well, I have no idea who that is, but you might be able to find out," she said closing the ledger. "At least it wasn't destroyed."

"Yes. Thank you so much for your help, Anna."

"You're welcome." She put the volume back on the shelf and turned to face him. "I hope you find it."

"Thanks…and thank you for taking the time to show me the manifest."

"Well, it's not something I'd normally do, but you seemed very interested."

"I am. I've been fortunate to have studied a few codex over the years and when I heard about this one, I just had to see it."

"Well, good luck," she said walking to the door. "I really should lock up and get ready for the next tour."

"Of course. Thanks again."

He left the office and headed back to his car. He'd learned far more than he thought he might. At least he had a name to go on, and with luck, Dave could track down what happened to it after that. It sounded like it might be in a private collection somewhere, and that made it a lot easier to steal.

Chapter 16

Monastery of Santa Maria de Huerta
Spain 1597

Alonso was up early the following morning. He'd packed as much parchment and quills as he could into the small chest, along with his meagre belongings. He snapped the chest shut and sighed. He couldn't change whatever awaited him, but prayed God would protect and guide him.

He stepped out into the hallway and was immediately hailed by two brothers. He knew Brother Jose quite well and greeted him with a smile. He only knew Brother Sancho by sight – he'd only been in the order for a short time.

"Brother Benito sent us to collect your chest. Is it ready?" asked Brother Jose.

"Yes," he said opening the door to his small cell.

"We'll take care of it for you," he said ushering Brother Sancho ahead of him.

"Thank you."

Alonso left them and made his way to the chapel for prayers. This would be his last morning in the chapel and the thought gave him an odd feeling. He was going to miss being here with his Brothers, and the uncertainty of his future was giving him a feeling of rising anxiety.

After his usual morning prayers, he prayed for his own well-being and his Brothers. All he could do was put his trust in God. He rose to his feet and walked to the end of the aisle.

"Goodbye, Brother Alonso," said Diego approaching him. "I'll miss you."

"Stay safe, my Brother," he replied as he tucked his hands into the ends of his sleeves, resisting the urge to hug Diego to him. "I'd write to you, but you don't read Latin."

"Perhaps Padre will pass on any news of you. Then again, probably not. I'm not supposed to know what you're doing," he whispered.

Alonso smiled and nodded. There was nothing else to say and Diego was right; Padre wouldn't share any information with him or anyone else. "Goodbye."

He left the chapel and returned to his cell to collect the travelling cloak Padre had given him only yesterday. He'd never had any need of one before. He took one final look around his room and walked out into the hallway, hastily avoiding bumping into Brother Benito.

"Good, you're ready. Meet me out by the stables."

"Yes, I'll go straight there."

Brother Benito kept on scurrying down the hall and Alonso headed for the side door near the garden. The chill morning air hit him as soon as he stepped outside, and he pulled his cloak around himself. The monastery was shrouded in light fog and Alonso shivered as he hurried down to the stables. He was glad of one thing, at least he wasn't expected to walk to Valencia carrying his sea chest.

As he neared the stables he could see a small cart had been hitched in readiness. It was usually used to cart produce and items made by his Brothers to the village to sell. He was sure Padre had a much better one for his use on the occasions that he left the monastery.

"You're in the back," said Brother Jose when he saw him. "Is Brother Benito not with you?"

"He had some matters to attend to," said Alonso eyeing the cart. "He'll join us soon."

Brother Jose nodded before climbing up onto the driver's seat. Alonso stuck his boot into the spoke of the wheel and hauled himself into the back of it. He was pleased to see his chest was already loaded and settled himself down on the floor of the cart. It was going to be a hard and uncomfortable journey. *The first of many* he thought to himself.

Brother Benito arrived five minutes later and with a quick glance in Alonso's direction, joined Brother Jose on the driver seat. They set off at a trot and the chill air swirled around Alonso's ears. He pulled the hood of his cloak over his head and groaned.

They travelled all day, stopping occasionally for prayer and arrived in the village of Calamocha at dusk. Alonso had difficulty moving after a day scrunched up in the cart. He groaned as he slowly climbed out of it and tried to get his legs to work.

"Wait here," said Brother Benito jumping down beside him. "Help Brother Jose to settle the horses."

He nodded as he joined Brother Jose, who was already unstrapping the horses. "Do that one first," he said indicating with one hand.

Alonso had no idea about horses or their hitching but did his best to follow Brother

Jose's instructions. There was already a chill in the air with signs that it would be a cool night. His fingers fumbled with the straps and Brother Jose pushed him aside.

"Let me do that. Grab the reins."

He gladly did as he was bid. Brother Jose worked deftly and in no time the horses were freed from the cart. Brother Benito returned a few minutes later with a smile on his face carrying a small basket.

"Take them into the barn," he said stroking the horse's muzzle. "The innkeeper has kindly let us sleep in the barn as well, and I have supper for us."

"I'm glad," said Brother Jose before leading the horses inside. "I'm starving."

Alonso followed them and was surprised at how warm it was inside. As soon as the horses were taken care of, the three of them settled down on a pile of hay. Brother Benito handed each of them some cheese and bread.

"We should reach Valencia by early afternoon tomorrow," he said before taking a large bite.

Alonso nodded. "Will the ship be ready?"

Brother Benito nodded. “It should be. Brother Jose and I will find somewhere to stay the night, but I’ll see you safely on board first.”

They ate the rest of their supper in silence, and Alonso was relieved to finally lie down to sleep after evening prayers. He was feeling both excited and uncertain at the prospect of a sea voyage. He’d never been on a ship before and had no idea what it would be like.

They left Calamocha early the following morning. The sun was up but the air was chill and Alonso huddled down in the back of the cart. By early afternoon, the sun was warm on his back and he admired the many olive groves they passed. They soon reached the outskirts of Valencia with its creamy-coloured houses and terracotta roofs. There was so much to see in the busy streets. Vendors selling all manner of things, carts loaded with produce and fish. There were so many people going to and fro. Alonso was mesmerised by it all.

His heart started racing when he spotted the first ship's mast poking up above the rooftops. *Would he soon be sailing on that one?* He wasn’t sure he was ready.

Half an hour later they reached the docks, and the huge ships came into full view.

The wharf was lined with cargo and bustling with activity. Soldiers were on guard duty and there was an air of anticipation. Alonso leaned out of the cart to get a better view of the harbour, and a galleon in full sail in the distance. He couldn't work out if it was coming or going.

Brother Benito was pointing and giving directions to Brother Jose, who carefully guided the horses through the throng. They came to a halt at the command of a soldier who looked them over with a steely stare.

"Good afternoon," said Brother Benito. "We're looking for the Santa Ana."

He waved his arm towards the end of the docks. "Second last. Keep to the right and stay out of the way."

Brother Benito nodded and Brother Jose urged the horses forward at a walk. Alonso sat back and sighed. He was nervous about the voyage ahead and what awaited him in the new world. He never imagined he'd ever leave the safety of the monastery, and his stomach was writhing.

A few minutes later Brother Jose brought the cart to halt and Brother Benito leapt down. "You two get Brother Alonso's chest and follow me." Without waiting for them, he headed across the docks to the Santa Ana and marched up the gangplank.

Alonso licked his lips and slowly climbed down from the cart.

"Are you alright?" asked Brother Jose coming around to the back of it. "You don't look well."

"I'll be fine," he replied with a weak smile.

Brother Jose shrugged and slapped him on the back. "You're a braver man than me."

They grabbed the chest between them and followed after Brother Benito. There was no sign of him as they reached the top of the gangplank, and they stood there for several seconds, uncertain as to what to do.

"Get outta the way," a burly seaman yelled at them.

They quickly shuffled aside. Alonso's eyes were going in every direction trying to take in all of the ship. It was huge, with multiple decks and four masts. He could only imagine what it would be like below decks. He'd noticed the gunports as he'd come up the gangplank – he hoped they wouldn't need them.

"Come this way," called Brother Benito, who'd just appeared on deck.

He held open the door and gestured to them. Alonso and Brother Jose hurried towards him with the chest bumping between them. The interior was dimly lit and it took a few moments for Alonso's eyes to adjust to the gloom. They followed Brother Benito down a set of narrow steps and then another. At the bottom of the steps, he glanced over his shoulder at them before continuing down the shadowy hallway. It was barely wide enough for one man to walk, and Alonso had to hold the chest handle behind his back in order to follow.

At the end of the hall, Brother Benito stopped and knocked softly on the door. He opened it a moment later and disappeared inside. Alonso and Brother Jose followed as best they could. The chest clunked loudly against the door frame as they manoeuvred their way inside.

"Brother Alonso, this is Father Garcia. He's the ship's chaplain and you'll be sharing his quarters," said Brother Benito moving to the back of the small cabin to make room.

"Good afternoon, Father," said Alonso glancing around. It was a tiny cramped room, with two narrow bunks and a nightstand. In one corner was a small desk and a hard wooden chair. A lamp swung from the ceiling, barely illuminating the cabin.

"Put your chest under the bunk, Brother," said Father Garcia with a warm smile. "There isn't a lot of room but it's comfortable enough." He chuckled as he sat down on the nearest bunk.

Alonso and Brother Jose managed to shove the chest under the bunk, after much grunting and wriggling it about.

"Well, I wish you safe travels, Brother Alonso," said Brother Benito squeezing himself between the bunks and into the doorway.

"Thank you for seeing me safely on board," said Alonso straightening. "Safe travels to you both."

"Come, Brother Jose, I have other business to attend to before we return," said Brother Benito.

With a nod the pair left, and Alonso felt very alone. "Thank you for your generosity, Father. I'll try not to be a burden."

"I'm happy for the company, Brother." He got to his feet and ran his fingers through his greying beard. "Come." He walked to the door and glanced back at him. "You'll need to learn your way around, so you might as well start now."

Chapter 17

Manchester 1968

Lana and Di walked up the path to the front door, arm in arm. Di giggled as she wobbled sideways, almost landing in the garden bed. Lana pulled her back just in time, and then they both nearly lost their balance, which was followed by more giggling.

"Have you got the keys?" said Di fumbling in her purse and coming up empty-handed.

"I think so," said Lana dumping the entire contents of her bag on the front step.

"My God, you've got some crap in there," said Di with a giggle. "I hope you've got keys."

"Yeah, I'm sure I have," she said sifting through the pile of debris. "Ah…no, that's not them." She held up the small key that opened the box, and lights glinted off the crystal dangling from it. "It's such a pretty thing."

"Yeah, but it won't open the door. Here, let me look." Di shoved her aside and Lana lost her balance. She landed on her bottom on the step and burst out laughing.

"Sorry…oh, here they are." She dumped the pile of stuff back in Lana's bag before helping her to her feet.

"Thanks." Lana grabbed her bag and peered inside. It was a jumbled-up mess of stuff. She tossed the key in on top and zipped it up. "You've made a mess of my bag."

"Sorry," said Di with a shrug.

Di slipped the key into the lock with a look of surprise. "I didn't think I'd get it first go."

"Neither did I," said Lana giggling. "With the amount of gin you drank tonight, I'm surprised you can even see the lock."

"I'm not sure I can." Di laughed as she pushed open the door and the two of them went inside.

Lana slammed the door shut behind them and pushed the snib across. "We're safely locked in," she said grinning.

"Want a nightcap?"

"Ooh, what have we got?"

"I think Mum left a bottle of Pimm's in the cupboard."

"Alright," said Lana wobbling into the lounge.

Di tossed her bag on the couch and opened the liquor cabinet. “Yes.” She held up the bottle of Pimm’s for Lana to see. “I haven’t had this forever.”

“I don’t think I ever have,” said Lana kicking off her shoes.

“Well, tonight’s the night then.” She poured two small glasses and handed one to Lana. “Here’s to your new wealth.”

“Not if Uncle Rob gets his way.”

Lana and Di both looked at the ceiling as they heard a loud thump. They looked at one another with quizzical stares.

“I didn’t think Toby was home,” said Lana putting down her glass.

“Neither did I,” said Di heading out to the hallway with Lana at her heels.

“Is that you Toby?” called Di slowly walking towards the stairs. There was no reply. She turned and looked at Lana with alarm etched on her face. “I don’t think it’s Toby,” she whispered.

Lana’s heart was thumping madly as the two made their way to the foot of the stairs. Di grabbed the umbrella from the coat stand and put down her glass.

“What are you going to do with that?”

"I don't know, but I'm not going up there unarmed," said Di with a determined look.

Lana grabbed her arm. "We can't go up there. What if it's the burglar? My Dad said they might come here looking for my box." The fear was obvious in her voice. She hadn't actually taken her father's words seriously, but now, she was beginning to think he was right.

"Well, we can't just ignore it either," said Di shrugging her off. "I'm going up there. Are you coming?"

Lana looked from the ceiling to Di. She didn't want to go up there, but she couldn't let Di go alone. "Okay," she said in a tremulous voice.

Lana followed Di as they slowly climbed the stairs. Her heart was thumping madly in her chest by the time they reached the landing. She could hear noises coming from her bedroom, and all of a sudden she felt very sober. Di stopped and gestured with the umbrella towards Lana's room. She nodded and drew in breath before the two of them stormed in.

A man looked up in alarm as they burst in. He was sitting on Lana's bed with her box open in front of him with pages of parchment spread around. He dived off the bed and backed away from them towards the wardrobe.

"What the hell!" said Di brandishing her umbrella at the man. "Go…call the police, Lana."

Lana stood frozen on the spot as her eyes took in the scene in front of her. *Her father had been right.*

"Go," said Di with a note of urgency in her now high-pitched voice.

"Wait." The man held up his hands and his eyes pleaded with them. "Please, don't call the police," he said in a panicked voice, thick with a Spanish accent.

Lana dismissed Di's words and began gathering the pages together.

"Where did you get those?" said the man.

She ignored him as she shoved them back in the box and hugging it to herself she joined Di in the doorway.

"Please, Lana. Go and call the police," said Di not taking her eyes off the cornered man.

"I've been dreaming of you," said the man with his gaze squarely on Lana. "And you've been dreaming of me."

Lana paled and hugged the box tighter to her chest.

"Oh my God, is that some sort of pick up line?" said Di rolling her eyes.

"No," said Lana drawing in a breath. "I…I dreamed about him ransacking my Nan's house." *But how could he know that?*

"That's weird," said Di staring at her.

"I know," said Lana shaking her head.

"Please…you have a crystal I need. Give it to me and I'll leave and you'll never see me again," he said imploringly. "I promise, I never meant to scare you."

Di's eyes widened and she took a step towards him. "Who are you?"

The man went down on his knees and clasped his hands in front of him. "My name is Miguel." He drew in a breath and slowly let it out. "It's not easy to explain."

"Well, give it a go," said Di in an angry tone. "How do you know about the crystal?"

Lana stared at him. He couldn't possibly know about that. Her mind was whirring as she tried to understand.

"I'm a monk from the monastery of Santa Maria de Huerta in Spain," he said slowly. "I was sent to transcribe metal tablets that were discovered in a cavern. I…I found the crystal there."

“That doesn’t explain what you’re doing here,” said Di pointing the umbrella at the man’s chest.

“Wait,” said Lana. She put the box down on the bed and looked at him. “The box, the pages in this box, that’s what they’re about aren’t they?”

“Yes,” he said nodding. “I don’t know how you come to have them. I wrote them and sent them to Brother Alonso.”

“Don’t be ridiculous,” said Di with a scoff. “They’re hundreds of years old.”

The man groaned. “There’s an orb...”

“Oh my God,” exclaimed Lana staring at him. “We read about that.”

Di swung around and stared at her. “You mean this garbled crap is making sense to you?”

“Not exactly,” said Lana shaking her head. “Please, go on.”

“Well, I had one of those crystals in my pocket when I approached the orb. The humming got louder and I reached out and touched it. The next thing I knew I woke up. I was still in the room with the orb, but it was different.” He drew in a breath. “The crystal had shattered, and I soon realised when I left the caverns that I was in a different time. Your time.”

"Well, why didn't you go back to your time?" said Di with her voice dripping with sarcasm. "This is just ridiculous and I don't believe a word of it."

"I couldn't," he said in an anguished tone. "I searched the caverns for another crystal, but there were none. It didn't matter how many times I touched the orb nothing happened. I didn't think there was any way for me to return until I started dreaming about the old woman…your Nan." His dark eyes bore into Lana, "and then you."

Lana sat down on the bed and blew out her breath. "This is so confusing. What have dreams got to do with this?"

"Before, when I was in my time, I would dream of Brother Alonso. There's some connection between me and your crystal." He paused and shook his head. "I don't understand it, but when I started dreaming about your Nan I knew it was the crystal…that she had it, and if I could get it then I could return to my time."

"And so you searched her house for it?" said Lana as understanding dawned on her. "And then you dreamed of me and broke in here to get it?"

"Yes."

"Hang on just a minute," said Di brandishing the umbrella at him again. "If you're from some Spanish monastery, from God knows when, how come you speak such good English?" Disbelief was written all over her face and she squared her shoulders. "Explain that if you can!"

Miguel's shoulders slumped and his eyes pleaded with her. "It's not easy to explain."

"Give it go, or I swear I'll go call the police myself," said Di.

He nodded and let his gaze rest squarely on Di and her umbrella. "I found a box at the back of a shelf, hidden behind several tablets. The lid was covered in writing, which at the time, I didn't understand was one word - infinity, written in six languages.

"Inside, the box was divided into two compartments with a small multicoloured crystal lying in each one."

Lana's eyes widened. "Is that where my crystal came from?"

"Yes," said Miguel glancing at her. "I lifted one of the crystals from the box and light emanated from it. When I took the other one out, a bright light, like daylight, flashed between the two crystals in my hand.

"I put the box on my desk, and it was only later that I realised I could now read and understand the writing on the lid. I have no understanding of how, but I was gifted the ability to read the ancient language, and to understand your speech."

Di scoffed and rolled her eyes to the ceiling.

Lana shook her head. "What did you do with the crystals? How did I end up with one?"

"I put one in my pocket to keep for myself, and I sent the other one to Brother Alonso at Santa Maria de Huerta," he said looking bewildered. "I don't know how it came to be in your possession."

Lana and Di both jumped at the sound of the front door slamming. "Toby," said Di in a voice barely above a whisper. "Up here, Toby," she yelled over her shoulder. "We've got a burglar."

"Please, if you'll just give me the crystal. I can't get back without it," said Miguel, his eyes pleading with Lana.

"What's going on?" said Toby rushing into the room with alarm etched on his face. "Bloody hell!"

"It's alright," said Lana diving off the bed and stepping in front of him. "He's not going to hurt us."

"You won't believe what this guy's been saying." Di rolled her eyes to the ceiling.

"Go on," she said turning back to Miguel. "Tell him what you've just told us."

Toby glanced around the room. "I see you got your box back," he said before settling his eyes on Miguel, "go on then, what are you doing here?"

Miguel licked his lips and then relayed to Toby what he'd just told Di and Lana. "I know it sounds unbelievable, but I swear it's true. If I could just have the crystal. Please."

"This is insane," said Toby running his fingers through his hair.

"I know, but he knows too much," said Lana shaking her head. "Stuff he shouldn't know, couldn't know."

"Alright…let me think," said Toby.

He paced the room while Lana and Di watched him. Lana was inclined to just give the crystal to Miguel. It was a pretty thing but she had no use for it, and what if he was telling the truth?

Toby stopped pacing and looked at Miguel who was still kneeling on the floor. "Can you read the ancient writing?"

Miguel raised his dark eyes and Lana saw the truth in their depths. "Yes."

"Alright then. Lana, did your Dad translate all the pages?"

"I think so," she said reaching for a manilla folder sitting on her dressing table. "I haven't had a chance to look at it." She handed it to Toby, "He only brought them back this afternoon."

"Okay. No one can read this and if you can then I'll believe you," said Toby as he opened the box and lifted out a page. He then sorted through the pages in the folder and found the matching translation. He placed the parchment on the bed and covered the writing in Greek and Latin with another page. "Read this."

Miguel slowly got to his feet and approached the bed. "If I read this you'll give me the crystal?"

"We'll think about it," said Toby with a note of disbelief in his voice.

"Yes, we will," interjected Lana.

"Lana?" Toby turned and stared at her.

"We will," she repeated in a don't argue with me tone. "If he's telling the truth, Toby we have to."

"Maybe…but first read."

Miguel looked from Toby and back to Lana and nodded. "Thank you." He then turned his attention to the parchment sitting on the bed and read it out loud. "The interlopers have all but…overrun our defences. Our…crops have been…decimated and we have harvested all that we can."

He paused and looked at Toby, who was staring at him with his mouth agape. "Am I right?"

Toby drew in a breath and nodded. "Yes."

"Bloody hell," said Di.

Lana had a hundred thoughts all slipping and sliding over one another. Miguel had read the ancient writing, he knew about her dreams and he knew about the crystal. One fundamental thought kept rising to the surface – he was telling the truth.

"Do you believe me now?" said Miguel with his eyes squarely on Toby.

Toby ran his fingers through his hair and shook his head. "Honestly, I don't know what to believe. I don't know how you did that."

"He's telling the truth," said Lana yawning widely. "And I say we give him the crystal."

Di shook her head and dropped the umbrella by the door. "It's impossible."

Miguel shrugged. "It would seem to be impossible, and yet here I am. I just want to get back to my time…and the crystal is the only way."

Toby's face lit up and he stared at Miguel. "You know where this library is, right?"

"Of course."

"Take us to it. Show us and we'll give you the crystal."

Miguel stared around at the three of them. "I can't. I've taken a vow of silence."

"Surely that doesn't matter now," said Toby gathering the pages together and shoving them in the box.

"I believe God is everywhere," said Miguel matter-of-factly.

"Can we sort this out in the morning?" said Di yawning. "I'm beat."

Lana glanced at her bedside clock – it was 2 am. "I agree, we'll be able to think straighter in the morning."

Miguel slowly nodded. "Alright…"

"Come back in the morning and we'll talk," said Toby walking to the doorway. "Come, Miguel and I'll let you out the front door. No need to climb out whatever window you used to get in here."

A grin spread across Miguel's face. "Thank you."

Ten minutes later Lana climbed into bed and snuggled under the covers. It had been an eventful night full of unbelievable revelations. As she drifted off to sleep, her mind was full of what they might find if they managed to convince Miguel to take them to the library.

Chapter 18

Manchester 1968

Lana woke up and glanced at the clock. It was twenty-past nine, and she groaned as she dragged herself out of bed. She felt like she'd been run over by a bus. Her mouth was dry and her head was pounding. She jumped straight in the shower and let the hot water run over her body. The events of the previous night seemed like a dream. Her Nan had certainly opened a can of worms by giving her that box.

She threw on a pair of jeans and a jumper and headed downstairs to the kitchen. Toby was sitting at the table halfway through eating a bowl of cornflakes.

"Morning," he mumbled with his mouth half full.

"Hi," said Lana flicking on the kettle. She opened the third drawer down and pulled out the box of Bex powders.

"Headache?" said Toby with a grin.

"Yeah…I feel terrible." She swallowed the Bex and swished it down with water before preparing a mug of coffee. "Di and I tied one on last night."

"I thought you two were a bit tipsy."

"More than a bit." She grinned as she poured hot water into her mug. "But I soon sobered up when we discovered Miguel in my bedroom."

"I can't believe it…I mean time travel and all that," said Toby before spooning the last of his cornflakes in his mouth.

Lana sat down with her mug of coffee clasped in her hands. "As weird as it sounds, I believe him."

"Well, I'm not sure, but I hope we can convince him to show us the library…imagine, Lana. What a discovery. We could be famous."

"I don't want to be famous." Lana frowned. She was surprised at him and had expected him to be more excited about the history and all that, than being famous. "I think we should just help him and be done with it."

He grinned. "I'm just kidding, I don't want to be famous. And I think we should help him, but…" He leaned forward and stared at her. "I don't think you should just give him the crystal. If he can show us where this library is in exchange, then we should do it."

She nodded and sipped her coffee. *That would be so rad.* "Yeah…but it's a big if."

Toby looked up and grinned as a loud knock on the front door reverberated down the hall. "He's here." He hurried down the hall and returned a few moments later with Miguel. "We didn't properly introduce ourselves last night," he said smiling. "I'm Toby, this is Lana, and I suspect my sister Di is still in bed."

"Good morning," said Miguel looking nervously about.

"Sit," said Toby gesturing to the nearest chair. "I'll get us a coffee."

Miguel slowly eased himself into a chair and sat rigidly upright with his hands in his lap.

"It's alright," said Lana smiling. "We're going to help you."

Miguel relaxed somewhat. "Thank you doesn't seem enough…but, thank you," he said with a look of relief. "I'm so sorry I scared you and broke into your house. I was desperate."

"It's alright." Lana shook her head and grinned. "I'm sorry Di nearly stabbed you with that umbrella."

"You can't blame her," said Toby putting two mugs of coffee on the table.

"No, I guess not." Lana took another sip of her coffee and watched Miguel from under her lashes. She genuinely wanted to help him get back, but she also agreed with Toby.

"So…have you thought about our offer? You show us the library and we'll give you the crystal?"

"I have," he said slowly. "And I spoke with God on the matter."

Lana's eyes widened and she gave Toby a look of 'I think he's going to agree' from across the table.

"And what did you decide?" said Toby with an expectant look.

Miguel glanced from one to the other and drew in a breath. "I'd like you to understand why I can't just take you there. The ancient people who carved the caverns to keep their history and themselves safe, may still need our protection." He reached into his pocket and drew out a small intricately carved statue. He placed it on the table in front of Lana. "This is from the library."

"It's beautiful," she said with a note of awe. It was about four inches high and carved in such detail and painted in subtle colours. "Is he one of their Gods do you think?"

"No," said Miguel picking up the statue and turning it around. "See here. His name is carved on it. Attawal, their chief."

"Wow," said Toby. "Can I see it?"

Miguel handed him the statue and smiled. "They were under attack and Attawal ordered his people to retreat to the caverns. They were forced to find another time to go to where they would be safe. Attawal sent scouts through time until they found that place."

"Where did they go?" asked Lana.

"I don't know," said Miguel with a shake of his head. "And it's not so much where, but when. From their writings, I believe they went into the future, as I have done."

"Incredible," said Toby turning the statue over in his hand. "So, you think if you show us this library it will somehow affect these ancient people? In a bad way?" He put it back on the table and stared at Miguel.

"Yes. What if their library is destroyed, pulled apart and dissected? Would it not also disappear in the future? In the future where they have sought refuge?"

"I wouldn't want that," said Lana before taking another sip of coffee. "I'll just give you the crystal, Miguel and you can go home."

"Thank you," he said with a smile. "But, I think there's another way."

Toby's eyes widened. "What are you suggesting?"

"If you were to take a vow of silence, as I have done, then I could take you and show you where it is."

"What would that entail?" asked Lana with a furrowed brow. A vow of silence sounded really serious and something only monks and priests did.

"It's a vow made before God. It's not so much a promise to God, but to yourself. You make the vow that you will never speak of it or reveal it to anyone." He paused and a smile slowly spread across his face. "As you can see, I have already partly broken my vow."

"And if we do this, you'll take us?" said Toby with excitement lighting up his face.

"Yes."

"Wow, that would be amazing," said Lana grinning.

"It would," said Toby. "So, let's do it. We'll take the vow and then we can go. Whereabouts in Spain is it?"

Miguel smiled as he put the small statue back in his pocket. "You haven't taken the vow yet, but it's not in Spain. It's in Ecuador."

"Ecuador?" said Lana with an incredulous look. "How did you get here from Ecuador?"

"It wasn't easy," said Miguel with a shake of his head. "I had to sell a couple of things from the library to get some coin, which is why I have that small statue. Then I smuggled myself on board a cargo ship bound for England. I was discovered, but thankfully the sailor who discovered me had known difficult times. He helped me."

"Incredible," said Toby shaking his head. "I don't know how you got past customs. You don't have a passport do you?"

"I don't know what that is, but no, I don't have one."

"You need it to travel abroad," said Lana glancing between the two of them. "Toby, we can't go to Ecuador with Miguel if he doesn't have one. Can we?"

"No," said Toby shaking his head. "And he can't get one. He doesn't exist…or, at least, he's dead. Sorry, Miguel, I mean no offence."

"None taken."

"What are we going to do?" said Lana slumping in her chair. She wanted to go and see this amazing library made by ancient people. And she really wanted to help Miguel get back to his time.

"Morning," said Di rushing into the kitchen. "Sorry, I overslept."

"I'm not surprised," said Toby eyeing his sister. "You look better than Lana."

"I'm fine," she said glancing at Lana. "Headache?"

"Yes…and you should have one too."

Di grinned. “No, I never get a hangover. Anyone for coffee?”

“No, we’re good,” said Toby.

“I will,” said Lana holding out her mug to Di.

“So, what did I miss?”

“Everything,” said Toby.

Di filled the kettle and turned it on before swinging around and looking at the three of them. “What’s been decided?”

“Well, Miguel has agreed to show us the library if we take a vow of silence,” said Lana leaning forward and putting her elbows on the table. “But there’s a problem. He doesn’t have a passport and he can’t get one.”

“Why not?” said Di spooning coffee into the mugs.

“There’s the slight problem of he doesn’t exist,” said Toby with a groan. “And it doesn’t help that he’s not British.”

Di frowned. “Well, how did you get here? Oh, never mind…it doesn’t matter. Get him an illegal one. You know…there must be people who do that sort of thing, forgers and the like.”

Toby’s eyes widened and he stared at his sister. “I can’t believe you know about such things.”

"Good Lord, Toby, we don't all live in boring books and go to uni you know." She rolled her eyes to the ceiling. "There's bound to be someone that can forge a passport."

"And a Spanish one," said Lana sitting up straight. "They won't look so closely at a Spanish one."

"And where do we find a forger?" said Toby running his hands through his hair.

Di finished making the coffee and joined the others at the table. "In a sleazy pub. Barmen always know someone."

"Down at the waterfront," said Lana reaching for her coffee. "That's a bit seedy."

"If you mean dubious, then yes, the waterfront would be the place," said Miguel glancing around at them.

"Well, I think we should leave that to you boys to sort out," said Di sipping her coffee.

"Good idea," said Toby with a nod. "And you girls can work out how we're going to pay for four airfares to Ecuador."

"That's easy. Lana's Nan left her some money, and I'm sure she'd be happy if we used it to help Miguel," said Di raising her brows and looking at Lana.

"Yes, she would, but there's just one problem," said Lana putting down her mug.

"Uncle Rob's going to contest the Will and I don't know when, or even if I'll get any of it."

"Shit…can't you talk to your Dad about it? Get him to convince your Uncle Rob not to contest," said Toby.

"I don't know." Lana shrugged and blew out her breath. "I can try. But he's away on a business trip."

"Let's deal with one problem at a time," said Di. "You two sort out the passport problem and then we'll work out how we're going to pay for airfares."

Chapter 19

Santiago Guayaquil 1597

Alonso stood at the rail taking in the port of Guayaquil stretched out before him. After almost two months at sea, he was relieved to be finally getting back on land. Sea travel had not agreed with him and he'd spent weeks suffering from sea sickness.

White beaches and leafy trees framed the town of timber and stone buildings that stretched back from the coast. It looked like it was a busy port with several galleons moored with their masts bare. Alonso wiped his brow with the back of his hand and blew out his breath. It was far hotter than he'd imagined it would be. Without the stiff breeze filling their sails, it would be stifling.

"So, what do you think, Alonso?" said Father Garcia coming to stand beside him. "It's a fine sight for sure."

"It is." He glanced briefly at him and smiled. "Will you be returning with the Santa Ana?"

"Yes…but don't worry," he said slapping him on the shoulder. "I shall see you safely delivered into Father Acevedo's care."

"Thank you, Father."

"See that tower…it's in the middle of the town square," he said pointing to a tall stone lookout.

Alonso nodded. "Yes."

"Well, Father Acevedo's church isn't far beyond that, just to the left. It's a rather modest timber building with a school attached to it."

"A school? Does Father Acevedo teach?"

Alonso swung around as the ship lurched and the captain started yelling orders. Sailors scurried up the masts and began furling the sails.

"We best get out of the way," said Father Garcia urging Alonso forward with a prod in his back.

Alonso reluctantly headed back below decks. He would've liked to have stayed up there watching the sailors work and it was hot and stuffy below.

"It'll be a while before we're docked," said Father Garcia stopping at the bottom of the narrow steps. "Let's see if the cook has anything to eat. I'm famished."

Alonso smiled inwardly as he followed him to the galley. Father Garcia was often famished but on this occasion, he had to agree with him, he was rather hungry as well. The rich aroma of salt pork stew reached his nostrils as they entered the galley and his stomach grumbled.

"Ah…you have outdone yourself, Marcos," said Father Garcia sniffing the air. "It smells delicious in here."

Marcos' head popped out from behind the bulkhead and he grinned. "I knew you'd find your way here, Father. Sit, I'll get you both a bowl."

"I'm going to miss you, Brother Alonso," said Father Garcia easing himself onto a bench. "I've very much enjoyed your company."

"Thank you, Father." Alonso sat opposite him and smiled. "I wouldn't have survived without you."

"That's true." Father Garcia chuckled. "I hope the rest of your journey is without inconvenience."

Marcos placed two steaming bowls of stew before them and grinned. "Enjoy." He stuck a spoon in each bowl before retreating to the galley.

"Thank you," said Father Garcia breathing in the delicious smell.

"I hope it will be uneventful, but I expect it will be arduous," said Alonso spooning a mouthful of stew into his mouth. He chewed slowly, enjoying the sweet flavours. "I am nervous about what lies ahead."

"Understandable," said Father Garcia with a nod. "But I'm sure Father Acevedo will see you safely to your destination. Where are you going? You never did say."

"Ah…well, I'm sworn to silence on the matter," said Alonso with a shrug. "And, to be honest, I don't actually know precisely."

"Well, that makes it easy not to tell me something you shouldn't." He grinned before going back to his bowl of stew.

Half an hour later they returned to their small cabin, and Alonso dragged his chest out from under the bunk. He'd packed the few items he needed the night before, and all he had to do now was wait. He hoped he wouldn't have to wait long before disembarking. He would be glad to feel solid land under his feet again. He was anxious to meet with Father Acevedo and to get the journey over with, but, on the other hand, he was fearful of what he would find at the end of his travels.

***

Two hours later, Father Garcia and Alonso stepped onto the docks carrying Alonso's chest between them. After so long at sea, Alonso felt strangely odd standing on solid ground that didn't move. When he started walking, his knees trembled beneath him and he frowned.

Father Garcia glanced sideways at him as he wobbled. "You'll get used to it soon enough," he said with a chuckle.

"I hope so."

They wound their way through the narrow streets passing warehouses and vendors. Just beyond the lookout tower, Father Garcia turned left up a narrow alleyway which turned into stone steps going up between the houses. "Just up ahead," he said gesturing. "You can just see the bell tower from here."

Alonso nodded as he did his best to follow Father Garcia without losing his grip on the chest. The steps were steep and he had to lift the chest so that it didn't scrape. He was breathing heavily when they reached the top.

Father Garcia paused. “I just need to catch my breath.”

“So do I,” said Alonso panting.

“It’s a great view from up here.”

Alonso swung around and was rewarded with a view of the town below and the azure harbour shimmering in the sun. “It’s beautiful.”

They continued up a dirt path to a walled courtyard with two large iron gates that were standing open. “This way,” said Father Garcia leading the way inside. He dropped his end of the sea chest and groaned. “Well, this is it.”

Alonso put the chest down and wiped his brow. The trunk of a large leafy tree took up the centre of the courtyard, spreading its boughs to every corner. Around it, was a table with chairs with brightly coloured cushions. The shade was so cool and inviting. Father Garcia groaned as he eased himself into one of the chairs and wiped his face with his kerchief.

A native woman came bustling out of the whitewashed building that formed two sides of the courtyard. She smiled and waved her hands in the air. “Sit Father.” She then disappeared back inside. Alonso raised his brows.

"Sit, Brother Alonso. She'll fetch Father Acevedo to us."

Alonso sat and stared around the courtyard. "Is this his church?"

"No...no. This is his residence and orphanage, which are one and the same," he replied with a chuckle.

The woman returned a few minutes later carrying a tray which she put on the table. "Father is coming," she said in her thick accent. She took three small cups from the tray. "Coffee?"

"Si," said Father Garcia with a nod.

She poured three cups of black coffee and smiled before hurrying back inside.

"Have you had coffee before?"

"No," said Alonso peering at the dark liquid.

"Visitors are always welcome," called Father Acevedo as he stepped out into the courtyard.

Alonso was surprised at how young he was. He'd expected an older man, but he was very young – not much older than himself he thought. Two small boys were hanging from his robes, and he brushed them aside as he made his way towards them.

"Go…go," he said shooing them back inside.

Father Garcia got to his feet and smiled widely. “Father Acevedo, how nice to see you again. You remember me…yes. Father Garcia.”

“Of course,” he said as the two embraced.

“This is Brother Alonso,” said Father Garcia gesturing. “I believe you’re expecting him.”

“Thank you for receiving me, Father,” said Alonso rising to his feet. “I trust you received word from the monastery of Santa Maria?”

“Ah…yes,” he replied as it obviously dawned on him. “I received word a few weeks ago from the Abbot. I’m so sorry for the loss of Brother Miguel.”

“Thank you.”

“Sit…sit. I see Rosa has brought coffee. Excellent.”

Father Garcia and Alonso resumed their seats and waited for Father Acevedo to join them. He sat and picked up his cup. “I pray you’ve had a safe voyage?”

“Yes. It was uneventful,” said Father Garcia taking a sip of his coffee. “Hmm, delicious.”

“Do you know what happened to Brother Miguel?” said Alonso before taking a sip of his coffee. It was bitter but with a flavour he'd never tasted before. He liked it.

Father Acevedo shook his head. "They say the Muki killed him."

Alonso's brows raised quizzically and he stared at him. "Who's the Muki?"

"It's more like what. The Muki lives underground and is rumoured to be a fierce beast. I don't believe it actually exists, it's more like a myth." He paused. "I think he more likely died of a fever."

Alonso's heart jumped in his chest. *Is that what the evil in the caverns was?* He smiled and nodded and did his best to keep his face passive. He was fearful of what he'd find when he got there.

Father Garcia slapped him on the shoulder. "It's a myth, Brother Alonso. There's nothing to fear."

He nodded and took another sip of his coffee. He didn't think so. He knew there was some evil there and this would explain it.

"Are you returning to Spain on the Santa Ana?" asked Father Acevedo looking intently at Father Garcia.

"Yes. I expect we'll sail in a day or two once they've taken cargo on board," he replied with a nod.

“Good. I’ll prepare a despatch for the Abbot of Santa Maria to let him know Brother Alonso has arrived safely.”

“I’d be happy to see it delivered,” said Father Garcia draining his cup. “Well, I best get back. Safe travels, Brother Alonso.”

“Thank you, Father. I wish you a safe voyage as well.”

Father Garcia took his leave and Alonso retrieved the letter for Father Acevedo from his chest. “This is from the Abbot.” He handed him the sealed parchment and sat back down.

Father Acevedo looked at it in surprise as he unfolded and read it. Alonso watched him, but his face gave nothing away. He smiled as he folded it and slipped it into his pocket.

“I think your Abbot is concerned that I wouldn’t take care of you.” He smiled and drank his coffee. “I’ve sent for Mintaka and Wawae. They’ll guide you the rest of the way, but I don’t expect they’ll arrive for another few days. In the meantime, my home is your home.”

“Thank you.”

“I’m sure I don’t need to tell you that secrecy is of the utmost. If the authorities were to discover what we have discovered, they would take it all.”

"I understand, and I've taken a vow of silence."

"Good. Well, rest and recover your strength. You'll need it for what lies ahead."

Chapter 20

Manchester 1968

First thing Wednesday morning, Ian hot-footed it down to Dave's office. Peggy greeted him with a smile. "How was your trip?"

"Fine," he said with a nod. "Perhaps next time we might go up a notch with the accommodation?"

"Oh…a bit too cheap?" She grinned. "Dave's in his office and anxious to see you."

"Thanks." He knocked softly on the office door before entering.

Dave looked up from the other side of the desk with an excited look on his face. "Sit…sit. So, tell me all. What did you find out?"

Ian eased himself into the chair and wondered just where to start.

"Hang on," said Dave. He pressed the intercom button on his phone. "Peggy, get us a couple of coffees would you?" Dave turned his attention back to Ian and sat forward in his chair rubbing his hands together. "Alright…so tell me how it went."

"Well, you were right, the manuscripts were moved from the monastery, but they had a manifest that I managed to get my eyes on."

"Good job, Ian."

"Yes…and no," he said with a grimace. "The manuscripts were only listed by number, but I found two that had the words 'unknown' noted underneath them."

"Two?"

"Yeah, I don't know if it's two copies of one manuscript or two separate ones. At any rate, one was destroyed and the other was sent to the Vatican Library."

Dave sat back in his chair with a groan. "Well, that's that then. There's no way we can get our hands on it."

The door opened and Peggy came in carrying two mugs of coffee which she plonked on the desk. "Anything else?"

"No, thanks Peggy," said Dave with a wave of his hand.

Ian waited until she left and closed the door. "It's not in the Vatican Library anymore. It was sold in nineteen twelve to a man named Haas Kraus."

"Hang on while I write that down." Dave reached for a notepad and pen and began scribbling. "How do you spell that?"

"I think it's k r a u s, but I can't be sure. It was pretty illegible and that's my best guess." Ian sipped his coffee and groaned. "At any rate, it's not going to help us. I've got no idea how we'd track him down."

"Hmm," said Dave rubbing his chin. "There'd be a record of the sale somewhere, but you're right, we're not likely to get our hands on it." He drummed his fingers on his notepad. "Maybe if it was a big enough sale it might be mentioned in the Italian newspapers at the time."

Ian shrugged. "Maybe. Or if he's a well-known dealer in antique books and such he might be easy enough to find."

"Good idea. Leave it with me. I'll get Peggy to do some research and see what we can turn up." He gulped down half his coffee. "I'm not giving up," he said with determination.

Ian smiled. He didn't hold out much hope of finding it, but he wasn't giving up either.

***

It was late Friday afternoon. The phone rang just as Ian was thinking about calling it a day. "Ian Fuller," he said as he picked up the receiver.

"Ian. It's me, Dave."

"Hi Dave. Have you got something?"

"I have. Peggy's been busy calling booksellers, and she managed to get hold of a very helpful chap at Morten's. Anyway, it turns out Kraus was a big deal in the antique book business."

"Brilliant. So, do we know where he is?" Ian pulled his notepad closer and picked up his pen, ready to write down whatever information Dave had.

"We do…he's dead."

"Bugger." Ian dropped his pen and his shoulders sagged.

"It's not all bad, my friend," said Dave. "Apparently, he had a big business in London, so it might be possible to find out what happened to it after he died, presuming he still owned it."

Ian ran his fingers through his hair. "That's a bloody big if, Dave."

"We knew this wasn't going to be easy…we can't give up now."

"So, what are you suggesting?"

"First, we need to see if there's anything in the newspapers from back then. I'm hoping it might mention who he left his estate to. I'm sending Peggy down to the archives office in London next week."

Ian groaned. He didn't like to dampen Dave's enthusiasm, but this was an impossible task. "Alright…sounds good. Let me know how she goes."

"Will do. In the meantime, have a talk with Lana. She might know more than she's letting on."

Ian didn't think Lana knew anything else, but he agreed to Dave's plan anyway. "Okay, I'll talk to her."

"Good. Talk to you next week. Bye."

The phone went clunk and Ian hung up the receiver. He sat back in his chair. There had to be another way to find out where this damn library was. He wasn't holding out any hope of Peggy finding anything of use.

Chapter 21

Manchester 1968

Toby didn't usually frequent the seedier side of town, and his entire body was a jumble of nerves. Miguel looked far more confident striding along beside him and he wondered how the monk managed it. They'd come down to the waterfront near Salford and Toby was anxious to get their business done and to get out of there.

They walked slowly past the King's Arms. Toby didn't think it looked quite dingy enough for their purposes. Miguel appeared to agree as he shook his head and they continued.

Toby had the distinct feeling they were being followed. He glanced over his shoulder and looked sideways. There were very few people about but there was no one behind them and Miguel looked quite unconcerned. A bit further along he spied The Black Friars. A dingy-looking red brick building that seemed to ooze the wrong side of the tracks.

"What do you think?" he said gesturing with his chin.

Miguel surveyed the pub and nodded. "Maybe."

"Let's give it a go." Toby had only taken two steps towards the pub when someone called out to Miguel.

"Miguel, my friend." A tall, rather gangly-looking man, stepped out from the shadows with a wide grin on his face. "What are you doing here? Looking for a lift back to Ecuador?" He chuckled showing his even white teeth.

"Tom! Never mind me, what are you doing here? I thought you were staying aboard the Titan."

"Ah…a change of plans."

"This is Toby," said Miguel gesturing. "And this is Tom. He's the one I was telling you about."

"Nice to meet you," said Toby eyeing the man. *Had he been following them?* He pushed his suspicions aside and smiled. He'd helped to smuggle Miguel into England and Toby could think of no rational reason why he'd be following them.

"Same," said Tom nodding. "So, what are you doing down here, Miguel? Anything I can help with?"

Miguel shot Toby a quick glance. "Maybe. I need to find a forger to get a passport. It would be easier than trying to smuggle myself and my friends aboard a freighter."

"We thought we might find someone in the Black Friars," said Toby.

Tom chuckled and slapped Miguel on the shoulder. "Not the Black Friars my friend. Trust me, go to the King's Arms and ask for Nick."

"Thank you," said Miguel with a look of gratitude.

"Well, good luck," said Tom shoving his hands in his pockets. "I must be off, I'm running late." He leaned in and grinned. "I'm hoping to change my own fortunes tonight." He turned and headed into the Black Friars without a backward glance.

"I had no idea how we were going to find a forger, so it's good luck we ran into Tom," said Miguel as the two set off back towards the King's Arms.

Toby couldn't help but think that luck may have had nothing to do with it. He had no particular reason not to trust Miguel's friend, but something seemed off. It was all too convenient or something. He hoped he was wrong but he couldn't shake the niggling feeling in the back of his mind.

They soon arrived back at the corner and the King's Arms. Toby drew in a breath as they went inside. It was dimly lit and smelled of cigarette smoke and beer. Toby noticed a few people sitting in the shadows but no one paid them any attention. He walked up to the bar with Miguel at his side.

The burly barman looked them up and down with a scowl. "I ain't seen you two before."

Toby drew himself up to his full height and did his best to squash his nerves. "We're looking for Nick."

"Are ye just?"

He continued to scowl and for a brief moment, Toby thought he was going to order them out of the pub. Instead, he gestured with his eyes and brows to a dimly lit corner at the back of the pub.

"Thanks," said Toby giving Miguel a push.

They approached the table with some trepidation. A pall of smoke hung over it and through the gloom, Toby saw a man huddled in the far corner. He was wearing a hat pulled down over his forehead and Toby couldn't make out his features. Drawing in a breath he pulled out a chair and sat down. Miguel joined him a moment later.

Nick blew out a puff of smoke which swirled around Toby's head and he did his best to resist coughing. "What do you gentlemen want?"

"Are you Nick?" said Toby licking his lips.

He was silent for a moment. "I am."

"We're in need of a passport,' said Toby.

"For one of you?"

"Yes, for me," said Miguel in his Spanish accent.

Nick leaned forward and peered at him. "Spanish?"

"Yes."

He sat back and blew another puff of smoke. "Well, that'll cost more. Come back when you've got a photo and fifty pounds."

"Fifty pounds?" said Toby outraged.

"Take it or leave it."

"We'll take it," said Miguel rising to his feet and urging Toby to do the same. "Thank you."

The two left the pub and Toby managed to contain himself until they were out of earshot. "Do you know how much that is?"

"No," admitted Miguel with a sheepish look. "But now I know how much to sell the statue for."

"Don't be ridiculous. It's worth far more than that."

"Alright…how much would you suggest?"

Toby ran his hands through his mop of hair and groaned. "I don't know…but a lot more than that. Lana's father would have a better idea…he deals in antiques and such."

"Well, we'll ask Lana to ask him for us," said Miguel not put off in the least. "Now, what's a photo?"

Toby stopped and stared at him before grinning. "Well, it's sort of…um, it's a likeness."

"A likeness? You mean like a painting?"

"Not quite, but yeah, sort of like a painting." He slapped Miguel on the shoulder. "You're in for an experience."

***

Di was sitting on the couch with a box of tissues, sobbing, while Lana did her best to comfort her. Russell had dumped her and she hadn't taken it well at all.

"He's a cheating shit," said Di in between sobs. "And I can't believe I ever liked him."

Lana didn't know what to say, so she just agreed with her. She was sure Di didn't want to hear that he hadn't actually cheated on her, but he had met someone else. Someone he liked more than Di, or so he'd said.

"I'm not going to shed any more tears over him," she said sitting up straight and wiping her eyes. "Damn him."

"I agree," said Lana with a soft smile. "Don't give him the satisfaction."

"Yeah," she replied before breaking down into sobs again. "Damn it. I really liked him, Lana, and I thought he might've been the one."

"I know…I know, but it's best to find out now, isn't it?"

"Yeah, probably," she grudgingly agreed.

Lana had planned to go out with the girls from work tonight but instead was stuck at home with a distraught Di. It wasn't that she didn't feel for her, she did, but this was such a regular occurrence with Di. Every few months she met the man of her dreams and then it ended in tears - it always did.

Lana was relieved when the phone rang and she was able to extricate herself from the pity party. She hurried down the hall to the kitchen and picked up the receiver. “Hello, it’s Lana.”

“Hey, Kitten” came her father’s voice down the line.

“Dad. How was your business trip?”

“Okay…you know, a crappy hotel and meetings. How’s your week been?”

“Good…except we had a burglar last weekend.”

“What! Are you alright?”

“Yes, I’m fine Dad.” *Should she tell him, and where would she start?* “It’s a long story.”

“Are you home alone? I’m coming round.”

“No…it’s alright. Di’s home with me, and he didn’t take anything or hurt us or anything.”

“Toby’s not home I gather.”

“No. But really, we’re fine.”

“I don’t care, I’m coming round.”

“Alright…see you soon,” she said with a sigh. “Bye Dad.” She hung up the receiver and went back to the lounge room.

“Who was that?” asked Di looking at her with her tear-stained face.

“My Dad. He’s coming around. I told him about the burglar and he’s all worried.”

"Oh, God I don't want your father to see me like this," she said leaping up from the couch. "I'm going to bed."

"You don't have to do that."

She grimaced. "I'm not good company, Lana. I'll see you in the morning."

Di hurried from the lounge and Lana switched on the television before slumping down on the couch. *Poor Di.* She hoped she'd soon get over her broken heart. Of course, she couldn't understand why she constantly picked the wrong guys. Lana herself hadn't had a boyfriend in over a year and wasn't remotely interested in getting one.

Her father arrived twenty minutes later. He came into the lounge looking around like a burglar was about to jump out from behind the couch.

"Thank God you're alright," he said hugging her to him and placing a kiss on the top of her head. "So, what did the police say? Do they think it's the same guy?"

"We didn't call the police," she said pulling free of his embrace. "But, yeah it was the same guy."

"What?"

He looked puzzled, and Lana groaned inwardly. *This wasn't going to be easy.* "Sit down, Dad." She switched off the TV and turned to face him.

"I honestly don't know where to start." She drew in a breath and pinned her gaze on him. "You remember that weird dream I told you about?"

"Yeah," he said frowning at her.

"Well...I don't know how to explain this, but, he was dreaming about me as well. Apparently, it's got something to do with the crystal."

"What crystal? Kitten, you're not making any sense right now."

"There's this crystal that's attached to the key that unlocks the box. It's a pretty thing, but it's also like…um…like a time crystal. Miguel, that's his name, he needs it to get back to his time. That's why he broke into Nan's house and then he came here looking for it."

"Get back to his time?" he said shaking his head. "Are you sure you haven't been reading too much sci-fi?"

"No, Dad. He knows all kinds of stuff, and he can read the manuscript pages – the old writing that no one else can," she said with a note of frustration. "He wrote them!"

Ian sat back on the couch and stared at her with his mouth agape. She could see he was struggling to comprehend what she was saying, and she didn't blame him. The whole story was so far-fetched. "I swear, it's true and we're going to help him get back."

"How?" he said in a quiet voice.

"Well, we've got to get him a passport first." She sat down on the couch beside her father. "Then, we've got to get some money for airfares." She looked sideways at him. "Is there any chance that Nan's estate will settle soon?"

"No," he said shaking his head. "Your Uncle Rob's lodged a challenge. I don't know how long it'll take."

"Oh." She blew out her breath and her shoulders slumped. "I'm not surprised really, I thought he would."

"So, getting back to this man, Miguel," said Ian eyeing her. "How does this crystal get him back to his time? Presuming he's telling the truth that is."

"Well, first he's got to get back to…" She paused at the sound of thumping on the front door. "Oh, that'll be Toby."

She hurried to the front door and wrenched it open. "Forgot your key again?" she said in feigned surprise.

"Yeah, sorry," said Toby as he came inside followed by Miguel.

"How did you go? Did you find someone?" she asked as she closed the door.

"Yeah, but it's going to cost," said Toby with a grimace. "Fifty pounds."

"Yikes.'

Toby walked several paces before he noticed Ian sitting in the lounge. "Oh hey, Mr Fuller."

"Hi Toby," said Ian with a smile. "What are you buying for fifty pounds?"

Lana followed him into the lounge and sat back down. "A passport. This is Miguel," she said waving her arm in his direction. "This is my father."

"Hello," said Ian looking Miguel up and down.

Lana wondered what he was thinking, but his expression gave nothing away.

"Hello," said Miguel with a slight incline of his head. His eyes darted to Toby, then to Ian and back again.

Lana was puzzled by his actions and stared at the two of them.

"Ah…Mr Fuller, I wonder if you could help us?" asked Toby.

"Well, that depends," said Ian cautiously. "If you're asking for a loan, that's probably going to be no."

"No…not a loan," said Toby with a grin. "Miguel has a small statue he'd like to sell. It's really old and we thought you might be able to sell it for us."

"No," interjected Lana with a horrified look. "Don't sell it…it's beautiful."

"But we need money, Lana," said Toby with a shrug.

Ian appeared to ignore them both and rested his gaze on Miguel. "Have you got it with you?"

"Yes," replied Miguel reaching into his pocket. He drew out the small figure and looked at it briefly before handing it to Ian.

Ian blew out his breath and stared at the small statue as he turned it over in his hand. "This isn't European."

"No, it's from Ecuador," said Miguel. "Does that matter?"

"No, not at all. In fact, I've already got a buyer in mind." He squinted at it and looked up at Miguel. "It's got writing on the back. Do you know what it says?"

"Attawal," said Miguel with a smile. "How much can you sell it for, Mr Fuller?"

"Attawal?" Ian's brows raised and he quickly looked at Lana.

"I told you," she said with a smug look.

Lana smiled inwardly. It wasn't often she saw her father flustered, and he was currently breathing quickly and disbelief was written all over his face. He finally gathered himself together and drew in a breath.

"I'll have to consult with a colleague or two about it. It doesn't look Incan and that's unusual for that part of the world."

"I think it's pre-Incan," put in Toby.

"You may be right. Leave it with me and I'll see what I can find out about it and get you a price."

"Thank you, Mr Fuller," said Miguel with a satisfied smile.

Ian pulled a handkerchief from his pocket and carefully wrapped the figurine before putting it in his jacket pocket. "I'll get back to you as soon as I can."

"Well, hopefully, that's the money sorted," said Toby with a grin. "We still need fifty pounds to pay for the passport. Can you donate some cash to the cause, Lana?"

Lana groaned and nodded. "Yes. I can give you…say, fifteen pounds. Will that be alright?"

"Twenty-five would be better, but I'll take fifteen," said Toby with a resigned look at Lana. "I doubt Di can afford anything."

Ian shook his head and looked perplexed. "What are you planning?"

"Well, Miguel doesn't have a passport, and to get him back to Ecuador he needs one," said Toby matter-of-factly. "And, we're going with him, Di, Lana and me."

"Where? Lana, you said he had to get back to his time. I'm sorry, but this isn't making a lot of sense."

"I can't tell you," said Miguel in a low voice. "I've taken a vow of silence on the matter. Toby, Di and Lana have agreed to take one as well, otherwise, I couldn't take them with me."

Ian still looked rather confused, but he didn't say anymore but simply nodded his head. Lana looked sideways at him and wondered what he was thinking. No doubt, when they were alone, he'd question her further, she was sure of it.

Chapter 22

Santiago Guayaquil 1597

After a week of waiting in Guayaquil, Alonso was anxious to continue his journey. Father Acevedo had been most hospitable but he found the children noisy and on the whole chaotic. He'd soon discovered that Father didn't just run a school, but had six orphans who lived in the compound.

They had soon grown used to him and constantly chattered and even asked him to play games. He felt awkward and would rather they just left him alone. He had no idea how Father Acevedo managed them with a smile and a wave of his hands. He'd tried that and they'd laughed at him.

He was sitting in the shade of the tree in the courtyard contemplating the journey ahead. He knew it'd be hot and humid and he presumed there'd be a well-worn path to follow. He prayed they wouldn't meet any dangerous animals – that was probably his biggest fear. He drew in a breath and slowly exhaled. He was anxious to be there but wasn't looking forward to the pilgrimage.

He looked up at the sound of voices as two young men entered the courtyard. They were both wearing white calf-length trousers and ponchos; typical of many of the locals. One of them came forward and peered at Alonso before dropping his woven bag on the ground.

"You're the new Brother?" He gestured to his friend. "The new Brother."

"I'm Alonso," he said rising to his feet and smiling.

The young man grinned. "I'm Mintaka and this is Wawae."

"Thank you for coming for me," said Alonso with genuine gratitude. "You knew Brother Miguel?"

"Yes, we did," said Mintaka with a sad expression. "I'm so sorry he was killed. He was my friend."

Alonso nodded. "He was my friend too."

Father Acevedo appeared in the doorway and smiled. "I thought I heard voices." He walked over to the two men and embraced them. "I was getting worried about you two."

"Sorry, Father," said Mintaka. "We came as quickly as we could, but it was slow coming through the mountain pass."

"As long as you're alright," said Father with a dismissive wave of his hand. "Please sit, make yourselves at home. I'll ask Rosa to bring you some food."

"Thank you," said Wawae dropping his bag and slumping down in a chair.

Father Acevedo disappeared inside and returned a few minutes later and joined them at the table. "I see you've met Brother Alonso," he said easing himself into a chair. "He's anxious to be on his way I'm sure, but I think you should rest here for a day or two."

Alonso sat back down. "Whatever you think is best, Father."

"We can't wait too long," interjected Mintaka with a frown. "We encountered unseasonal rain over the mountains."

Father Acevedo rubbed his chin. "At least rest tomorrow, Mintaka. One day will make little difference."

"Perhaps," he said with a nod before turning to Alonso. "It will be an arduous journey for you, but Wawae and I will get you to Tayos."

“I’ll do my best to keep up.” The unknown always made Alonso nervous, and this journey was rather daunting.

“Do you have much to take with you?” asked Wawae.

Rosa came bustling out with a tray laden with corn cakes and fried fish which she put on the table with a groan. “Help yourselves,” she said wiping her brow.

“Thank you, Rosa,” said Father gesturing to Mintaka and Wawae.

They wasted no time in reaching for a corn cake each and stuffing it in their mouths.

“I don’t have much,” said Alonso. “A chest, mainly filled with parchment, quills and ink.”

“We won’t be able to take that with us,” said Mintaka with his mouth half full.

“I’ll get you a satchel for your parchment and a bag to put your things in,” said Father with a smile. “You’ll find it easier to carry.”

***

After a day of rest, Alonso rose early and dressed. He went out into the sultry morning air of the courtyard to wait for his companions. Father Acevedo had provided a leather satchel for his parchment, and a woven bag, which he was now slinging over his shoulder. He was surprised at how comfortable it was. He looked up and smiled as Mintaka and Wawae stepped out into the courtyard.

They were quickly followed by Rosa. “For the journey,” she said handing each of them a wrapped parcel.

The aroma of corn cakes hit Alonso’s nostrils and he smiled. “Thank you.” He put them in his bag and let his gaze settle on Mintaka and Wawae. He’d learned that Mintaka had once been one of Father Acevedo’s orphans. He now ran errands and would be the one trusted with delivering his pages, as he had done for Brother Miguel.

“We have a long day ahead of us. Are you ready to go, Brother Alonso?” said Mintaka tucking his corn cakes into his bag.

“Yes.” He nodded and with one final glance around the courtyard, he followed his companions out onto the dusty path. Three sturdy ponies were tethered near the gate and Alonso stopped and stared. He’d never ridden a horse and had expected they’d be going on foot. He was more than a little apprehensive.

“Here, give me your satchel,” said Wawae taking it and stuffing it into a saddle bag. "There's no room for your bag." He turned to face Alonso and frowned. "Are you alright?"

Alonso's eyes flitted from Wawae to the pony. "I've never ridden."

"It's easy…here, I'll help you get on," said Wawae grinning.

Mintaka was also grinning as he mounted his pony. "You'll soon get used to it, my friend."

With Wawae's help, Alonso climbed onto the back of the pony and gripped the pummel until his knuckles shone white.

"Relax," said Wawae patting the animal. "Gather the reins up and don't worry…she'll just follow Mintaka."

Alonso nodded, not convinced that he was going to stay seated on the animal. He gathered the reins in his hands while still keeping a firm hold of the saddle. "Don't go too fast."

"Grip with your knees," said Wawae as he mounted his pony.

Mintaka laughed before clicking his tongue and his mount began walking down the dirt path. Alonso's pony followed and he held on even tighter. Mintaka led the way as they headed down the road to the main thoroughfare. From there they rode in a southerly direction until they reached the edge of town. Alonso was glad to see there was a wide dirt path leading inland which Mintaka took. The road wound its way up the sloping hills surrounding Guayaquil, and Alonso was relieved that Mintaka was only going at walking pace and he was quickly getting used to the pony's gait.

As they climbed further upwards and put more distance between them and the coast, Alonso was glad of the shade afforded by the leafy trees. After a few hours, the breeze had disappeared completely and without the shade, it would've been very hot. They appeared to be heading in a south-easterly direction and he could see the snow-capped mountains ahead of them.

"I hope we're not climbing those mountains," he called to Mintaka.

Mintaka laughed and turned his head over his shoulder. "No…there's a mountain pass, my friend, although we won't make that today."

Alonso nodded, relieved by the news.

By midday, the road had narrowed to no more than a path wide enough for two people to walk side by side. It wound its way up the side of the mountain for several miles before levelling out. Alonso's legs were aching from gripping the pony's sides and he relaxed a little to ease their cramping. They stopped on the side of the path for a rest and a bite to eat for half an hour before setting off again.

They hadn't seen too many other people on the road. A shepherd with a small herd of goats had passed them shortly after their stop. A group of farmers carrying large sacks on their backs had lumbered by and a family carrying all they possessed. It was late in the afternoon before Mintaka stopped again under a clump of scrawny trees.

"We'll camp here the night," he said dismounting and stretching.

Alonso slid down from his pony and stood there for a moment as his body reoriented itself. His hips and thighs were stiff and aching and he knew he'd be even sorer tomorrow. Wawae tended the ponies while Mintaka set a small fire and produced a poncho for Alonso.

After a meagre supper of bread and cheese and an uncomfortable night wrapped in a poncho by the side of the road, Alonso was yearning for a comfortable bed.

"How long will it take us to get there?" he asked as they set off on the second day.

"Eight or nine days," said Mintaka picking up the pace. "Don't worry, we should reach Cuenza before nightfall."

"And a comfortable bed," said Wawae reading his mind.

The humidity from the coast had disappeared and been replaced by a cool mountain breeze. Alonso expected it to get hot by midday and hoped they'd be through the mountains and going down the other side by then.

They made it to the pass, which wove its way up and around the mountain, before midday. The ponies easily traversed the rocky path at a sedate pace. As they began to ride down the other side, the valley below beckoned to Alonso. It was a vista of green trees and jungle for as far as the eye could see.

They stopped at the bottom of the steep path for their midday meal and Alonso was glad to be out of the saddle. He wondered if his legs would ever feel normal again. Mintaka produced some delicious pastries from his saddlebags, which he said Rosa had prepared for them.

After a brief rest, they continued on towards Cuenza. The terrain had changed completely from the other side of the mountain, which had been sparsely treed and rocky. Now, they travelled under a canopy of trees in a wide valley that was sheltered from the hot afternoon sun.

It was nightfall before they arrived in the small village of Cuenza. Alonso was exhausted from another day on the road and didn't pay too much attention to where they'd stopped. It was only after he'd dismounted that he realised they were at someone's home.

"Don't forget your poncho, Alonso," said Mintaka grabbing a parcel of food from his saddlebags. "Wawae will tend to the ponies."

Alonso retrieved his poncho and followed Mintaka into the ramshackle building. He was rather dismayed to discover it was a barn – so much for Wawae's promise of a comfortable bed. Bales of hay had been spread out at one end of it and the smell of llamas assaulted his nostrils. Mintaka threw his poncho on the hay and settled himself on top of it.

He spread the parcel of food out in front of him and smiled. "Eat, Alonso, before you fall asleep."

Alonso wasn't that hungry and would've preferred to lie down and sleep, but he forced himself to eat a few mouthfuls. This was not how he thought he'd be spending the night. He'd imagined a well-tended inn with a hot meal and a comfortable bed.

No sooner had he curled himself up in his poncho than he was asleep, from utter exhaustion, and his surroundings mattered not.

Chapter 23

Manchester 1968

Ian was up before dawn on Sunday morning, having spent a sleepless night with a thousand thoughts racing around in his mind. What he'd learned last night still didn't make a lot of sense to him, but one thing he was sure of – the Spaniard knew the whereabouts of the library.

He prepared a pot of tea, and while it was brewing, he stared at the small statue. It was proof, and he was sure Dave would agree with him. The prize was so close he could almost taste it. He lifted the figure and inspected it closely. It was made of pottery and finely carved and parts of it had been painted in subtle colours. Pottery didn't tend to be that valuable, certainly nowhere near as much as metal objects.

He imagined the library of metal tablets, glinting in the dim light and what they would be worth. It was unimaginable. *Priceless*. He put the figure back on the table and grinned.

"You, my little friend, are going to make us rich," he said out loud as he walked the two steps to the bench and poured himself a mug of tea.

He picked up the phone and dialled Dave's number and waited while it rang at least half a dozen times. *Come on, pick up*. A couple more rings and then finally Dave's sleepy voice came down the line. "Hello."

"Dave, it's me Ian."

"Shit…I thought someone had died. Do you know what time it is?"

"Time…now that's interesting. You'll want to get your arse out of bed and over here as fast as you can," said Ian ignoring the angry tone in Dave's voice. "I have big news, my friend. I have a statue from the metal library in my possession, and I know how we can get to it."

There was silence for several seconds. "You spoke to Lana? I bloody knew it. She knew more than she's been letting on."

"It's even better than that, Dave. Get over here."

"I'm on my way."

Ian grinned as he hung up the receiver and sipped his tea. He had yet to formulate a plan but he was confident between him and Dave they'd work it out. All they had to do was get themselves to Ecuador with Lana and the rest of them. *That might not be so easy*. He dismissed the thought and took another sip of his tea. He'd have to speak to Lana again. Not a lot of what she'd told him made sense and he needed to understand exactly what she was going to do. A pang of guilt shot through him which he quickly buried. She'd never know – at least she wouldn't if he was careful.

Fifteen minutes later there was a knock on the door, quickly followed by Dave bellowing. "It's me…let me in for God's sake."

Ian grinned as he opened the door and Dave hurried inside. "Alright, I came as fast as I could. Where is it?"

"On the table," said Ian smiling inwardly as he closed the door. "Would you like a cup of tea?"

"God no…coffee," said Dave settling himself at the table. "So, tell me everything, starting with how you know this came from the library."

Ian turned on the kettle and prepared to make a mug of coffee for Dave while he told him about the events of the night before. He poured the coffee and put it on the table in front of Dave before sitting down opposite him.

"According to this Miguel, the writing on the back of that statue says, Attawal."

"Attawal?" asked Dave looking at him. "That's from the pages." His eyes had widened and he had an incredulous look on his face.

"Exactly," said Ian grinning. "If we are to believe him, then he knows where this library is, and he can lead us to it…there's just one problem."

"Just the one?" said Dave slumping back in his chair. "I think you're being optimistic."

"Perhaps, but the kids need money to get to Ecuador, and they want to sell this statue to finance their trip," said Ian leaning forward. "Dave, if we can't get them enough money then they're not going to be able to go. And we need them to go if we're going to tag along and discover where this library is." He glanced from Dave to the statue and back again. "Think about it…this is huge, and we can't let it slip between our fingers."

"I agree, but these things aren't worth that much," said Dave picking up the statue and turning it over in his hand. "It's pre-Incan and therefore a rarity, but it's not worth much more than two or three hundred pounds."

"We can't actually sell it," said Ian taking it out of Dave's hand and placing it back on the table. "We can't have something like this hitting the market…too many questions my friend."

Dave slowly nodded and sipped his coffee. "What are you suggesting we do then? We'll have to buy it ourselves," he said answering his own question. "Are they all planning on going? Shit…that'll cost a bomb."

"Yeah. I reckon they'll need at least twelve hundred pounds."

"Alright…alright," said Dave putting down his coffee and running his fingers through his hair. "Let's think about this. They need money to go, and you're suggesting we tag along somehow…that's going to cost as well. I can probably put up the twelve hundred…it'll be bloody worth it!"

Ian sat back in his chair and grinned. He was glad Dave was quick to catch on, and also glad he'd put up the bulk of the money. "Thanks. I'll fund my own way, and I'll lend Lana anything extra she might need," said Ian nodding. "We just have to work out how we can follow them without them knowing it. That's going to be tricky, and I'm not sure how we'll do it."

They spent the next few hours going over ideas on how they might accomplish their goal. Dave was all for him getting himself on the same flights as them and dogging their footsteps, and Ian following a day behind. Ian thought it was too risky. *What if they lost them*? They had no idea where they were going and how would he even know where Dave was?

"Look, the simplest plan is for me to go with them," said Ian in exasperation. His frustration was beginning to show and he did his best to restrain himself. "I'll tell Lana that I'm worried about her going to such a place. I'll accompany them as far as they'll allow, and then you and I will track them from there."

"Alright," said Dave finally conceding. "But, I'll get there ahead of you. I don't plan on being left behind on this."

"Good idea. As soon as I know where we're going and when, you can arrange to get yourself there ahead of us."

"Right, let's do this," said Dave grinning. "I'll get you the twelve hundred tomorrow when the bank opens."

"Brilliant," said Ian heaving a sigh of relief. "And the good thing is, Lana's never met you, so even if you're spotted it won't matter."

"Yeah, as long as we aren't seen together," said Dave with a serious look. "We can't afford to stuff this up, Ian. We're only going to get one shot at it."

"Don't worry, we're not going to stuff it up. This is going to be life changing."

Dave got to his feet and tucked the statue into his pocket. "I get to keep this then," he said patting his pocket and grinning.

"Yeah, I suppose so."

Ian was sorry he didn't get to keep it, but seeing as Dave was putting up the money, he could hardly argue.

***

By lunch time Monday, Ian had formulated his plan to approach Lana about accompanying them. He'd have the money for them by tonight and he was confident she wouldn't say no. He leaned back in his chair as he imagined the treasure they'd find. He'd be set for life. He sprang forward in his chair as the phone rang. He grinned as he picked up the receiver.

"Ian Fuller." He'd been expecting Dave's voice to be on the other end, but it wasn't.

"Mr Fuller, good afternoon. It's Alan Robinson, your mother's lawyer."

"Yes, I remember. How can I help you?"

"Well, actually I thought I might be able help you, Mr Fuller. I'm not sure if you're aware that your brother has lodged a challenge against Mrs Fuller's Will?"

Ian groaned inwardly. "Yes, he told me."

"Do you and your daughter plan on defending the challenge?"

Ian hadn't given it any thought whatsoever and was a bit surprised that they'd need to defend their claim. "I don't know, Mr Robinson. I have no idea how these things work."

"Right, well, may I suggest we meet to discuss it. I can fit you in on Wednesday morning if that will suit?"

"No…my daughter works and won't be able to get away. Can you make it lunch time?"

"Hmm, let me see," said Mr Robinson. He was quiet for several seconds. "How about twelve thirty on Thursday?"

"Yes, that'll work."

"Excellent. Well, I'll see you then."

"Thank you," said Ian before hanging up the phone.

This was the last thing he needed to deal with right now, and he wished he could just ignore it. But…he had no intention of letting Rob get away with what should be Lana's.

***

Lana was drying the last of the tea dishes just as there was a knock at the door. Di grinned and whipped the tea towel out of her hand.

"That'll be your father. Go…I'll finish these."

"Thanks," said Lana hurrying down the hall to the front door. She wrenched it open and smiled widely at her father.

"Hey, Kitten." He hugged her before stepping inside. "How was your day?"

"Great." She closed the door and followed him down to the kitchen.

"Hi, Mr Fuller," said Di swivelling around to greet him.

"Hi, Di."

"So, how did you go, Dad?" said Lana getting straight to the point. "Did you manage to sell it?" She slumped down in the chair at the table. "I'm kind of sorry if you did."

"Yeah, I did," he said reaching into his jacket pocket and pulling out a wad of cash. "And, I got a very good price for it. I'm sure Toby and Miguel will be happy. Aren't they here?"

"No, they've gone to pay for the passport," said Di wiping her hands and joining Lana at the table. "This is getting so exciting!"

Ian put the cash on the table in front of them. "Well, when they get home, tell them I got twelve hundred pounds for it."

"Wow…I didn't think it'd be worth that much," said Lana eyeing the money. "That should be enough to pay for all our flights to

Ecuador." She grinned before standing up and hugging her father. "Thanks, Dad." She kissed his cheek before sitting back down.

"I'm happy to help," he said sitting down. "Now, there's a couple of other things I want to discuss."

"Oh…I'll leave you to it then," said Di leaping to her feet.

"No…no need, Di," said Ian pushing her back down. "This first part involves you too."

"Oh?" Di plonked herself back down and looked at him.

Ian cleared his throat and smiled. "I'm worried about you all going off to Ecuador by yourselves. It's not like England over there…so, I was thinking I should come with you…to keep an eye on you."

Lana smiled. That was so like her father, to be all worried about her going off to South America. But, she wasn't going alone.

"You don't have to do that."

"But I want to, Kitten. I'd feel happier knowing you're safe."

Di raised her eyebrows and gave Lana a private look that said 'what a drag', and Lana had to agree. Having her father tag along would definitely cramp her style and would take the fun out of the whole adventure. She shook her head.

"I'm not a child, Dad, and I'm not going by myself. Anyway, it'll be fun…just the four of us."

Ian smiled and nodded, but Lana thought she saw something else behind his brown eyes – *was it determination*?

"You won't even know I'm there," he said reaching out and squeezing her hand. "Please, you don't know how dangerous it could be."

"We'll be careful, Mr Fuller," put in Di with a shrug. "At any rate, Miguel's only letting us go with him if we take a vow of silence or whatever. I don't think he'd want anyone else coming."

"That's right," said Lana retrieving her hand. "I promise I'll be careful Dad and we won't do anything silly. Alright?"

He was quiet for a few moments before he finally nodded. "Yeah, alright." He smiled at them both. "Promise me you'll be really careful?"

"I promise," said Lana relieved that he'd given up on the idea. She couldn't think of anything worse that her father tagging along. "Now, what else did you want to talk about? You said there were a couple of things?"

He blew out his breath. "I got a phone call from Alan Robinson today…you know, your Nan's lawyer."

"Ah…I'll leave you to it," said Di jumping to her feet. "Bye, Mr Fuller."

She hurried from the kitchen and Lana heard her footsteps going down the hall.

"Has Uncle Rob changed his mind?" asked Lana with a hopeful look.

"No, and according to Mr Robinson we'll need to defend our position." He ran his hands through his hair and groaned. "I have no idea how these things work, but Mr Robinson wants to discuss it with us. Twelve thirty Thursday. I hope you can make it."

"Yeah, I can make it," she said slowly. "Why do we have to defend ourselves? Surely, what Nan put in her Will should stand."

"Honestly, I don't know," he replied with a shake of his head. "But, I'm sure Mr Robinson will fill us in on Thursday." He paused and appeared to contemplate for a moment. "I…I'd really prefer to come with you to Ecuador. Please, won't you reconsider? I'll take Miguel's vow or whatever."

Lana knew he'd given in too easily and she groaned inwardly. She didn't want him there keeping an eye on her…following her every move. She could think of nothing worse. "No, Dad. I want to go with Toby, Di and Miguel on my own. Okay?" She smiled. "I promise I'll be fine and I'll tell you all about it when I get back."

"I'll just be there to keep an eye on you, I promise not to get in the way," he said in an insistent tone.

Lana always had difficulty saying no to her father, but on this issue, she dug her toes in. "Please, Dad don't make this any harder. I don't want to hurt your feelings, but I don't want you to come with me."

He sighed and smiled. "Alright…I can see you're not going to change your mind."

"No, I'm not." Lana was determined and prayed her father would drop the subject.

He nodded and got to his feet. "No bad feelings, Kitten. I get it."

She smiled as she stood up and hugged him. "See you on Thursday then."

"Yeah."

She saw him to the door and sighed with relief when she closed it behind him. She hoped that would be the end of the matter.

Chapter 24

Manchester 1968

Toby felt the flutter of nerves in his stomach as he pushed open the door to the King's Arms. Miguel's presence at his back gave him the courage to enter the dingy pub. It was still early; not yet nine o'clock, and he fully intended to hand over the cash and get out of there without delay.

His eyes went straight to the dimly lit corner at the front of the pub where he expected to see a pall of cigarette smoke. The table was empty and Toby groaned. He glanced at Miguel and shrugged before approaching the bar.

The barman sidled along as soon as he saw them. "What'll it be?"

"We're looking for Nick," said Toby with a glance over his shoulder. "Is he around?"

"Two pints?" he replied quirking his eyebrows.

"Sure," said Toby licking his lips. "Is Nick here tonight?"

"You're the two guys who want the passport, aren't ye?" he asked as he poured two pints.

"Yes," said Toby wishing the man would just answer the damned question.

"Nick doesn't normally do business on a Monday, but I'm sure he'll make an exception." He put the two pints of beer on the bar and grinned. "That'll be a crown."

Toby pulled out his wallet and paid him. "Thanks."

The barman nodded and wandered down to the end of the bar and disappeared out the back. Toby relaxed somewhat as he picked up his beer.

"Cheers, my friend," he said raising his glass.

Miguel looked at him, puzzled.

"It's what you do when you have a drink together," said Toby grinning.

"Oh…well, cheers," said Miguel lifting his glass. "I've never had beer."

"Well, there's a first time for everything." Toby gulped down his beer.

Miguel followed suit and then a wide grin spread across his face. "Hmm, nice."

Toby glanced around the nearly empty room. There were only a couple of other patrons sitting in a dimly lit corner. He leaned against the bar and drank down more of his beer.

“Do you think Mr Fuller will have sold my statue yet?” asked Miguel eyeing him.

Toby shrugged. “Maybe. Don’t worry, he’ll definitely get you the best price. I just hope it’s enough.”

“What do we do if it isn’t?” said Miguel sipping his beer. “I don’t have anything else to sell.”

Toby turned to face him and rested his hand on his shoulder. “It’ll be enough to get you home.” He removed his hand and smiled. “Even if we can’t go with you, I know Lana will give you the crystal…you don’t need to worry.”

Miguel nodded and gulped down more of his beer. “Thank you…that eases my mind somewhat.”

They finished their beer and still, there was no sign of Nick or the barman. Toby walked up and down the bar and peered at the swinging door. He was anxious to get this over and done with and was considering calling out when the door opened and Nick appeared. With a glance in their direction, he ambled over to the table in the corner and slumped down in the chair. Relief flooded through Toby as he nudged Miguel and the two of them made their way over to the dimly lit corner. Toby pulled out a chair and sat down before reaching for his wallet.

Nick eyeballed them from under the rim of his hat before lighting a cigarette. The puff of smoke hung in the air between them like a cloud, but Nick remained silent. Toby licked his lips and pulled fifty pounds in small notes from his wallet.

"Fifty pounds," he said putting them on the table and sliding the small pile towards Nick. "For the passport."

Nick casually collected the cash and counted it before shoving it into his pocket. "Photo?"

Miguel pulled a strip of four photos from his pocket and put it on the table in front of Nick. "I hope these will do."

Nick took another drag on his cigarette and blew smoke across the table before picking up the photos. He grinned. "Been to a photo booth I see. Name?"

"Miguel Perez."

Nick got to his feet and put the photos in his pocket with the cash. "Come back in a week…not Monday." Without another word, he ambled back towards the bar and disappeared through the swinging door.

Toby let out his breath and sat back in his chair. *Thank God that was over*. He smiled weakly at Miguel. "Come on, let's get out of here."

***

Lana put the money her father had given her on the table in front of Toby and Miguel and smiled widely. "That's twelve hundred pounds…and it should be enough to get us all to Ecuador."

Toby let out a whistle as he eyed the cash. "That'll definitely be enough. We just have to wait until we get Miguel's passport next week and then we're set to go." He grinned as he slapped Miguel on the back. "You're going home, my friend."

Tears welled in Miguel's eyes as he glanced at Toby before settling his gaze on Lana. "Please thank your father for me…I can hardly believe it."

"I'll tell him," said Lana with a soft smile. "But first, we need to get airfares booked, and I thought you could do that, Di, you've got more time than any of us."

Up until this point Di hadn't been paying any attention, and she pulled her nose out of the magazine and peered at them. "What?"

"Can you book the airfares?" said Lana rolling her eyes. "You've got Friday off work…you'd have time to go to the travel agent. Yes?"

"I suppose so," she replied slowly closing her magazine. "Where are we going exactly?"

"Good point," said Toby nodding. "Where are we going, Miguel?"

Miguel shifted uncomfortably in his seat. "You have yet to take your vow of silence."

"Oh, with all the excitement I forgot about that," said Lana with a frown. "How do we do that?"

"You must vow before God that you will not speak of it to anyone," said Miguel matter-of-factly. "Do you have a church?"

"Of course. We could do it at St Mary's," said Lana nodding. "Will we need Father O'Malley do you think? If not, we could all go this Sunday."

Miguel shook his head. "Father O'Malley won't be necessary. This is a promise you'll make to God."

"Alright, let's do it this Sunday then," put in Toby with a grin. "In the meantime, it would help if you could tell us where we're going. What's the closest big city?"

Miguel looked unsure as he glanced at them, but then Lana noticed his expression softened and he nodded. Lana was delighted that he trusted them, although what choice did he have? Without her crystal, he couldn't get back to his time.

Miguel smiled. "Guayaquil…it's the nearest port. From there, we have to go inland."

"Alright, do you want to write that down, Di?" said Toby nudging his sister.

"No," she said scowling at him. "I'll remember."

"How long will we need do you think, Miguel?" said Toby ignoring Di who continued to glare at him. "Did it take you long to get to Guayaquil?"

"Several days…possibly two weeks for you to go to…where we're going, and then to get back to Guayaquil," said Miguel tapping his finger on his chin.

"Two weeks?" said Lana slumping back in her chair. "I didn't think I'd need to take that long off work."

"You'll need at least three," said Toby shaking his head. "I expect we'll get flights direct to New York, but then we'll need a couple of stopovers to get down to Ecuador. We don't want to cut it too fine."

"No, you'll want time to explore this library," added Di with her voice dripping with sarcasm. "I'm not going to bother taking holidays, I'm just going to quit. They've already cut my hours and I'm not fussed about it anyway."

"That's all very well for you," said Toby looking disgruntled. "I'm right in the middle of exams. I can't possibly get away until the end of the month."

"Yeah, but then you've got about five weeks off," said Lana not showing any sympathy for him. "I'll have to put in for holidays."

"Do you want to do this or not?" said Toby scowling at them.

"Yes," said Lana blowing out her breath.

"Right, well, we need a firm plan," said Toby leaning forward in his chair. "We'll take our vows on Sunday, Miguel will get his passport next week…so let's book flights for the first week in July, allowing two weeks in Ecuador." He stared around at the three of them and waited until they all nodded their affirmation. "Brilliant. Let's do it."

Lana sat back with a satisfied expression on her face. Finally, they were getting somewhere and she could hardly wait.

"Well, I'm glad that's done," said Di getting to her feet. "I'm going to run a bath. See you tomorrow."

"Night," Toby called to her as she headed out the door.

"I better get going too," said Miguel standing and pushing his chair under the table. "I'll call in again on Friday night."

"Okay," said Toby with a nod.

"I'll walk you to the door," said Lana leaping to her feet.

She followed him out of the kitchen and down the hall to the front door. "Miguel."

He stopped and looked at her. "Yes."

She glanced over her shoulder. "I had a dream about you last night."

He smiled. "We're still connected through the crystal. I dream of you sometimes as well."

"Well, it's just that…there was another man with you," she said licking her lips. "Did someone else time travel with you?"

He looked puzzled for a moment and then he grinned. "No, that would be Tom. He helped smuggle me into England, and I ran into him again."

"Oh?"

"He invited me to stay with him, which was most kind of him," he said reaching for the front door handle. "It's much better than the hostel I was staying at."

"Oh…well, that explains it then."

"There's nothing else to it," he said with a grin. "Good night, Lana."

"Good night."

She closed the door behind him and leaned against it. She was rather disappointed in his explanation.

Chapter 25

Manchester 1968

Lana arrived at Robinson and Son's just before twelve thirty. She hurried inside and was relieved to see her father was already there. She smiled and plonked herself down on the chair next to him.

"Hey, Dad."

"I'm glad you made it," he said wrapping his arm around her shoulders and squeezing. "Are you alright?"

"Yeah, I'm fine. Just a bit apprehensive." She smiled and shrugged. "I wish Uncle Rob wasn't doing this…I feel like it's so disrespectful to Nan."

"I know." He removed his arm and rubbed his hands together. "I wish he'd leave it be, but he's convinced that you've had a hand in her Will," he said. "I know you didn't," he hastened to add.

"Thanks, Dad."

They sat in silence until the receptionist called to them a few minutes later.

"Mr Robinson will see you now."

Lana stood and followed her father down the hall to Mr Robinson's office and closed the door behind her. Mr Robinson smiled and gestured to them to sit. She sat down on the edge of the nearest chair and folded her hands in her lap. She licked her lips and did her best to dismiss the anxiety that was rising from her stomach.

"Good afternoon," said Mr Robinson with a warm smile. "I wish we were meeting under happier circumstances, but I'm glad you could both come." He opened the folder that was sitting on his desk in front of him and shuffled through a few papers. "As you know, Mr Robert Fuller has lodged a challenge against Mrs Fuller's Will. He's applied for the beneficiary percentage to be split seventy percent to him, and thirty percent to you, Mr Fuller."

"What?" said Ian leaning forward.

Mr Robinson raised his head and looked directly at Ian. "He's claiming that Miss Fuller manipulated your late mother into leaving her forty percent of the estate. And, he's also claiming that portion for himself, citing that he has cared far more for your mother than you have."

"That's outrageous," said Ian glancing wide-eyed at Lana.

Lana didn't know what to say. She could hardly believe that he was applying for more than half of her Nan's estate. Surely, her father was entitled to half.

"Well, I would agree with you, Mr Fuller. Your mother was fully aware of what she was doing when she made her last Will, and I'm prepared to testify to that. However, in order to succeed, I recommend that you both prepare evidence to support your claims."

Ian sat back in his chair and with a look of disbelief on his face. "What sort of evidence?"

"Before we get to that, I need to know if you would like me to represent you?" He clasped his hands together and leaned his chin on his hands. "A hearing date has been set for the twenty sixth of June."

"Yes…yes of course we'd like you to represent us. Wouldn't we?" said Ian turning to Lana.

"Yes," she replied nodding. "I should be able to make it. I'm going overseas in early July." An odd expression crossed her father's face and Lana frowned. "If I can't, you can attend the hearing for both of us, can't you?"

"Yes, Kitten," he said with a smile that didn't quite reach his eyes. He turned his gaze back to Mr Robinson. "What evidence will we need?"

"Right, well for you, Mr Fuller, anything you have that indicates you cared equally for your mother. How often you visited, what assistance you gave her, that sort of thing." He sat back in his chair. "Of course, we already have evidence that your mother believed you were equally deserving. She left you and your brother equal shares of her estate."

"And what about me?" asked Lana.

"Your claim is a little more difficult," said Mr Robinson with a frown. "Do you have any letters or photographs that show you had a special relationship?"

"Nan used to take me on holidays and she always took photos. We'd send a postcard to Dad and I think she kept a diary," said Lana compressing her lips. "She always sent me a birthday card and we spent lots of time together."

"Did she have the same relationship with her other grandchildren?" he asked.

Lana shook her head. There was only ever the two of them on holidays, and she didn't think Nan took Pat and Morris to Blackpool. "I don't think so. My mother died when I was young and Nan did her best to fill the gap."

"Excellent. If you can provide any photos, letters and postcards of the two of you.

Also, see if you can locate your grandmother's diary. That could prove to be invaluable, for both of you." Mr Robinson closed the folder in front of him and smiled. "I believe we have a good chance of defending against this challenge."

"I certainly hope so," said Ian blowing out his breath.

"Well, I'll leave it to you to gather what evidence you can and drop it off here, at the office. I'll be in touch, Mr Fuller, with details of the hearing and anything else."

Ian nodded and rose to his feet. "Thank you, Mr Robinson."

They left the office and were silent until they got out onto the footpath. Ian wrapped his arms around Lana and kissed the top of her head.

"Don't worry, Kitten. We'll win this," he said before letting her go.

"I hope so. It's so unfair what Uncle Rob's trying to do," she said smiling weakly.

"Yeah. Are you free Saturday morning? I can meet you at Nan's house at around ten and we'll search out some photos and stuff."

"Okay." She kissed his cheek and smiled. "I've got to get back to work. I'll see you Saturday."

***

Saturday dawned grey and overcast which matched Lana's mood. She wasn't looking forward to going through her Nan's things – it felt so wrong. But, what Uncle Rob was trying to do was even worse. Her boots clacked on the footpath as she made her way around the corner and down the street to her Nan's house. She found herself silently counting her footsteps as she walked up the path to the front door. Drawing in a breath she reached for the handle. *Was her father here yet?*

The door swung open answering her question, and she stepped inside. "Hey, Dad."

There was no reply. She shut the door and dumped her bag on the hall table as she removed her coat. "Dad?" she called a little louder folding her coat and putting it on top of her bag.

A moment later he appeared at the foot of the stairs. "Hi, Kitten."

"Are you alright?"

He looked rather frazzled like he'd been running his hands through his hair, which was standing on end. And he looked a bit shocked.

"Not really…it looks like Rob's beaten us to it."

"What?"

"The box your Nan used to keep her letters and keepsakes in is gone," he said with a shrug. "And her jewellery box."

Lana stared wide-eyed at him. She could hardly believe what he was telling her. "What about her diary and photo albums?"

"I don't know, I haven't got to them yet. Come and see for yourself."

Lana followed him upstairs to her Nan's bedroom. She paused on the threshold as memories came flooding back. She could see her Nan lying against the pillows as she took her last breath. She'd held her hand and felt the life go out of her. Lana's eyes welled with tears as she struggled to push the memory aside.

Her father, noticing her frozen in the doorway, wrapped her in his arms without saying a word. She leaned against him and buried her face in his shoulder as she let her tears go. She missed her so much, and being back here was a lot harder than she'd imagined it would be. After a few moments, she pushed away from her father and wiped her eyes with the back of her hand. Now was not the time for grief.

"I'm alright," she said with a sob. "I'll be fine."

Her father squeezed her arm and grimaced. "I know, I miss her too."

Lana compressed her lips and managed a nod. "Let's see if her diary's still here."

Ian glanced around the room. "Any idea where she kept it?"

"No…I only ever saw her writing in it," said Lana glancing at the dressing table. A clean rectangular space where the jewellery box once sat stood out from the dusty surface. She couldn't believe Uncle Rob had taken it. "She would've kept it hidden away, I'm sure."

Ian was already rummaging through the bedside table. "It's not in here." He stood there looking around the room for a moment. "Why don't you look for it, and I'll go see if the photo albums are still in the closet?"

"Alright."

Her father hurried from the room and Lana slumped down on the end of the bed. *Oh, Nan, I miss you.* She sat there for several minutes before getting up and opening the top drawer of the dressing table. Her Nan's stockings and a cute little bag of potpourri were all she found. The next drawer was full of underwear, and Lana just felt around, not wanting to rummage through her Nan's undies.

A thorough search of the dressing table turned up nothing. There was only one other possible hiding place, and that was the wardrobe. She was sure her father would've already looked there, and anyway, she knew the bottom of it was a jumbled-up mess.

She made her way back downstairs, where her father was sitting on the floor surrounded by several photo albums.

"Oh, good he didn't take them," she said smiling.

"Well, not all of them. How did you go? Anything?"

"No."

"It looks like Rob's taken any albums that had photos of you and Nan." He pulled the last album out from the bottom of the closet and opened it. "Yeah, this one's all of us when we were kids."

"What? He's taken them too?" Lana slumped down on the floor beside her father. "What are we going to do?"

Ian blew out his breath as he began to put the albums back into the closet. "I don't know."

"Maybe Nan kept things in other places. We'll have to search the whole house," she said getting to her feet.

Ian shook his head as he put the last album in the closet and stood up. "There's no point, Kitten. Rob would've searched everywhere and taken anything we could use."

"I can't believe it. This is so unfair. If Nan was here, she'd give him what for."

"If Nan was here, we wouldn't need these things." He closed the closet door with a clunk. "Fancy a cuppa before we go?"

"Yeah…coffee for me."

Chapter 26

Ecuador 1597

After six days on the road, Alonso was body weary and saddle sore. They'd left the jungle behind them yesterday, and according to Mintaka would reach the village of Maria de Nieva by nightfall. This time, he'd promised a proper bed and a hot meal. Alonso dared not hope, but the idea had imbued him with enthusiasm for the afternoon that lay ahead.

The terrain was now mostly open grassland, with the mountains to their right and many small farms dotting the landscape. They'd stopped at one such farm at midday, and the inhabitants had kindly shared their meal with them. Alonso still had the taste of the spicy empanadas in his mouth, and he wasn't sure he liked it.

The afternoon wore on in a monotonous fashion and Alonso, who was half asleep in the saddle, was taken by surprise when Mintaka called to him.

"Look, Alonso, up ahead…do you see…Maria de Nieva."

He straightened himself and looked to the horizon. A smattering of low buildings were visible, not far ahead of them, on the other side of a wide river. “I see,” said Alonso grinning. “I hope you haven’t lied to me, Mintaka.”

“He hasn’t lied,” said Wawae trotting up beside him. “They have a very comfortable inn, with real beds.” He grinned as he urged his mount into a trot.

Alonso did the same and the three of them hurried to the edge of the river. Mintaka came to a halt in front of a rickety-looking rope bridge. Several planks were missing, and it sagged more than usual in the middle.

“We walk from here,” said Mintaka dismounting and taking the reins in his hands.

Alonso followed suit and eyed the bridge with some trepidation. It didn’t look very safe to him.

“We cross one at a time,” said Mintaka. “I’ll go first.”

Without waiting for a response, he urged his mount forward, clicking his tongue and pulling the reins taut. Alonso watched as Mintaka slowly made his way across the bridge. It creaked and groaned under the weight, and Alonso thought the pony was going to baulk in the middle of it. He tossed his head showing the whites of his eyes. He could hear Mintaka crooning softly to the animal. He held his breath while Mintaka navigated the other half and finally stepped onto solid ground.

"Alright, your turn, Alonso," he called.

Alonso took a firm grip of the reins as he urged his pony to walk onto the bridge. He fixed his gaze firmly on Mintaka. Taking one step at a time, he did his best to ignore the groaning bridge beneath him and the fear that was writhing in his belly. His pony was pulling against him, but he held firm until he stepped onto the riverbank on the other side. He prayed he wouldn't have to ever do that again.

A few minutes later Wawae joined them and they mounted their ponies and set off again. They were soon at the outskirts of the village, and Alonso was surprised at the size of it. Unlike the other villages they'd passed through, which were no more than a group of houses, Maria de Nieva had a church, a small market and, most importantly, an inn, that from the outside looked quite sizeable.

Alonso dismounted and stretched his weary body before handing the reins to Wawae, who grinned at him.

"Feeling sore?"

"Very," said Alonso with a grimace. "How much further is it?"

"Maybe, another day and a half," said Mintaka dismounting. "You can rest when we get there, my friend."

"You should wear your poncho," said Wawae looking Alonso up and down. "You'll blend in better."

Alonso was a little alarmed at needing to blend in, but he kept his thoughts to himself. He nodded and retrieved his poncho from the saddlebags along with his satchel. He'd been writing a letter to Padre whenever he had the chance, and he thought he'd have time to add a little more to it tonight.

"We'll meet you inside, Wawae," said Mintaka. "Take care of the ponies."

Wawae nodded as he gathered the reins for the three ponies and headed off around the back of the inn. Alonso slipped his poncho on before following Mintaka into the low timber building.

The room wasn't well lit and it took a few moments for Alonso's eyes to adjust to the dim interior. There was a small counter at one end of the large open room, with wooden tables and chairs scattered about. Several groups of people stopped and stared as they entered before going back to their own affairs.

"Sit down, Alonso. I'll arrange our rooms and some food," said Mintaka gesturing to a table.

Alonso nodded before selecting an empty table and easing himself onto the bench seat. He put his satchel down beside him and glanced around the room at the other people. He noticed some were giving him furtive glances and he lowered his eyes and stared at the table as Wawae's words played over in his mind.

Mintaka joined him five minutes later and put three mugs on the table. "Horchata tea," he said settling himself on the bench opposite Alonso.

Alonso smiled. "Thank you." He'd had the tea before and took a mouthful, relishing the fruity taste of it.

"I've arranged two rooms for tonight," he said. "I'll share with Wawae and you can have a night without his snoring." He grinned before picking up his mug.

Alonso was surprised when Wawae joined them. He hadn't been gone long enough to tend to the ponies and settle them for the night. Mintaka shared his astonishment.

"What have you done with the ponies?" said Mintaka raising his eyebrows.

"They've got a young stable hand," said Wawae easing himself onto the bench beside Alonso. "For a few coins, he's taking care of them."

"Oh, well I'll see if I can get us supper then," said Mintaka getting up and walking over to the counter.

"Are you looking forward to a good night's sleep?" said Wawae sipping his tea.

"I am. And I'm expecting to," said Alonso with a grin. "Mintaka's got me a room to myself…so, no snoring from you."

Wawae feigned innocence and then slapped Alonso on the back. "In that case, I expect you'll be riding like the wind tomorrow. We might even get to Tayos before nightfall."

Alonso knew he was joking with him and laughed. He'd only fallen off his pony twice, which was more good luck than good riding. He could handle a short trot, but even that scared him.

They retired to their rooms after supper and Alonso pulled out his parchment and writing implements and settled himself at the small table in his room. He planned on adding to his letter to Padre tonight with the news that he would reach Tayos in another day. He would be glad to get there. The journey had been more arduous than he'd imagined, and his whole body ached.

He spent the next half hour describing his journey to Padre, before sitting back with a satisfied smile. He stretched his hand and sighed before repacking his satchel. He hadn't shared his fears of what he might find in Tayos. Miguel's death was still a mystery. No one seemed to know what had killed him, but he knew there was some evil at work. Fear squirmed in his belly at the thought and he quickly pushed it away.

He knelt, bowing his head as he began to recite his evening prayers. He prayed for God's guidance and blessing, and that he'd keep him safe. When he finally finished with 'amen', he felt more at ease. The frightening thoughts had faded and God was with him.

When he climbed into bed he moaned with delight. He hadn't slept in a proper bed since leaving Guayaquil, and after finding his favourite sleeping position, he went straight to sleep.

He could hardly believe it when he woke in the morning. He'd slept the whole night through, and the gloomy grey of dawn was only just now peeping through the slats on the window. He stretched, rolled out of bed and groaned as his back complained about being once again upright. Another day or two in the saddle stretched before him and he anticipated reaching his destination. How nice it would be to finally have this all behind him.

Gathering his thoughts, he prepared for the day ahead and with his satchel under his arm made his way out to the salon. He hoped there might be time for a mug of tea before leaving. Mintaka gestured to him as soon as he entered, and he joined him at one of the tables.

"I got you a mug of tea," he said pushing it towards him. "Wawae's saddling the ponies and then we'll be off."

"Thank you," said Alonso taking a mouthful.

"Mintaka! Mintaka!" yelled Wawae as he came rushing through the door.

Mintaka swivelled around and stared at Wawae, who had a look of alarm on his face.

"The ponies…they're gone," he said hurrying over to them. "Someone's taken them."

"What?"

Mintaka leapt to his feet and hurried out the door with Wawae right behind him. Alonso grabbed his satchel and went after them. He arrived around the side of the inn just as they disappeared into a ramshackle barn. He followed them inside. Mintaka was staring around the small stables like he expected the ponies to appear out of thin air.

"Where's the stable hand?" he asked.

Wawae looked startled for a moment, before looking to the ceiling. "I expect he's asleep in the loft. I don't know, I haven't seen him this morning."

Mintaka wasted no time in climbing the ladder which led to the loft. He paused at the top of it before climbing back down. “He’s not there. Damn it, Wawae. Are you sure he worked here?”

“He said he did.” Wawae shook his head and looked bewildered.

“I’m sorry…it’s not your fault,” said Mintaka with a groan. “But, we’ve not only lost our mounts but the food we had for the rest of the journey.”

“Maybe there’s some explanation,” said Alonso looking at the empty stalls. “We should ask the innkeeper if he knows anything.”

“Hmm…we should, but I doubt it,” said Mintaka. “It looks like we’re walking to Tayos from here.”

They went back inside the inn and Mintaka spoke at length to the innkeeper. He confirmed that he didn’t employ a stable hand, and whoever Wawae had left the ponies with, had obviously stolen them. It was unlikely they’d be able to track them.

“He probably took them as soon as you turned your back, Wawae,” said Mintaka as they left the inn. “Father Acevedo will be most disappointed in us.”

“I’m so sorry,” said Wawae looking forlorn.

They called in at the market where they managed to buy enough provisions to get them to Tayos, and then they set off on foot. Alonso was grateful that the weather was mild – at least it wasn't too hot or rainy.

Chapter 27

Manchester 1968

Lana and the others arrived home from church at around three o'clock. They'd taken their vow of silence and Lana was surprised at what a spiritual experience it had been. She hadn't been expecting to feel any different, but she did. It was like a weight had been added to her and the gravity of her vow had settled itself snugly into her being. It was a very odd feeling.

"Coffee?" asked Toby taking off his coat and hanging it on the stand at the foot of the stairs.

"Yes, please," said Di kicking off her shoes with a groan.

"Yes," said Miguel.

"Me," said Lana following Toby and Miguel down the hall to the kitchen. "I'll give you a hand."

"So, Lana, I never got a chance to ask you how things went yesterday," said Toby as he filled the kettle and turned it on. "Did you get everything you need?"

"No…Uncle Rob had beaten us to it," she replied, taking four mugs from the cupboard. "He's taken the letters and photos, and even Nan's jewellery box. We searched everywhere, and we couldn't find her diary either, so I expect he took that too."

"Bloody hell. What are you going to do?" said Toby spooning coffee into the mugs. "You can't let him get away with it."

"I don't know…what can we do?"

"What's a diary?" asked Miguel from the table.

"It's a book you write in," said Di plonking herself down at the table. "You know, like a…book."

"Oh, well done Sherlock," said Toby with a scoff.

Di poked her tongue out at him before turning her back.

"Did you look under the bed?" asked Miguel with a quizzical expression.

Lana glanced at him. "I didn't, but I expect Dad did. Why do you ask?"

Miguel shifted uncomfortably and bowed his head. "Well…it's just that…well, there's a box under the bed. It's got old shoes in it, and under them are books."

Lana gaped at him.

"I…I," he stammered.

"You saw them when you searched her house, didn't you?" said Lana finding her voice.

“Yes,” said Miguel with a sheepish look. “I’m sorry.”

“Oh, thank you.” Lana rushed over to him and grabbing his face between her hands, kissed him on the forehead.

Miguel reddened.

“Do you think they’ll still be there?” said Toby putting two mugs of coffee on the table.

“I don’t know,” said Lana lifting the telephone receiver.

She dialled her father’s phone number and waited impatiently while it rang. “Ian Fuller,” came her father’s voice down the line.

“Dad…it’s me.”

“Hey, Kitten. What’s up?”

“Did you look under the bed yesterday?”

“Yeah, there was just a box of old shoes under there.”

Lana’s heart skipped a beat. “Did you look in it? Under the shoes?”

“No. Why?”

“According to Miguel, there are books under the shoes. Nan’s diary might be amongst them.”

“That sounds like something she’d do. Leave it with me, I’ll head over there right now and check it out.”

There was no mistaking the excitement in his voice and Lana found herself hoping that Uncle Rob had also overlooked the box of shoes.

"Thanks, Dad. Let me know."

"Don't worry, I'll call you back. Bye."

"Bye."

She hung up the receiver and turned and grinned. "He's going to go over there to take a look. Thank you so much, Miguel," she said sitting down. "We might still have some hope of beating Uncle Rob."

"I hope they're still there," said Miguel picking up his mug of coffee.

"I can't believe he cleaned the place out," said Di. "What a rat."

"I know, I can't believe it either," said Lana sipping her coffee.

Uncle Rob certainly wasn't who she'd thought he was. He'd always been kind, not generous, but she'd never seen this side of him before. She just hoped her Nan's diary was hidden in the bottom of the box.

"Now," said Toby joining them at the table with his mug of coffee. "Did you get to the travel agents on Friday, Di?"

Di looked at the three of them and shrugged. "No. I wasn't sure of the dates and stuff. I'm not working on Wednesday - I'll go then."

“Whatever dates you can get for the first week of July,” said Toby getting up and perusing the calendar hanging on the back of the door. “So, the fourth or fifth would work.” He looked over his shoulder at Lana. “Will that work for you?”

“I don’t know…what days are they?” she asked.

Toby pulled the calendar off the wall and handed it to Lana. She scanned the calendar and shook her head. “No, Monday the first would be better for me. I’ll need to take three weeks off work, and it’s better to start on a Monday.”

“Okay, Di, see if you can get flights on the first, and return flights that land us in Manchester no later than the... What do you think, Lana?”

“The Nineteenth,” said Lana handing the calendar back to Toby.

“Alright, I’ll do it on Wednesday,” said Di before gulping down her coffee.

“I really appreciate you all helping me,” said Miguel with a serious look. “I don’t know how to thank you.”

“Taking us with you will be thanks enough,” said Toby slapping him on the shoulder. “I can’t wait to see this library. It’s going to be totally rad.”

"Can you tell us where we're going?" said Lana with an enquiring look. "We've all taken our vow of silence now."

Miguel smiled and nodded. "Very well. From Guayaquil, we'll head southwest to a place called Cueva de los Tayos."

Lana and Toby were hanging on his every word. It sounded so exotic to Lana's ears and she imagined an ancient monument or something marking the location. Then they'd go underground, probably into catacombs or crypts. She was excited and a little scared all at the same time. She could hardly believe her family had been hiding this secret for centuries.

"It's a very deep cave system with a wide opening that goes straight down," said Miguel motioning with his hands. "There's a hidden entrance to the underground library near the opening." He paused and sipped his coffee. "I can't explain it more than that. You'll have to wait and see it."

"Wow, I can hardly wait," said Toby.

***

Ian let himself in the door, shoved the keys back in his pocket and closed it behind him, flicking the snib in place. He headed straight up the stairs to his mother's bedroom, taking a moment to stare at the spot where her jewellery box should've been. He still couldn't believe Rob's actions. Rob had always been his annoying younger brother and Mum's favourite. He grimaced.

He was still thinking about Rob when he bent down on his hands and knees and peered under the bed. He grabbed the cardboard box with both hands and pulled it out. He'd never been jealous that Rob was his Mum's favourite. He'd always felt he was more like his father, not just in looks, but in personality. Like Ian, he'd always sailed a little close to the wind and occasionally on the wrong side of the law, but he was sure his mother didn't know that about him. Ian had always been discreet and she couldn't see past Rob anyway.

The box was full of old worn shoes which he quickly tossed aside, anxious to see what lay at the bottom. Pulling the last few shoes out he saw them – not just one notebook, but several. He reached for one and flipped it open.

> *Lana came for tea last night. It was so good to see her. She still doesn't have a boyfriend, and I do hope she finds the right one soon. I want nothing but happiness for her. She's always been such a joy to me.*

Ian grinned. “We’ve got you, little brother.”

There were four more in the box which he pulled out and placed on the floor beside himself, before putting the other one on top. He tossed the shoes back into the box and shoved it under the bed. Gathering the diaries under his arm, he got to his feet and headed downstairs to the kitchen. He put them on the table and grabbed the receiver from the wall phone near the dresser. The ringtone buzzed in his ear and he smiled as he dialled Lana’s number.

She answered immediately. “Is that you Dad?”

“Yes, it’s me. I’ve got them,” he said laughing.

“Oh, I can hardly believe it. Them? How many are there?”

“Five. I’ve read a bit of one, and I can tell you this is all we’ll need,” said Ian letting his gaze rest on the pile of diaries. “I’ll get them to Mr Robinson tomorrow. I’m confident we’ve got all the evidence we need to beat Rob.”

“That’s fantastic.”

Ian froze as he heard the front door open, followed by voices wafting up the hallway.

“I’ve got to go, Kitten. I’ll call you later.”

"Okay, bye Dad."

He hung up the receiver, scooped the diaries off the table and tucked them under his arm. Drawing in a breath, he walked to the doorway and wasn't at all surprised to see Rob and Rose standing at the foot of the stairs.

"Back to take more of Mum's stuff I see," said Ian.

Rob looked at him in mild surprise. "I could say the same about you, brother."

"Hello, Rose," said Ian walking slowly towards them.

"Good afternoon, Ian," she said in a small nervous voice as her eyes flitted between the two brothers.

Ian was seething on the inside at their gall. It was not enough to take any evidence Lana could use, now they were back to take more of what was not theirs. "Just bear in mind, that whatever you take you'll only have to return when you lose your challenge." He continued walking to the front door, anxious to be out of there.

He heard Rob's laugh behind him and his back stiffened.

"We both know I'll win," Rob continued. "Not to worry, you get thirty percent either way."

Ian closed his eyes and breathed in through his nose. *Don't bite*! He reached for the handle and pushed the door open. "I'll see you in court," he called over his shoulder, before stepping outside and slamming the door shut.

His insides felt like jelly as his anger quickly subsided. He had the diaries, there was no way Rob could win.

Chapter 28

Manchester 1968

Di teased the last bit of her fringe and plastered it in hairspray before peering at herself in the mirror. Smiling with satisfaction she left the bathroom, grabbed her shoulder bag and headed out the door. Her heels clicked on the footpath as she walked down to the bus stop.

She'd thought about not going to Ecuador with the others. She despised the outdoors, and the idea of trekking through a jungle wasn't her idea of fun. But, even she found herself intrigued by this stupid library of metal tablets. *Whoever heard of a library without books*? Anyway, she had no intention of missing out on what she hoped would be a fun holiday.

She caught the bus down to High Street where the distinctive red Lunn Poly Holiday Shop took up pride of place. She inspected her reflection in the window before pushing open the door and going inside. The shop was empty of customers and a smiling travel agent immediately greeted Di with a sunny 'good morning'.

"Good morning," said Di gazing around the shop.

There were racks of glossy brochures depicting sunny beaches and tantalising destinations. Di wished she was going to those places rather than Ecuador.

"Were you looking at going somewhere particular?" asked the travel agent.

"Ecuador," said Di.

"Ooh, that sounds exciting," she said gesturing to the chair beside her desk. "Take a seat and we can discuss it if you like."

"Thanks," said Di sitting down. "There are four of us going, and we want to go on the first of July, if possible."

"Okay…let's see. Where did you want to fly into? Quito?" She flipped open a brochure that showed the various jet routes from England to the world.

"No, Guayaquil."

"Oh, BOAC doesn't fly into Guayaquil. Let me see," she said closing the brochure and grabbing another one. She flipped through several before she looked up and smiled. "But KLM does."

"That will do," said Di quite unconcerned with what airline they'd fly on.

"Alright. By the way, I'm Marj." She pointed to her name badge and smiled.

"Hi. I'm Di, Di Markwell."

"So, you want to book four airfares to Guayaquil?"

"Yes, please," said Di.

"And what about accommodation? I've got a brochure here you can look at to get some ideas." She opened a drawer and fossicked through a pile of brochures before extracting one. She put it on the desk in front of Di. "Have a look through and see what you think. I don't think there are a lot of options."

"Thanks." Di flipped through the brochure, not really paying too much attention to the options. "Can I take this with me and discuss it with my friends?"

"Yes, of course, that's the idea," said Marj with a smile. "It'll take me a couple of days to work out your itinerary, so there's no rush."

"Oh." Di realised she was quite ignorant of how these things were done. Of course, she'd been overseas, to Ibiza last summer, but she hadn't done the booking herself. "I can come back on Friday."

"Perfect. I should have your itinerary sorted by then. And, if there's anything you're not happy with I can always change it, until we confirm the booking that is."

"Okay, thanks."

"When you come back on Friday, I'll need to know the names of your travelling companions. You can bring their passports as well if you like, or you can leave them until the tickets are ready to be collected. Whatever you prefer," said Marj with a smug smile. "Oh, and I'll need a deposit."

Di was starting to regret that she'd agreed to make the travel arrangements. It was a lot more complicated than she'd imagined it would be. She stood up and smiled.

"Okay. I'll be back on Friday with all of that."

"Great…see you then."

Di left the shop feeling somewhat overwhelmed by the whole thing. She had no idea what accommodation they'd need. Obviously, something in Guayaquil and then at Tayos, or whatever the place was they were going to. Maybe she could shove this onto Toby. She didn't like being responsible for it at all.

***

Lana left Di to dry the last of the tea dishes and plonked herself down at the table. "Was this the only brochure they gave you?"

"Yeah," said Di grabbing the tea towel that Lana had dumped on the bench. "That's all she had for Ecuador."

Lana flipped open the brochure and after reading the contents, turned to the page for Guayaquil. There were only two accommodation options, and Lana didn't think it would matter which one they chose. "Did she say anything about how we'd get to Tayos?"

"No…but to be honest I didn't ask," said Di with a shrug. "It was a lot harder than I thought it'd be."

Lana looked at Di and smiled. "You're doing a great job." She closed the brochure. "Anyway, I'm sure Miguel will know how to get to Tayos, and where we can stay along the way."

There was a knock at the door and Di looked quizzically at Lana. "Are we expecting anyone?"

"Probably my Dad," said Lana getting up and heading out of the kitchen.

She reached the end of the hall and opened the door. "Dad, I thought I might be you."

"Hey, Kitten," he said giving her a quick hug as he came in the door. "Sorry, I haven't been around."

"That's okay." She closed the door and followed him down the hall to the kitchen.

"Hi, Di," he said with a smile. "Any chance of a cup of tea?"

"Yeah, I'll do it," said Lana reaching for the kettle.

"Ah, I see you've been to the travel agents," he said picking up the brochure. "Are you all booked then?"

"Just about," said Di hanging the tea towel on the rack. "She'll have our itinerary ready on Friday."

"Excellent. Let me know when you've got it so you can give me all the details," he said easing himself into a chair. "I at least want to know where you're going and when."

"Don't worry, Dad, I will," said Lana putting a tea bag into a large mug. She was thankful he hadn't insisted on coming with them, and if knowing the itinerary kept him happy, well she'd oblige. "So, Dad, tell me about the diaries. Have you spoken to Mr Robinson about them?"

"I have," he said grinning. "Your Uncle Rob doesn't stand a chance at winning. Actually, I ran into him and Aunt Rose at the house on Sunday."

"What?" said Lana turning abruptly to face her father.

"Yeah, I presume they were taking stuff," he said with a shrug. "I got rather angry and left."

"I don't blame you," she said putting the mug of tea on the table in front of him. "They've got no right taking Nan's things."

"Don't worry, Kitten. Once we defeat his challenge, they'll be forced to bring everything back."

"I can't believe what your uncle's doing," said Di sitting down and picking up the brochure. "It's so wrong."

"I know," said Lana sitting beside Di. "I don't know why he's doing this. He's always been so kind to me."

"Kind, maybe," said her father with a grimace. "But he's never been generous." He sipped his tea. "Enough of Rob. Where are you thinking of staying?"

"There's only a couple of options," said Di flipping to the page headed Guayaquil. "Hotel del Parque or Oro Verde."

She turned the brochure around so Ian could see. "They both look about the same," she said with a shrug.

Lana looked up as she heard the front door open. "That must be Toby and Miguel," she said smiling at Di. "I hope they got the passport."

Toby and Miguel arrived in the kitchen a few moments later, and Toby dumped a pile of canvas backpacks on the table. "Miguel and

I went to the army disposal shop and got these," he said grinning, "they'll be perfect."

"Did you get the passport?" asked Lana.

"We did," said Miguel pulling it from his pocket and waving it about.

"These are so ugly," said Di pulling a face as she inspected one of the backpacks. "I'm not using that."

"Suit yourself," said Toby with a shrug. "You can trek through the jungle with a suitcase under your arm if you like."

"Trek through the jungle?" said Ian in an alarmed tone. "Where are you lot going?"

"We can't tell you," said Lana reaching out and squeezing his arm. "Don't worry, we'll be fine." She wished Toby hadn't mentioned the jungle. The last thing she needed was her father being worried about where she was going.

"Hey, I see you went to the travel agents today," said Toby scooping the brochure off the table. "Did you book everything?" He flipped through the brochure before looking at Di with a questioning look.

"I did," she said with a smug smile. "I'll have the itinerary on Friday…oh, and I'll need all your passports."

"Great," said Toby dropping the brochure back on the table. "This is going to be so rad, I can hardly wait."

"Why don't you come for tea on Friday, Miguel?" said Lana picking up one of the backpacks. "Di will have the itinerary and we can work out the finer details."

"Thanks, I will," said Miguel with a grin. "I can't thank you all enough. I can hardly believe I'll be going home soon."

Toby slapped him on the back and grinned. "We're just as excited. Hey, why don't I pick up pizzas on my way home on Friday?"

"Good idea," said Di with a nod. "That'll save us cooking."

***

Lana ran home from the bus stop and was panting with a stitch in her side by the time she reached the front door. She half bent over as she reached into her bag for the door key. Of all the days for Mrs Clausen to ask everyone to do overtime. She'd been thinking about tonight all day. Di would have the itinerary and in less than two weeks she'd be jetting off to South America. Of course, the whole library thing was intriguing, but going to such an exotic destination was going to be so exciting.

She unlocked the door and hurried inside, pushing the snib across as soon as she closed it. “I’m home,” she called as she dumped her bag on the hall table.

“In the kitchen,” came Di’s reply.

She grinned as she headed down the hall to the kitchen. The three of them were there, with pizza boxes open on the table and cans of beer in front of them.

“Sorry, we started without you,” said Toby with his mouth half full. “Grab yourself a beer.”

“Thanks, I will.” Lana grabbed a can off the bench before sitting down. “So, did you get to the travel agents? I hope you did because I’ve been thinking about it all day.” She slid a slice of pizza onto a plate and took a big bite. It was cheesy and delicious and she sighed with contentment.

“I did,” said Di with a grin. “Actually, it wasn’t as hard as I thought it was going to be. Marj, the travel agent, was just so helpful. Here, this is for you.” Di tossed a copy of the itinerary across the table at her. “It’s all booked, so don’t find anything to complain about. Okay?”

“Okay.” Lana grinned as she grabbed the itinerary and began to read.

"I hope you've got your holidays booked," said Toby eyeing her from across the table.

"I have…I've got three weeks off, and I can't wait," said Lana raising her eyes to look at Toby. "Let me read this thing."

Lana took another bite of pizza while she read through their itinerary. She mentally calculated how many days it was going to take to get to Guayaquil. A stopover in London, New York, then Curaçao before arriving in Ecuador. Four nights there and four nights back. That was already eight days before they even got to Tayos.

"It's going to be tight," she said pushing the itinerary aside. "How long will it take to get to Tayos from Guayaquil?"

Miguel shrugged. "I'm not sure…I think it will only take us a couple of days, maybe three."

"It'll be fine," said Toby before gulping down his beer. "Eight days travel, plus a bit of time difference, maybe six days to Tayos and back. That still leaves us a week to explore the library…more than enough time."

"I thought you said we'd be trekking through the jungle?" said Di. "That'll take more than a couple of days." She looked alarmed at the thought.

"There's only a little bit of jungle," said Miguel with a grin. "There was a bus…I didn't get on it…I was scared." He shrugged and looked sheepish. "I'm not scared anymore."

"Well, I'm glad to hear it, because I'll be going by bus," said Di emphatically.

"Can I give this itinerary to Dad?" asked Lana tapping her finger on it. "He wants to know where I'll be at any given moment."

"Sure," said Di with a shrug. "I'm sure I can get you another copy when I pick up the tickets."

"Great, thanks."

The rest of the evening was spent going over and over their plans until Lana wanted to scream. Toby could be so pedantic sometimes, and he wanted every little detail locked in and agreed upon. She climbed into bed feeling exhausted, but excited for what lay ahead.

Chapter 29

Monastery of Santa Maria de Huerta
Spain 1597

Pedro had searched everywhere he could think of, and still, he'd found nothing of any significance. He was sure there was more to it than the pages of odd writing he was supposed to transcribe. *Why else was there all this secrecy*? It made no sense to him. He knew Brother Alonso was hiding something, he just didn't know what.

It was late when he left the scriptorium. He'd deliberately waited until everyone was at supper. He cautiously made his way down the hall to the dormitories, keeping to the shadows and glancing every which way. He'd done his own fair share of spying and knew there were eyes everywhere.

He paused outside Brother Alonso's room, pressing himself hard up against the cold wall. He waited, barely breathing until he was sure no one had followed him. He quietly opened the door and slipped inside.

He groaned at the darkness of the room; he couldn't see a thing. He fumbled around on the nightstand until his hand landed on the tinderbox. He grinned as he lit the lamp and waited for it to sputter to life. The room was barely furnished with a table, which held a bowl and ewer, and a small chest of three drawers. A narrow bed and nightstand completed the room.

He pulled open the top drawer – it was empty. Groaning with frustration he opened the next one and then the bottom drawer. They were all empty. His eyes flitted around the small cell as he tried to think of where Brother Alonso might hide something, anything. He ran his hands under the nightstand thinking something might be tucked under it, but he came up empty handed.

He turned his attention to the narrow bed and lifted one corner of the mattress. Nothing. He wasn't ready to give up just yet, and he rummaged through the bedclothes and lifted the mattress in every corner. He sat down on the bed and ran his hands through his hair. He was sure Brother Alonso had something to hide, he knew it in every fibre of his being.

On several occasions he'd seen him late at night, creeping through the halls when he thought no one saw him. He'd never had reason enough to report his comings and goings to Brother Benito, but he had always been suspicious of him. He stood up and bent down to peer under the bed. It was dark and he couldn't see a thing. Grabbing the lamp, he bent down again peering into every corner. He was about to give up when a small corner of parchment caught the light. It was tucked in between the bed slat and the mattress with just a small piece peeking out. He grinned as he grabbed it and pulled it free. He unfolded it and read the sprawling writing.

It is done, and you can be assured she will keep it safe. Diego.

It wasn't much, but it was far more than he'd found to date. It was odd that it was written in Spanish rather than Latin. He sat back on the bed holding the small piece of parchment between his fingers. When he thought about it further, he'd often see Brother Alonso and Brother Diego in conversation. *But what was she keeping safe for Brother Alonso?* Pedro tucked the piece of parchment into his pocket and extinguished the lamp. He smiled as he left the room.

***

As soon as morning prayers were dispensed with, Pedro made his way to the scriptorium. He lingered for a few minutes outside the door, before heading out to the garden. He walked along the covered walkway with deliberate steps and down the path to the carpenters workshop. He paused in the doorway, and drawing in a breath, he went inside. He caught sight of Diego just inside the door and approached him.

"Brother Diego, a moment of your time," he said in a low voice.

Diego looked momentarily surprised, but quickly hid his feelings. "Good morning, Brother Pedro. How can I assist?"

Pedro took a fleeting look around the workshop and leaned in closer to Diego. "I'd like a private word, Brother."

Diego's face was unreadable as he nodded and walked from the workshop. Pedro followed him outside and down the path to a covered arbour.

"What do you want?" Diego's voice was guarded and full of distrust.

Pedro pulled the small scrap of parchment from his pocket and read it aloud. He watched Diego's face intently. Diego's expression remained unchanged and Pedro groaned inwardly. "I know who she is," he said in a low voice.

Diego licked his lips and stared at Pedro. "I'll ask again. What do you want?"

Pedro laughed. "I think you know very well what I want. What is your sister keeping safe for Brother Alonso?"

"Nothing. That's an old note. Now, if there's nothing else, I have a lot to do."

"Forgive me if I don't believe you," said Pedro carefully folding the note and slipping it back into his pocket. "Perhaps, you'd like to explain it to Brother Benito? I'll give you a day or two to decide."

With a smug smile he turned and walked back down the path to the covered walkway, leaving Brother Diego alone under the arbour. Pedro was confident in what decision Brother Diego would make, and finally he'd know what Brother Alonso was up to.

***

Diego's heart was beating hard against his chest as he watched Pedro walk down the path. His mind was racing as he tried to think of what to tell him. He had to protect Alonso and Maria and he currently had no idea how he was going to do that.

He slowly walked back to the workshop, all the while running various scenarios over in his mind. He was sure he could come up with some benign reason for the note, but Brother Pedro would be unlikely to drop the matter.

Diego did his best to put all thoughts of Brother Pedro aside as he set to work. But he couldn't push it from his mind and by the time he left the workshop for the day, he was frantic to find a solution.

He spent longer than usual at evening prayer, hoping that God would give him the answer he needed. When he finally got off his knees and left the chapel, he was no closer to knowing what he was going to tell Brother Pedro. God had not eased his mind or provided any answers.

He retired to his dormitory and spent the night tossing and turning. He wished Alonso was here, or someone he could turn to, but he couldn't tell anyone. If Padre found out that Alonso had broken his vow, then they could both be expelled, maybe even excommunicated. By the time he swung his legs over the side of his cot, he was in a cold sweat. One plan had been playing over and over in his mind since dawn, but it was a terrible idea. It went against his conscience and he was sure God would not absolve him of it. *What choice did he have*? A hard knot had formed in the pit of his stomach and he felt ill.

He readied himself and walked down to the chapel for morning prayers. As soon as he entered he saw Brother Benito who had not yet knelt for prayer. Drawing in a breath he approached him.

"Brother Benito, good morning," he said nodding his head.

"Brother Diego."

"I seek an audience with Padre," said Diego, almost regretting his words as soon as they left his lips. "Today, if possible."

Benito raised one dark eyebrow and stared at him. "That can possibly be arranged. Or perhaps I can better assist you?"

"No." Diego shook his head and forced a smile. "Thank you for the kind offer, Brother Benito, but I must speak with Padre on this matter."

"Very well. I will arrange it…but he's a busy man. I will let you know when he can see you."

"Thank you."

Diego inclined his head before stepping aside and attending to his prayers. He recited his prayers from memory, while his mind was busy thinking about his meeting with Padre. It was too late to back out now, and the thought of what he was about to do, left him with a feeling of dread and mounting panic.

Chapter 30

Monastery of Santa Maria de Huerta
Spain 1597

Pedro set his page aside and drew in a breath. He hadn't been able to concentrate on his work since finding the note from Diego. And, although he was anxious to confront him again, he knew he had to be patient. Given enough time, Diego would come to only one conclusion, and that was to tell him what Alonso had been doing.

Even he had trouble imagining what Alonso had given to Diego's sister for safekeeping. *What could it possibly be*? He kept coming back to one conclusion – it had to be something Brother Miguel had sent him from the new world. He ran his hands through his hair and groaned. Nothing made any sense but he knew there was something more to it. His instincts told him there was much more going on than he understood. And Diego was the key.

He slid the page he was transcribing towards himself and stared at it. He had no idea what it said and Alonso couldn't have understood it either. *So why the vow of silence and the secrecy that Padre insisted upon?* He smiled as he picked up his quill – he would soon know.

He spent the afternoon trying to push all thoughts of Alonso and Diego aside without success. He finally gave up and left the scriptorium well before suppertime. He locked the door behind him and wandered the corridors, hoping to encounter Diego. He could wait no longer.

There was no sign of his quarry and he could feel the frustration building inside him, ready to explode at any moment. He drew in several deep breaths and closed his eyes as he leaned against the panelled wall. Patience, he reminded himself. He stood there, breathing steadily for several minutes until he felt the calm return to him. He opened his eyes, and there was Diego, walking down the corridor alone. He smiled inwardly as he slowly approached him.

He knew Diego had seen him; Diego stopped and stared in his direction with his face unreadable. Pedro was undaunted as he sidled up beside him.

"So, Brother Diego, have you reached a decision?" he said in a low voice, glancing furtively down the hall.

"I have," said Diego in a flat tone. "I'll meet you in the courtyard after supper and tell you whatever you want to know."

A smug smile spread across Pedro's face as he nodded. "Don't be late."

Tucking his hands up his sleeves he continued walking with slow deliberate steps. Finally, he would know the truth and he was confident, that whatever he learned would result in Brother Alonso's expulsion.

***

Diego's heart was racing and he drew in several deep breaths to calm the feeling that his legs were about to collapse beneath him. He needed to see Padre, right now, and yet he'd received no word from Brother Benito. Panic gripped him as he hurried down the hall towards the Abbot's office. He said a quick prayer beseeching God's help as he came to a halt outside his office. He sat down on the hard bench and prepared to wait for as long as was needed.

Every few seconds he glanced up and down the hall, ready to leap off the bench if he should see Pedro coming. Ten minutes later, there was no sign of anyone and Diego was sure he was going to be sick. He stood up and was preparing to leave when the Abbot's door opened and Brother Benito stepped out. He smiled.

"I was just about to send for you, Brother Diego," he said with a nod. "Padre will see you now."

"Thank you."

Diego let out a long breath as he went into the Abbot's office, closing the door softly behind him. It was too late now. He had to say what he'd come to say, knowing full well it would blight his soul for eternity.

Padre was busy writing and only briefly glanced at Diego. "Take a seat, Brother Diego, I'll be but a moment."

Diego sat on the edge of the hard chair and folded his hands in his lap. He'd been running this meeting over in his mind all day, and imagining how the conversation would progress. Now that he was here - he wished he wasn't.

"Now, you have a matter you wish to discuss?" said Padre putting down his quill and peering at Diego.

Diego nodded and licked his lips. "Yes, Padre." He thought his heart was about to beat out of his chest and the squirming in his stomach was like a nest of vipers. "It's Brother Pedro. He…I thought you should know …he's."

Padre smiled and leaned forward. "I find it best to start at the beginning, Brother Diego. Take a breath and calm yourself."

"Yes." He drew in a breath and slowly let it out. It didn't do anything to calm him. "I feel compelled to tell you, although it is not my wish to break Brother Pedro's confidence, he has…he has broken his vow of silence, Padre."

"This is a serious accusation, Brother Diego. Do you have proof?"

"I do. He has shown me the pages sent by Brother Miguel. I can describe them in detail if you like." He paused and lowered his eyes. "He then threatened me to keep silent on the matter. He has asked me to meet him in the courtyard after supper, but I am afraid, Padre."

He raised his eyes and looked intently at Padre as he tried to convey the truth of his words. Padre stared at him for several moments, his steely eyes boring into him. Diego thought he was going to be sick at any moment and swallowed the rising bile in the back of his throat.

"Speak of this no one," said Padre rising to his feet, his gaze not leaving Diego's face. "Go about your business and meet with him as planned. Do not fear, Brother Diego, I will be there with Brother Benito. You understand?"

"Yes, Padre."

"Good. Now go."

Diego stood. His legs felt weak beneath him, but he drew himself up to his full height and bowed to the Abbot. It was done, and it couldn't be undone. He opened the door and as he stepped out into the hall, he heard Padre calling for Brother Benito, who glanced at him with a puzzled look before disappearing inside.

Whatever happened now was out of Diego's hands. He just prayed he wouldn't lose his nerve and he'd be able to see it through to the end. The dining room beckoned, although he doubted he'd be able to eat a bite.

***

Pedro finished his supper and sat back in his chair, his eyes firmly fixed on Diego, who was sitting at a bench with his back to him. He could feel the excitement coursing through him and was anxious for their meeting.

He watched as Diego slowly rose from his bench and appeared to glance at Padre and Brother Benito. Pedro smiled inwardly. His threat of sharing the note with Brother Benito had got him the result he wanted. He never had any intention of following through with it, but Diego didn't know that. Pedro was delighted he hadn't seen through the ruse, and now he would know all about Brother Alonso.

Without looking in Pedro's direction, Diego left the dining hall and Pedro waited just long enough so as not to be obvious, before following him. The corridor was deserted, with most of his Brothers either in the dining hall or having made their way to evening prayers. Pedro took his time, walking casually down the corridor to the doors leading out to the courtyard. He paused briefly before pushing them open.

The courtyard was in shadows, but he spied Diego standing by the large urn which took up pride of place. He grinned as he approached him.

"Let's not dally too long, Brother Diego," he said in a low voice. "First, I'd like to know what your sister is keeping safe for Brother Alonso?"

"Straight to the point I see," said Diego compressing his lips into a thin line. "Nothing of importance, except to Brother Alonso. He has a gold cross, given him by his mother, which he was afraid of losing in the new world."

Pedro scoffed and took a step back. "What about the pages? What was he doing?"

The doors to the courtyard opened and Padre appeared in the doorway. "A lovely evening," he said with his gaze resting on Pedro.

Pedro's heart leapt into his throat and he took another step back from Diego. "Padre?"

"Brother Benito wishes to see you, Brother Pedro, as do I."

It took a moment for the Padre's words to sink into Pedro's mind, and before he could gather his thoughts, Brother Benito arrived and stood beside Padre. Pedro stared at Diego who was pale and looked like he was about to faint. Pedro's mind was racing as he tried to make sense of what was going on. *Did Brother Diego have something to do with this*? He dismissed the thought and smiled as he approached Padre.

"Of course, Padre."

"In my office, Brother Pedro," said Padre. He stepped aside to make room for Pedro to walk between him and Brother Benito.

As Pedro began walking down the hall, followed by Brother Benito, he heard Padre tell Diego to come as well. He was now firmly convinced Diego had said something, what exactly, he didn't know. His mind was whirring as he made his way to Padre's office. Whatever Diego had said or done, he needed to counter it, and quickly.

He entered Padre's office and stood waiting. Padre and Brother Benito joined him a moment later and Padre eased himself into his chair behind his desk.

"The key to your scriptorium, and the drawer please, Brother Pedro," said Padre holding out his hand, palm up.

"Yes, of course, Padre." He reached into his pocket and retrieving the keys dropped them into Padre's outstretched palm.

"Fetch the pages, all of them, Brother Benito," said Padre handing him the keys.

"Yes, Padre."

Brother Benito turned and left, closing the door behind him and Pedro drew in a deep breath.

"Padre, whatever Brother Diego has told you, I'm sure I can explain." His heart was beating fast as he tried to think.

Padre clasped his hands together and leaned forward. "Sit down, Brother Pedro."

He sat down on the hard wooden chair and folded his hands in his lap.

"Certain accusations have been made against you, and I intend to determine if they are true."

"By Brother Diego?" said Pedro.

"Yes," said Padre pinning him with his steely gaze. "He claims you've broken your vow of silence."

"What? I swear I have not." He was breathing heavily as he tried to get his mind to think. *What was Brother Diego up to?* He groaned inwardly as he realised he may have underestimated him.

"We shall soon see," said Padre leaning back in his chair.

They sat in silence while they waited for Brother Benito to return. The longer he sat waiting, the more Pedro started to relax. Diego couldn't possibly have proof that he'd spoken to him about the pages. It had been a private conversation; no one had overheard them, he was sure. He slowed his breathing and sat back in his chair.

Brother Benito returned ten minutes later with the pile of Brother Miguel's pages. He placed them on the desk in front of Padre, putting the keys on top.

"Call Brother Diego," said Padre.

He nodded before opening the door and summoning him. Diego walked in, staring straight ahead and stopped beside the desk.

"Padre," he said with a nod.

"Now, Brother Diego, please describe the pages in detail."

Diego licked his lips and drew in a deep breath. "Most are just writing in a strange language," he said. "But, there is one which depicts naked women surrounded by a green haze, and another shows people lying prone with what looks like light around them."

Pedro drew in a sharp breath and stared at him. “Padre, I swear I didn’t show him any of this.”

Padre ignored him as he carefully looked through the pile of pages, putting each one aside in turn. He was halfway through the pile before he stopped and looked at Diego.

“Thank you, Brother Diego, you may go,” he said putting the pages back into one pile. “Speak of this to no one.”

“Yes, Padre.” He bowed his head and drew in a breath. “Shall I take a vow of silence?”

Padre nodded. “That would be best.”

“I’ll do it at once,” he said before opening the door and hurrying out.

Pedro stared after him and then turned his attention back to Padre. “You must believe me, I didn’t show him. It must’ve been Brother Alonso,” he said as he reached into his pocket and drew out the scrap of parchment. “I found this, Padre.”

“You now try to cast aspersions on Brother Alonso?” asked Padre standing up and leaning over the desk. “You will retire to your room and stay there until I decide what to do with you,” he said glaring at him. “See that he stays there, Brother Benito.”

"Yes, Padre," said Brother Benito grabbing Pedro by the arm. "Enough of your lies."

Pedro stood up and frantically tried to think of what else he could say. Padre was still glaring at him, and so, with an incline of his head, he allowed Brother Benito to drag him from the office.

Chapter 31

Manchester 1968

Ian entered his small apartment, flicking on the light switch as soon as he closed the door. He could barely contain his excitement as he crossed the room and put Lana's itinerary on the bench. Picking up the phone receiver he dialled Dave's number.

After a few rings, Dave picked up and Ian grinned. "I've got it."

"Oh, good evening, Ian. Got what?" came Dave's sarcastic voice down the line.

Ian wasn't about to let Dave dampen his spirits. "Lana's itinerary."

"Oh, shit," said Dave quickly changing his tune. "Brilliant. Where and when?"

"Guayaquil in Ecuador. They fly out on the second of July," said Ian rapping his fingers on the benchtop. "We need to talk. Lana won't have a bar of me going with her, so we'll have to change plans."

"Ecuador? I thought it'd be in Europe somewhere."

"Yeah, so did I, but when you think about it, the Spanish were in South America. It makes sense."

"I guess so," said Dave in an unconvinced tone. "Can you come down to my office in the morning?"

"Yeah, I'll be there first thing," said Ian. "We can't stuff this up, Dave."

"I know, I know. This is going to put us on the map."

Ian could hear the excitement in Dave's voice and he grinned. "See you tomorrow. Bye."

He hung up the phone and picking up the itinerary he kissed it. "You little beauty."

Ian was up early on Monday morning and at nine o'clock he made a beeline for Dave's office. He'd spent the night thinking over how they might discreetly follow Lana and her friends until the location of the library was revealed. Miguel was key and would be their primary concern.

Peggy greeted him as soon as he entered the office. "He's expecting you," she said waving her hand in the direction of Dave's office. "I'll get you two some coffee."

"Thanks," said Ian grinning as he pushed open the door to Dave's office and went inside.

"Ian…close the door and let me see it," he said without preamble. "I haven't been able to stop thinking about this all bloody night."

"Me either."

Ian closed the door and eased himself into a chair before pulling the itinerary from his pocket. He carefully unfolded it and spread it out on the desk in front of Dave.

"We'll need to get cracking," he said.

"Don't worry, we'll be right," said Dave running his eyes over the itinerary.

Dave pulled his notepad closer and picked up his pen. "So, what's the plan then?" He looked up at Ian with one brow raised. "You say Lana won't let you go with her?"

"No, she's adamant. So, you'll have to get yourself on the same flights as them, and I'll get down there a few days ahead of you."

"Alright," said Dave as he scribbled down dates and flight numbers onto his notepad. "Any idea where they're staying in Guayaquil?"

"Not yet. They're still deciding between a couple of hotels. As soon as I know, I'll let you know. I thought you could stay in the same one as them, and I'll book in somewhere else." Ian leaned forward and clasped his hands together. "The important thing is that they don't spot me."

"Agreed, but how will you know when we leave? Presumably, the damned library isn't hiding in Guayaquil."

"No, but Lana wouldn't tell me where they're going, so you're going to have to follow them."

The office door opened and Peggy came in with two mugs of coffee. She placed them on the desk and smiled. "Anything else?"

"Yes," said Dave ripping the page from his notepad. "Get yourself down to the travel agents, not Lunn Poly, and get me booked on these flights."

"You want me to go now?" she said taking the notepaper from him.

"Yes, God damn it."

"Okay, I'll switch the phone through to you then."

"Fine," said Dave waving her off with his hand. "Go."

As soon as Peggy left, Dave sat back in his chair and ran his hands through his hair.

"There's just one big problem. How will you follow us? You won't know when we leave Guayaquil."

"Ah, I spent all of last night thinking about that," said Ian picking up his coffee and taking a long sip.

"And?"

"Well, I thought maybe we could hire someone as a go-between."

Dave nodded. "That could work." He sipped his coffee and groaned. "If only we knew where we were going."

"She won't tell me." Ian shrugged. "So, if I employ one of the locals, I'll have them meet you at the airport and you can have them report back to me when you leave. I'm thinking they'll only spend one night in Guayaquil before heading off." Ian gulped down his coffee and sat back in his chair. "I can't think of any other way to do this."

"Neither can I. You better get there at least three or four days ahead of us then."

"In that case, I better get onto it." Ian grabbed the itinerary and shoved it back in his pocket before getting to his feet. "I'll let you know once I'm booked."

"Great…God, this is going to be so worth it, my friend."

"It better be. It's costing us a fortune."

Dave grinned. "Nothing like the fortune we're going to make."

Ian smirked as he left Dave's office. Their plans were coming together nicely, and it was just a matter of time before they were not only rich but famous. He could imagine the news headlines now.

***

Over the next few days, Ian got his flights booked and made his apologies to Mr Robinson that he wouldn't be able to make the court date. He'd be flying out next Tuesday, and while he felt bad leaving Lana to deal with Rob, he had bigger fish to fry. All he had to do was tell her, and as he made his way along the street towards her house, he rehearsed his speech.

Toby opened the door almost as soon as he knocked. "Hey, Mr Fuller," he said waving a piece of toast in the air. "Lana's in the lounge."

"Hi, Toby. How are you doing?" he said stepping over the threshold.

"Good…excited. Did Lana tell you, we're all booked and ready to go?"

"She did," said Ian grinning. "I'm just a bit jealous I'm not going with you."

Toby shrugged before closing the door. "Too bad, Mr Fuller."

"Hi Dad," said Lana poking her head out of the lounge. "I thought I heard your voice. Is everything okay?"

“Yeah…I’ve just got a bit of bad news. I won’t be able to make the court date.” He did his best to look disappointed and sorry.

“What? But you have to!” She looked alarmed as she stared wide-eyed at him.

“I know, I’m sorry Kitten, but I’ve got to go on an urgent business trip, I leave on Tuesday,” he said looking crestfallen. “I’ve been working on this big deal for months, and I can’t miss it. I tried to get my colleague to go instead, but he’s got an auction on Wednesday.” He blew out his breath. “I’m really sorry.”

Lana’s shoulders slumped and she nodded. “I get it, but I’m not sure I can do this on my own.”

Ian gathered her into his arms and kissed the top of her head. “Maybe Di would go with you?”

“Yeah,” she said pulling free of his embrace. “I’ll ask her. When will you be back?”

“Not until the following Monday. So, I’m going to miss seeing you on the train as well.”

“That’s okay,” she said with a smile. “Gee, I won’t see you for about a month.”

“Hey, how about I take you down to the pub for tea? It’ll be our last night together for a while.”

She grinned. "I'll just grab my bag."

Chapter 32

Ecuador 1597

Alonso stopped and groaned as he switched his bag to his other shoulder. Their progress on foot was slow, and the weight of the few provisions they'd bought at the market was getting heavier. They'd been on the road since yesterday morning and Alonso had no idea how much further it was to Tayos. He prayed they'd reach their destination today.

"Are you alright?" asked Mintaka coming to a halt a few yards ahead of him.

"I'm fine," said Alonso with a grimace.

"I can carry your bag for a while," said Wawae reaching for it.

Alonso surrendered it with gratitude. He was only now beginning to appreciate their lost ponies. "Thank you."

A short time later the road narrowed to little more than a worn path that required them to walk in single file. It wound its way up through the hills and by the time they reached the top, Alonso's legs were screaming for relief. On the other side, the jungle stretched in every direction; a sea of tree canopies. He took his bag back from Wawae as they began the difficult walk down the other side. The path was rocky and his feet kept slipping and sliding.

The path widened again when they reached the valley floor and Alonso trudged along beside Mintaka. He just kept putting one foot in front of the other, even though his whole body was crying out for him to stop.

It was late in the afternoon when Mintaka finally came to a halt in a small clearing beside the path. He dropped his bag and sat down with a groan. “We’ll stay here the night.”

Alonso sighed as he collapsed beside him, removing his bag and dumping it down beside Mintaka’s. *Another day, how many more?*

“I’ll gather some firewood,” said Wawae putting his bag down and grinning.

Wawae appeared to be none the worse for two days of hiking and Alonso admired the young man’s endurance.

“We don’t have far to go,” said Mintaka leaning forward to stretch his back. “But you look exhausted, my friend.”

Alonso smiled. He was glad to hear they didn’t have far to go, and Mintaka was right, he was exhausted.

After a simple supper, Alonso wrapped himself in his poncho and did his best to find a comfortable spot to sleep. The ground was hard and unforgiving, but he was too exhausted to care.

They set off again soon after dawn and after several hours came to a wide river lined with trees and vines. A narrow rope bridge spanned the expanse, which was in a much better state than the one they'd previously crossed. Mintaka paused on the other side and adjusted his bag.

"Only a mile or so to go, my friend," he said slapping Alonso on the shoulder.

Alonso grinned. "I shall say a prayer of thanks as soon as we arrive."

They continued down a winding path, that, from time to time, disappeared completely. Alonso was grateful that Mintaka knew the way, he'd never find it on his own.

Mintaka stopped and pointed through the trees. "See the cave opening over there?"

Alonso gasped as he spotted the large cavernous opening in the ground, not far from them.

"It goes straight down," said Mintaka as he began walking towards it. "But, do not fear, you won't have to climb a vine ladder down there."

"I'm glad," said Alonso following behind him. "I'm more than a bit terrified of such an idea."

Mintaka laughed.

They skirted around the edge of the opening, staying well enough back, but even so, Alonso's stomach felt most peculiar every time he looked into it. There was no longer any discernible path, as they walked beyond the opening to a rocky outcrop where there was a smaller cave opening. Alonso followed Mintaka inside.

Not far into the cave, Mintaka stopped beside a large pot that had several torches lying beside it. He picked one up and dipped it into the pot of oil. A few moments later it sputtered to life, illuminating the depths of the cave.

Mintaka continued deeper into the cave, where the ground soon started to fall away into a steep descent. Alonso steadied himself against the cave wall before following Mintaka deeper underground. A feeling of dread in the pit of his stomach grew more the deeper they went. Miguel had died here and he wasn't sure he was brave enough to face the evil that he knew dwelled here.

The ground levelled out again and a passage went off to the left, but Mintaka continued straight ahead. They wound their way further down, with other openings appearing to the left and right. Mintaka turned right, and Alonso wondered how deep underground they were going to go when all of a sudden the ground levelled out. The narrow passage widened into a small cavern where the cave came to an abrupt end.

Alonso looked around in surprise. He'd expected the tunnel to continue until they reached the library. There was no indication that there was anything more beyond this point.

"Do you see it, Brother Alonso?" asked Mintaka grinning.

Alonso looked puzzled. "I see nothing, Mintaka."

"The ancients were masters of illusion," said Wawae as he moved towards the side of the cavern, running his hand over the rock wall.

Alonso was perplexed. The cavern walls all looked the same, rough rock and shadows created by the torchlight. Nothing stood out as being any different from any other part of it. Mintaka walked to the opposite side of the cave and grinned before he appeared to disappear into the rock. Alonso gasped and stared at where he had vanished; he still couldn't see any sort of opening, only the dim glow of the torch.

"Come," said Wawae pushing him gently on his shoulder blade.

Alonso tentatively walked towards the glow and to his surprise, he could see where there was a fold in the rock wall which had at first appeared to be solid. He stepped between the two walls and found himself in a smooth narrow tunnel with steps leading down into the depths.

"Wawae's right, they were masters of illusion and carving, as you will soon see," said Mintaka with a grin. "Come, we're almost there."

Alonso was amazed and intrigued by their mastery. He knew what to expect at the bottom of the stairs, he'd seen it on many occasions in his dreams. He followed Mintaka down the steep steps, marvelling at the smooth rock walls.

The stairs wound their way ever deeper into the earth, until finally they reached the bottom where the cave widened into a large cavern. The walls were like the colour of burnished deep brown wood. Alonso ran his fingers down the wall. It was smooth and cool to the touch as if it had been polished like a rare stone. Mintaka lit a metal brazier which illuminated the cavern, showing two passageways leading off to the left and right. At the end of the cavern was a large tunnel that disappeared into the darkness.

"We'll take you to your workroom first," said Mintaka before heading down the passage on the right.

Alonso nodded and followed him into the darkness. He lit another brazier which lit up the passage, showing a large wooden door set into the wall. Mintaka pushed it open and disappeared inside. Alonso went in after him.

"This is where Brother Miguel did his work," said Mintaka lighting two wall lamps which immediately lit the small room.

It was simply furnished with a desk and chair with shelves lining one wall. Ink pots and parchment covered one end of the desk, with a half-completed page of writing sitting in the middle. A large gold tablet was sitting on one of the shelves, along with an assortment of quills and two bound manuscripts. Alonso dropped his satchel on the desk and walked over to the shelf and stared at the tablet. It was just like the ones he'd seen in his dreams, except there'd been a whole room of them. He ran his finger over the tablet, which was engraved in the strange writing. It was beautiful to behold.

"What do you think?" said Mintaka.

Alonso pulled himself away from the gold tablet and smiled. "I can imagine Brother Miguel working in here," he said with a note of sadness in his voice. He stared around the small room and nodded. "It will suit my needs."

"I imagine this is difficult for you, Brother Alonso," said Wawae joining them. He put his hand on Alonso's shoulder. "We miss him too."

Alonso compressed his lips and nodded. He could almost feel Miguel's presence here, but it was the fear of the evil in the place that gnawed at the pit of his stomach.

"Come," said Mintaka walking to the doorway. "I'll show you where you'll sleep tonight. And then…" He turned and grinned, "we'll show you the main hall and the library."

They left the room and walked further down the passageway. Mintaka lit another brazier and Alonso could see there were a number of doors set into the walls.

"These are the dormitories," said Mintaka pushing open one of the doors. "We've made this one more comfortable since Brother Miguel came."

Alonso went into the room, which was larger than he'd imagined with enough room for at least a dozen beds. There were three pallets and Mintaka dropped his bag on the nearest one.

"Wawae and I will share with you when we're here," he said. "Leave your bag here, Brother Alonso."

He nodded as he put his bag down, glad to be rid of the weight of it. He stretched his back and rubbed his shoulder. He followed Mintaka and Wawae back out of the room and down the hall the way they'd come.

"How big is this place?" asked Alonso as they arrived back in the first passageway.

"It's huge," said Mintaka. "Down there's the kitchen and steps that go down to an underground lake. In the other direction, there are storerooms and all sorts. Rooms full of pottery and statues and other things." He grinned. "And this way…is the library."

Alonso followed him down the large tunnel which soon opened into an even wider one. Mintaka lit several wall torches as he went, illuminating the cavernous space. Alonso stopped and gasped. Huge carved statues, half man half beast lined the walls, their eyes glinting in the flickering light. He'd seen them before, in his dreams, but they were even more frightening in real life, but nonetheless impressive. He continued walking slowly, his footsteps echoing in the large chamber. His heart started racing when he spied two massive double doors at the end of the room. They were ten feet tall with bands of metal and large gold handles.

"Stop," said Alonso as Mintaka reached out to open the doors.

Mintaka turned and looked at him with a puzzled expression. Alonso was breathing heavily and he could feel the sweat dripping down his back. He wasn't ready for what lay on the other side of the door.

"It's alright, Brother Alonso. There is nothing to fear," said Mintaka in a soft voice.

Alonso drew in several deep breaths. "There is some evil in there and it's where Brother Miguel died." He took several steps back. "I'm not ready."

Again, Mintaka looked puzzled as he shook his head. "No…we don't know where Brother Miguel died. He was never found, but I'm sure there is nothing to fear in the library."

Alonso closed his eyes and breathed in steadily through his nose. He knew he'd have to face it, *how else would he transcribe the tablets?* He bowed his head and ushered a prayer. Opening his eyes, he nodded. He expected to hear the booming voice warning them as soon as Mintaka touched the door handle, but there was only silence. He was relieved and perplexed.

Mintaka pushed the huge doors open wide and Alonso stood rooted to the spot while Mintaka lit several wall torches and a large brazier.

Alonso could see the glint of gold in every direction from the large tablets that covered the shelves lining the room, but his eyes were glued to the orb sitting on a pedestal in the middle of the cavern. It wasn't lit, or humming, as it had been in his dreams, but still, it scared him to his core.

Chapter 33

Manchester 1968

Lana looped her arm in Di's as they climbed the steps to the front of the court. Di glanced sideways at her and smiled.

"Nervous?"

"Yeah," replied Lana with a nod. "I wish Dad was here."

"Well, I'll do my best to take his place," said Di reaching for the glass door and pulling it open.

"Thanks."

The foyer was bustling with people, some scurrying about with briefcases in hand. An imposing staircase with a curved banister went straight up from the middle of the room. Glancing around, Lana finally spied a reception desk set to one side. She nudged Di and they joined the short queue of people.

"Good morning," said the young receptionist when it was their turn. "Name?"

"Lana Fuller."

The young woman ran her finger down a large ledger in front of her. "Fuller versus Fuller?"

"Yes," said Lana with a sinking feeling in the pit of her stomach. She wished she was just about anywhere else other than here. It was made all the more stressful because her father was away on a business trip. *What if she said the wrong thing?* She could only hope that Mr Robinson would do all the talking.

"Court three," said the receptionist. "Straight down the hall on your right. There's a waiting area where you can sit."

"Thanks," said Lana.

They slowly made their way down the panelled hall until they came to two large double doors with 'Court 3' emblazoned on it in gold lettering. Several chairs were lined up against one wall and Lana was relieved that her uncle wasn't sitting there waiting. The last thing she wanted to do was sit and wait with him, knowing what he was trying to do.

They both sat down and Di patted Lana on the shoulder. "It'll be alright. There's no way your uncle can win this."

"Honestly, right now, I don't care," said Lana with a sigh, "I just want it over with."

Di nodded and drew in a breath. "Yeah, I can understand that."

They sat in silence for about ten minutes, before Lana spied Mr Robinson, and another man, hurrying down the hall towards them. She nudged Di before getting her to feet.

"Miss Fuller, good morning," said Mr Robinson coming to a halt in front of her. "This is my associate, Mr Clements."

"Good morning," she murmured as a pang of anxiety shot through her.

"Come with me," he said before continuing down the hall. He opened a door and waited for Lana and Di to catch up to him. "We don't want you waiting out there."

Lana entered the small meeting room. There was a long table in the middle with chairs all around. Mr Robinson put his briefcase on the table and waited for Mr Clements to enter and close the door.

"Now, we're in luck," he said smiling. "We've got Judge Growcott. He's a fair and intelligent man and I expect he'll see straight through this case. And, we're the first to be heard this morning."

"Oh, that's good news," said Lana, relieved that it would all be over soon.

"Yes. We should also take the other side by surprise. I only presented your grandmother's diaries to the court yesterday afternoon, which means your uncle's lawyer won't have had time to see them."

"Is that good?" she asked.

"Trust me, Miss Fuller, yes, that's good," he said picking up his briefcase. "You two wait here until we're called. I'll send Mr Clements to fetch you."

"Okay," said Lana nodding.

The two men left and Lana slumped down into the nearest chair. She felt quite ill, but also hopeful that they would win the case. Her Nan wouldn't believe what was going on, and she knew she'd be angry at Uncle Rob for what he was trying to do. If only her father hadn't had to go on his urgent business trip. She knew she'd feel so much better if he was here.

After half an hour of nervous waiting, the door opened and Mr Clements popped his head in. "We're on."

Lana's stomach did a flip-flop at his words and she stared wide-eyed at Di before standing up. They followed Mr Clements out the door and into the courtroom. Her uncle glanced over his shoulder at her and she swallowed.

"Sit here," said Mr Clements indicating to the seats right behind the desk where Mr Robinson was sitting.

Lana sat down and looked around the timber-panelled room. There were two clerks sitting at the front of the court, shuffling papers and doing whatever it was they were supposed to be doing. Her uncle and his lawyer were thankfully on the other side of the room and she stared straight ahead, not wanting to make eye contact with him. She noticed her aunt and cousins were seated behind her uncle. She closed her eyes momentarily and breathed in heavily through her nose. If only her father was here.

The minutes ticked by until finally one of the clerks stood up. "All rise, His Honour Judge Growcott presiding."

Lana stood as the judge entered the chamber, as did everyone else in the court. He looked serious and she couldn't help but wonder if Mr Robinson was right about him. As soon as he took his seat everyone sat down and Lana followed suit, all except Uncle Rob's lawyer.

"Your Honour, I present the case for Mr Robert Fuller in his claim against Mrs Mary Fuller's last Will and Testament."

"Yes, Mr Miller, I have read through your client's evidence," said Judge Growcott as he shuffled through several pages. "He's also claiming on behalf of his children, I understand?"

"Yes, Your Honour," said Mr Miller.

"That all seems reasonable on the basis of their relationship to Mrs Fuller. In my mind, an allowance for them would be in order."

"Thank you, Your Honour."

Lana stared at Di and mouthed the word, 'What?'. This wasn't what she'd expected, and she knew Pat and Morris had never visited her like she had. Nan had never taken them on holidays like she'd taken her. She was puzzled and more than a little worried. *What evidence did they have?*

"However, it is clear to me that Mrs Fuller held both her sons in equal regard," said the Judge looking up from his papers and looking directly at Rob. "You haven't satisfied me that you're deserving of a larger portion of the estate. Therefore, the portion of the estate shared between Mr Robert Fuller and Mr Ian Fuller will be of equal shares."

Mr Miller whispered something to Uncle Rob and Lana saw her uncle nod and whisper something back to him. She grasped Di's hand and smiled weakly at her.

"My client never intended to take anything away from his brother, Your Honour," said Mr Miller in a loud voice. "He would be satisfied with equal shares."

The Judge nodded and returned to his paperwork. The court was silent for several minutes while he wrote and referred to the evidence. Finally, he looked up again. "Do you have anything further to add, Mr Miller?"

"Your Honour, I believe my client has presented sufficient evidence to support his claim that Miss Lana Fuller is not deserving of a larger share of his mother's estate. He has shown that he was a caring son and that any relationship between Miss Fuller and his mother, was nothing beyond the normal relationship between a grandmother and her grandchild. We trust the court will deliberate on the evidence," he said before sitting down.

Lana's heart sank. *How could he have evidence to support such a claim*? Everyone knew that she shared a special relationship with her Nan. Everyone.

The court fell silent again while Judge Growcott continued writing. Several minutes passed before he set his pen aside and looked up. "Mr Robinson, I understand you prepared Mrs Fuller's last Will?"

Mr Robinson stood up. "Yes, Your Honour. Mrs Fuller has been my client for many years, and I have prepared several Wills for her in that time."

"Hmm. In your affidavit, you claim she was of sound mind and well aware of what she was doing?"

"That's right, Your Honour."

"I also see from the evidence you've presented, that you believe Miss Lana Fuller had a relationship with Mrs Fuller not shared by her other two grandchildren. Can you explain that?"

"Yes, Your Honour. Miss Fuller's mother died when she was very young, and Mrs Fuller developed a special bond with her granddaughter. They went on holidays together and spent time with one another that Mrs Fuller didn't indulge upon her other grandchildren."

"I see." Judge Growcott went back to writing and shuffling through papers.

Lana had no idea which way the Judge was going to go. One minute he seemed to be agreeing with Uncle Rob, and the next it sounded like they would win. It was perplexing and harrowing.

"Mr Robinson, do you have a copy of a previous Will you could share with the court?"

"Yes…I thought I included that, Your Honour. Please…one moment."

Mr Clement started flipping through papers and pulling more from his briefcase. The two of them spent several minutes searching through the pile of paperwork before Mr Robinson held up a piece of paper. "I have a copy here, Your Honour."

One of the clerks walked down and took it from Mr Robinson and delivered it to the Judge. He perused the document for several minutes, and Lana fidgeted nervously in her seat. She just wanted this to be over.

"Do you have anything further to add, Mr Robinson?" asked Judge Growcott.

"No, Your Honour." He resumed his seat.

The Judge continued writing and then gathered several papers together in front of him. "I find that Mrs Fuller was well aware of her intentions, and not influenced in her decision making," he said. "However, I believe she may have overlooked several key points."

Lana glanced at her uncle. He looked disappointed in the Judge's words, which gave her hope that he wouldn't succeed. *But, what were the key points that he thought Nan had overlooked?* There was a growing nauseous feeling in the pit of her stomach, and she drew in a deep breath and slowly let it out.

"In her previous Will, Mrs Fuller made certain allowances for Miss Patricia Fuller and Mr Morris Fuller that she omitted in her last Will. I conclude this to be an oversight," he said drawing in a breath. "I therefore award them both the sum of five hundred pounds."

Lana almost held her breath while she waited for the rest of his verdict. At least it wasn't likely that he'd cut her out completely, but maybe she'd just be awarded a lump sum.

"Also, in her previous Will, Mrs Fuller bequeathed twenty percent of her estate to her granddaughter, Miss Lana Fuller. I find that in the period of time between her writing of these two Wills, certain circumstances changed. This is enough for me to conclude that with her granddaughter reaching her majority, she decided, knowingly, to bequeath her a larger portion of her estate."

Di nudged her and grinned. "You're going to win," she whispered.

Lana didn't want to pre-empt the Judge or get her hopes up, but it certainly sounded like her Nan knew exactly what she was doing.

"Therefore, the remainder of Mrs Fuller's estate will be divided as per her wishes. Forty percent to Miss Lana Fuller, thirty percent to Mr Ian Fuller and thirty percent to Mr Rob Fuller."

Judge Growcott gathered his papers together and handed them to the clerk.

"All rise," said the clerk.

Lana's legs felt like jelly when she stood up. She could hardly believe they'd won the case and Uncle Rob had lost. She could feel his eyes boring into her, and she stared straight ahead, not daring to even glance in his direction. Judge Growcott left the chamber and Mr Robinson turned to face her with a wide grin across his face.

"Congratulations, Miss Fuller," he said.

"Thank you," she murmured.

"Give me a moment to gather my papers, and I'll meet you in the meeting room that we were in earlier," he said with a nod. "I suggest you don't engage with your uncle."

She couldn't agree more and had no intention of speaking to him. She nodded before Di and her left the court and hurried to the meeting room. She had no idea what would happen next, but at least it was over, and she could now look forward to going to Ecuador without this hanging over her head. She couldn't wait to share the news with her father, but that would have to wait.

Chapter 34

Guayaquil 1968

Ian sighed with relief as the plane touched down on the tarmac in Guayaquil. After three days of travel, most of which he'd spent cramped up on a plane, he was glad to have finally reached his destination. He'd been trying to push thoughts of Lana and the court case aside, and the guilt he felt at leaving her to deal with it, hadn't left him.

He now turned his thoughts to what lay ahead. He grinned as he got up from his seat and retrieved his backpack. He slowly made his way to the exit and down the boarding stairs to the tarmac. The heat of the late afternoon sun hit him with a wave of humidity. He hurried across the tarmac to the terminal building and into the cool interior. He'd known it was going to be hot in Ecuador, but the thick humid air had immediately sapped his energy.

After going through customs, he found himself a cab and climbed in, instructing the driver to take him to the Hotel Galeria. He settled back as the cab started down the road. He'd been running over in his mind how he was going to hire the go-between for him and Dave, and he hoped it wouldn't be too difficult. He had at least a week to get things sorted before Dave and Lana arrived. He was confident that would be enough time.

It was only a couple of miles from the airport to the bustling centre of Guayaquil, and to his hotel, which was close to the centre of town. Ian got out of the cab as soon as it pulled up outside his hotel. He paid the driver and wiped the sweat from his brow.

Large leafy trees framed the front of the hotel, and Ian relished the shade they provided as he walked to the main entrance. The building looked a bit run down and was nestled among other, equally shabby shops and bars. It was perfect. He checked in and settled into his rather basic accommodation.

The next morning, after a quick breakfast, he headed to the main reception desk. The same man who'd checked him in yesterday, greeted him with a toothless grin.

"Good morning. I wonder, do you know where I could hire a driver? You know, someone to show me around."

"Si…Jota runs deliveries, he may be able to help you. Or, I could call you a cab?"

"No, I need a driver for a couple of weeks. Where would I find this Jota?"

The old man scratched his whiskered chin. "Down at the Barrio in Las Penas, in the old part of town," he said with a nod. "He lives next door to La Paleta, there's a sign."

"Okay, how do I get there?" said Ian with growing frustration at the man's vague directions.

"From here, head straight down Juan Montalvo Fiallos. You can't miss it."

"Okay, thanks," said Ian with a nod.

He left the hotel and wandered along until he saw a sign indicating the street he needed. The day was already warm, promising to be just as hot as yesterday, and he was glad of the shady trees lining the street. He followed the street until it came to an intersection, where it ended. Ahead, he could see steps leading down a narrow alleyway. There was no sign of any place called, La Paleta, just older houses. He presumed he'd gone the right way, and so with a shrug, he headed down the steps between the houses.

At the bottom of the steps, he noticed a bar situated opposite with a big sign out the front – La Paleta. He grinned as he looked around for Jota's delivery business. A handwritten sign tacked to a green gate, half hanging off its hinges, which simply said, *'Jota's Entrega'* with a phone number caught his eye. He carefully pushed open the gate, which groaned and dug into the dirt. He finally jiggled it open only to find a rusty old shed with a big red closed sign hanging from the handle. He groaned.

He was in the midst of jiggling the gate closed when a van pulled up. Almost immediately, a young man sprang out of the van and approached him.

"*Te puedo ayudar*?" he asked.

Ian stopped and stared at him. "No Espanol." He had no idea what the young man had just said to him. "Are you Jota?"

"I am," he responded with a thick accent. He grinned as he pushed the gate open. "This is my business. Can I help you?"

Ian was relieved the young man spoke English and he eyed the van with optimism. It was old, with dull paintwork and a dent in the front fender. Perhaps Jota wasn't such a good driver, but his van would be rather inconspicuous.

He walked towards Jota. "I want to hire you as my driver."

Jota looked puzzled. "For a delivery?"

"No, no," said Ian drawing in a breath. "I need a driver for a couple of weeks. Someone discreet."

Ian was sure he saw Jota's eyes light up and he smiled inwardly. "I can pay you well."

Jota grinned and shook his head. "I'd like to help, but I've got a lot of deliveries to do."

"I don't need you until next Thursday."

"Next Thursday? Si…yes, I can do it," said Jota with an excited laugh. "You said you'd pay me well."

"Yes…I can pay you…say…one hundred sucre now, and then I'll pay you more once you start driving for me."

"Okay," he said slowly eyeing Ian as though he was summing up how much he could charge him.

"How much for two weeks?" said Ian tiring of hedging around.

"Sixteen hundred." Jota frowned. "You said you wanted somebody discreet."

Ian's eyes widened. He could pay a driver in London for that sort of money, but there was too much at stake to argue. "Alright," he said reaching for his wallet. He drew out one hundred sucre and handed it to Jota. "My name's Ian Fuller and I'm staying at the Galleria. Meet me there on Thursday morning."

"I'll be there," he said pocketing the money. "You won't be sorry."

Ian prayed he wouldn't regret his decision.

***

Thursday dawned hot and sunny, and Ian settled himself in the courtyard under the shade of the cassia tree. He realised he'd been a bit stupid not to stipulate a time for Jota to meet him. Now, all he could do was wait around until he got here.

It was nearly midday, and Ian's anxiety was growing. Dave was arriving this afternoon, and if Jota didn't work out, he didn't have a backup plan. He groaned as he ran his fingers through his hair. Everything was riding on Jota working out.

Ian wandered inside and into the lobby. It was deserted. With a groan he walked out the front door and stood on the path, looking up and down the street. He was about to return to the cool of the courtyard when Jota and his shabby van pulled up. He sighed with relief.

Ian watched while Jota jumped from the van and walked up the path.

"Good morning, Mr Fuller," he said with a grin.

"It's only just morning," said Ian with a frown. "I was beginning to think you weren't coming."

Jota shrugged. "I said I'd be here."

"Come, I have much to tell you," said Ian before heading back inside.

The two made their way out to the courtyard and settled on the bench. Ian stretched his legs out in front of him, crossing his ankles, he reached into his shirt pocket.

"I need you to meet my friend, Dave, at the airport this afternoon," he said handing Jota a photo of Dave. "His plane arrives at three thirty from Curaçao."

Jota took the photo and glanced at it before tucking it into his pocket. "Okay. I can do that."

"Good," said Ian feeling a little more confident. "Take him to his hotel and wait."

"Wait?"

"Yes." Ian blew out his breath and nodded. "We need to follow a group of young people, wherever they go. They're arriving on the same plane as Dave. We don't know where they're going, but Dave will find out. Your job is to come back and tell me, and then tomorrow we'll follow Dave and them…you and me."

"Are you doing something illegal?" asked Jota scratching his head. "It doesn't matter, I can do it," he hastened to add.

"No, nothing illegal. We just don't want them to know we're following them, and so we need to be secret about it," said Ian. "When we get to where we're going, you'll need to find Dave and wait for more instructions. Do you understand?"

"Yes," he said with a grin. "This is like being undercover. It should be fun."

Fun wasn't the first word that came to Ian's mind. The plan had so many holes in it, but it was the best they could come up with. He only hoped they weren't travelling for too many days or it would be impossible to keep track of them.

"Alright. I'll see you later on, once you know where we're going," said Ian.

Jota stood up and grinned. "You can count on me, Mr Fuller. I won't let you down." He stared at Ian for a moment as if deciding something. "I'll need more money."

"When you come back with the instructions from Dave, I'll pay you."

"Si…yes," he said nodding. "I'll be back."

Jota left and Ian stood up and straightened his trousers. God, he hoped Dave would be discreet.

Chapter 35

Monastery of Santa Maria de Huerta
Spain 1597

Brother Benito was furious. Not just with Pedro's ineptness but with his own stupidity for trusting him. He opened the door to Pedro's cell and shoved him inside before following. He slammed the door shut and stared at him.

"Please, Brother Benito, you must believe me, I didn't show Brother Diego anything," pleaded Pedro.

Benito drew in several deep breaths and nodded. "Well, if you didn't, then Brother Alonso did. But never mind that now. Show me the parchment you tried to show Padre. What is it?"

Pedro pulled the scrap of parchment from his pocket and handed it to him. "I found it in Brother Alonso's room." He then told him about his conversation with Diego and what he'd told him, which amounted to nothing of any importance.

"You should've brought this to me," said Benito frowning as he read it. "It's too late now." He shoved it in his pocket as he paced the small cell.

"What will happen to me now? Please, Brother Benito, you must help me."

Benito stopped pacing and blew out his breath. "I will plead your case to Padre, but I cannot guarantee that you won't be exiled," he said. "Do as Padre has ordered, and leave it to me, Brother Pedro."

"Thank you, Brother Benito."

"Did you find nothing else? I presume you searched the scriptorium thoroughly?"

"I did. There was nothing. But Brother Diego knows something, I'm sure of it. He was wary when I confronted him about what his sister is hiding."

Benito groaned. If only Pedro had come to him instead of trying to force Diego's hand. Now, there was nothing he could do. Pedro had given Diego plenty of time to warn his sister, and no doubt, whatever it was she was hiding, was now out of his reach. And, he was left with Pedro, who he could no longer trust.

"Leave it in my hands, Brother Pedro. I will do all I can for you and attempt to uncover the truth," said Benito wrenching the door open. "Do not do anything to anger Padre further."

Benito left, closing the door behind him. He leaned against it for a moment while he tried to think of what his next move should be. Pedro had ruined everything.

***

Benito spent the following day trying to find a solution to his biggest problem – Pedro. Whatever Alonso had been involved in was now well beyond his reach, as well as his opportunity to implicate Padre and push his advantage. That too was gone. He'd spent months spying and plotting Padre's downfall, and it had all amounted to nothing. He just had one loose end to tie off.

He waited patiently outside the kitchen. His supper could wait until he'd taken care of Pedro. The door opened and Brother Marcos appeared carrying a bowl of stew.

"Is that for Brother Pedro?" he asked with a smile.

"Yes, Brother Benito," he replied.

"I'll take it to him," said Benito reaching for the bowl.

"Thank you," said Marcos handing it to him along with a spoon.

Benito nodded before turning and walking towards the dining hall. He glanced back over his shoulder; Marcos had already retreated back into the kitchen. He hurried down the corridor until he was out of sight of the dining hall and stepped into the shadows. Retrieving a small vial from his pocket, he deftly removed the lid. He stared at the bowl of stew in his hand for a moment, and then, without another thought, sprinkled the contents onto the stew. He put the lid back on and slipped the vial back into his pocket. There was no turning back.

Benito closed his eyes briefly before continuing down the hall to Pedro's room. He knocked softly on the door before entering. Pedro leapt from his cot as soon as he saw him.

"What news, Brother Benito?" he said bowing slightly.

Benito put the bowl of stew on the nightstand without looking at Pedro. "I've spoken to Padre and pleaded your case," he lied. He was breathing heavily and he closed his eyes for a brief moment before turning to face Pedro. "I believe he will apply a penance upon you, but not exile."

"Thank you, Brother Benito," said Pedro falling to his knees. He kissed the hem of Benito's robe before looking up at him. "I won't let you down again."

"I know you won't," Benito said placing his hand on Pedro's shoulder. "Eat your supper, Brother Pedro. I shall return with news in the morning."

Benito's heart was racing as he left the small cell and closed the door. He walked briskly back down the corridor to the dining hall. He shortened his stride and entered the hall at a sedate pace and slowly made his way to the head of the room. He bowed to Padre before sitting on the bench beside him.

"I was beginning to wonder where you were, Brother Benito," said Padre reaching for a piece of bread. "All is well I hope?"

"Yes, Padre. I simply wanted to make sure Brother Pedro had his supper."

"Hmm…I'm not sure he deserves your kindness," he said with a frown. "How is he?"

"He's contrite, but I fear he's lost all hope."

"Well, I pray he's seeking God's guidance and forgiveness."

His voice was steely and showed no signs of compassion. Benito nodded and began eating his supper. It was good that Padre wasn't ready to forgive Brother Pedro. He would not likely ask too many questions.

After supper, Benito went to evening prayers in the chapel with the rest of the order. He knelt and bowed his head, unsure of exactly what he was going to say to God. *Ask his forgiveness?* That seemed somewhat hypocritical of him, and right at this moment, he didn't want forgiveness. He wanted Pedro dead.

He retired to his room after prayers and paced up and down in an agitated state. He tried to settle and read his Bible, but he couldn't push thoughts of Pedro aside. *Was he dead*? He prayed the apothecary hadn't lied to him.

It was nearly midnight before he ventured out of his room. He stood in the dark hall, listening, before setting off for Pedro's room. Hugging the wall and staying in the shadows, he slowly walked the short distance down the hall. He paused outside Brother Pedro's door, and after glancing up and down, he quietly entered.

Closing the door, he surveyed the scene. The candle had burnt nearly out but he could see all he needed to in the flickering light. He carefully stepped over the bowl of spilt stew. Pedro was lying prone on the floor and Benito only glanced at him long enough to know he was dead. He took the small vial from his pocket and placed it on the nightstand. He truly was sorry it had come to this, but he'd been left with no choice. He quietly left and returned to his room.

***

Benito returned to Pedro's room after morning prayers, mainly to satisfy himself that he was indeed dead. The room was just as he'd left it the night before, and with a grimace, he closed the door. He sought out Brother Pablo, who generally treated the sick, who announced that they were too late.

"I shall advise Padre," said Benito with a solemn nod. "Will you take care of our dear Brother?"

"Yes, of course, Brother Benito."

Benito left and made his way to Padre's office. He stopped outside the Abbot's door and drew in a breath. He knocked softly, and without waiting for a response, he opened the door and entered.

"Brother Benito?" said Padre looking up in surprise. "I wasn't expecting you."

"My apologies, Padre. I come on an urgent matter," he said easing himself into the nearest chair. "It's Brother Pedro…I went to check on him this morning, only to find he'd taken his own life."

"God save us," Padre said sitting back in his chair with a shocked expression.

"I called for Brother Pablo but we were too late."

Padre leant his elbows on the desk and rested his forehead on his clasped hands. He was silent for several minutes, and Benito wondered if was praying. He sat watching him, not knowing what else to say. Finally, Padre raised his head.

"First, Brother Miguel and now Brother Pedro; God rest their souls," he said pulling down the corners of his mouth. "With Brother Alonso in the new world, I cannot think what else to do except to bring this whole affair to an end."

"You mean transcribing the pages, Padre?"

"Yes. Brother Benito. We have lost three of our best scribes and we cannot risk losing another. I will have to think about how we can continue this work."

Benito nodded. "What about the secrets they hold, Padre? We surely need answers…for Spain."

"Indeed, we do, but we shall set it aside for now," he said with a note of finality. "It will be weeks before Brother Alonso sends us anything. Time enough to work out what to do."

"Very well, Padre," said Benito rising. "Shall I call the Brothers together in the chapel?"

"Yes…yes," said Padre nodding. "We shall hold a vigil for Brother Pedro. Please send for me when you're ready."

"Yes, Padre."

Benito bowed and left Padre's office. Just as he'd thought, Padre hadn't asked him any questions at all. He sighed as he closed the door behind him.

Chapter 36

Guayaquil 1968

Lana settled herself and clipped on her seat belt. They were on the last leg of their journey, and she could hardly wait to land in Guayaquil. After three days of travelling, she'd had quite enough of airports and customs checks. Di plonked herself down in the seat beside her and groaned.

"I hope this is going to be worth it," she said with a frown. "A week lazing by the pool in Ibiza would've been so much more fun."

Lana smiled. "Next year. I promise, we'll go and spend a week in the sun."

"Hmph…I'll hold you to that."

The plane started to taxi across the tarmac and Lana drew in a breath. Finally, they were on their way, and in a couple of hours, they'd be in Guayaquil. She wondered how Miguel was going. He'd been terrified on the train trip to London and had been sick on the Atlantic crossing to New York. She'd tried to imagine how this must be for him. Thrust into the twentieth century with all manner of strange machines. She didn't blame him for being terrified.

The flight to Guayaquil was short and uneventful, and Lana was looking forward to checking into their hotel and getting a decent night's sleep. They'd decided on the Hotel del Parque, and she hoped it would be clean and half-decent. Although, she reasoned, they'd only be staying one night. They planned to start the journey to Tayos in the morning. Her mind wandered to what they would find when they got there. *What would happen when Miguel went back through time?* She could hardly grasp that he was going back to the sixteenth century. The whole idea was unbelievable.

The plane touched down and they slowly made their way off, down the boarding stairs, and across the tarmac. Lana was last to get through customs, but she immediately spied her friends as soon as she came through the doors. Di was so easy to spot with her psychedelic backpack of blue and lime green. The ones Toby had bought at the army disposal shop had been too ugly and boring for Di. Lana giggled as she made her way over to them.

"Good, you're here," said Toby, who had his map out and was perusing it. "We need to get tickets for the bus to Yuquianza tomorrow."

Lana rolled her eyes. They'd been over their plans so many times that they were almost imprinted on her brain. But, Toby still recited them like everyone else had forgotten.

"We need to get to our accommodation for tonight," said Lana slipping her arms through the straps of her backpack. "It shouldn't be too hard to find the bus."

"Maybe, but we can't leave it to chance." Toby folded his map and shoved it into his pocket.

"Perhaps we can find out about it over there?" said Di pointing.

"I think that's just car rentals," said Toby glancing over.

"No…not that one, the tour desk next to it."

Without waiting for another response from Toby, she began walking towards what looked like a tourist information counter. Lana shrugged and followed her, and by the time she caught up with Di, Toby and Miguel were right beside her.

"Good afternoon," the young woman behind the counter greeted them with a wide smile. "How can I help you?"

"Can we book bus tickets here?" said Di leaning on the counter. "To...where are we going?" She turned and looked at Toby.

"Yuquianza," said Toby stepping forward.

"Hm…I can book you on the bus to Cuenca," she said reaching for a timetable. "See, it leaves tomorrow morning at nine o'clock." She marked it with her pen and smiled. "Then, to get to Yuquianza, you'll have to wait until Monday."

"Monday?" said Lana with a frown. "Can't we get there before then?" They'd planned their time so carefully, and having to spend the entire weekend in Cuenca was going to ruin them.

"No, sorry," she said shaking her head. "That bus doesn't run on the weekend."

"Well, we'll just have to wait," said Toby with a shrug. "Don't worry, Lana. We'll take that into account on our way back."

Lana nodded. *What else could they do?* They didn't have enough money to rent a car, and anyway, driving on the wrong side of the road would be terrifying.

***

Dave came through the doors from customs and glanced around, trying to spot Lana and her friends. He grinned when he saw them standing beside the tourist counter. Lana's friend had such a brightly coloured backpack, that she stood out from the crowd. He began walking over, with the plan to queue behind them and eavesdrop on their conversation.

"Dave?" said a young man stepping in front of him with a wide grin on his face.

Dave stopped. "Yes."

"I'm Jota, and I work for Mr Fuller. He said I'm to take you to your hotel."

"Great." Dave grinned. So, Ian had found a driver and all he had to do was find out where they were going. He glanced towards the counter and then back at Jota. "Wait for me…over there."

Dave hurried across to the counter where another couple of people had already joined the queue. He groaned inwardly as he pretended to browse through the stand of postcards. He was close enough to hear their conversation, but he hoped discreet enough for them not to pay him any heed.

"So, you're all booked on the bus for tomorrow morning," he heard the young woman say.

"Great. Can you book us on the bus to Yuquianza on Monday as well?"

Lana's friend glanced over her shoulder at Dave and he smiled before picking up a postcard and giving it his undivided attention.

"I can. I'll need to make some phone calls to complete the bookings for you. Can you come back in twenty minutes?"

"Yes, thanks," said Toby.

Lana and her friends moved away, and Dave put the postcard back and stood waiting behind the other couple. As soon as they were done with their enquiries he stepped up to the counter.

"Good afternoon," said the young woman with a smile. "How can I help you?"

"I couldn't help but overhear, you've arranged a bus to Yuquianza for that group of young people," he said with a smile. "I also want to go to Yuquianza."

"Oh, that is a coincidence." She smiled as she grabbed a timetable and put it in front of Dave. "As I've just explained, you'll need to catch the bus to Cuenca, it leaves at nine o'clock tomorrow from Rio Grande. And then wait until Monday for the bus to Yuquianza. Will that be alright?"

"Yes, perfect," said Dave.

"That will be three hundred sucre. If you could come back in about half an hour?"

"No problem. Thank you."

He paid the woman and picked up the bus timetable. He wandered back passed the car rental counter to where Jota was sitting. He sat down beside him.

“We have to wait for my bus tickets,” said Dave eyeing the young man. “So, tell me, did Mr Fuller tell you what we’re doing?”

“Si…yes,” said Jota leaning in close to Dave. “We’re going undercover.”

Dave was a little surprised by Jota’s obvious enthusiasm. “Yes…well, I suppose we are. Where’s Mr Fuller staying?”

“At the Galleria,” said Jota in a low voice. “Do you know where we’re going? Mr Fuller said I was to report back to him once you knew.”

“I do, but I’d rather tell him myself,” said Dave sitting back in the seat. He was sure Ian trusted Jota, and it wasn’t that he didn’t, but he also didn’t want any misunderstandings. “Once I’ve got my tickets we’ll go to my hotel, and then you can take me to the Galleria.”

“Okay,” said Jota with a shrug.

Dave and Jota left the airport an hour later, having secured his tickets and exchanged some traveller's cheques. Dave looked at Jota’s rather shabby van with a dubious eye. He hoped Ian knew what he was doing. He tossed his bag in the back and climbed into the front seat beside Jota. It was just as shabby on the inside, perhaps more so. The roof lining was completely missing and the seat was lumpy and uncomfortable. He was glad he wouldn’t be driving halfway across the country in it.

They headed into town and Dave checked into his hotel before they drove the short distance to the Galleria. Jota parked the van and the two of them got out and walked into the hotel. There were a couple of people sitting in the lobby, but there was no sign of Ian. An old man was manning the reception desk, who grinned at Dave as soon as he approached him.

"Good afternoon," he said and then his face lit up. "Jota. Did you want Mr Fuller?"

"Si," said Jota with a nod. "This is his friend, Dave."

"Oh." He grinned again before picking up the telephone. He dialled and a moment later he said. "Mr Fuller, I have two visitors here for you." He nodded and hung up the receiver. "Mr Fuller will meet you in the courtyard."

"Thank you," said Dave.

"This way," said Jota opening the door at the rear of the lobby.

Dave followed him out onto a covered veranda that opened onto a shady courtyard. Dave stepped down from the veranda and eased himself onto a bench under the tree. Jota joined him and a minute later Ian appeared from the other side of the veranda.

"Dave," he exclaimed as he hurried towards them. "You made it."

Dave grinned as he got to his feet. "Yes. And I see you've got yourself a driver. Well done. The first part of our plan is coming together."

Jota beamed.

Ian smiled and nodded. "Do I take it that you know where we're going?"

"I do indeed. First to Cuenca, and then on Monday to Yuquianza. After that, I've got no idea…yet."

"Hang on, I'll go grab my map so we can see where that is," said Ian before turning and going back the way he'd come.

He returned a few minutes later with a map in hand. He unfolded it and spread it out on the bench seat. Dave stared at the map as he tried to find Cuenca. After a moment he put his finger on it.

"There's Cuenca," he said. "We'll be there for the weekend."

"Okay…I hope it's a big enough place for me to stay out of sight." Ian grinned. "Don't worry, Jota and I will spend the weekend in our hotel if we have to."

"Well, you might have to," said Dave as he continued to study the map. "It'll ruin everything if you're seen."

"Don't worry," said Ian slapping him on the back. "I'll stay out of sight."

"Ah…there's Yuquianza," said Dave with a whistle. "Where the hell are they going? There's nothing but jungle down there."

"Maybe they're going to Tayos," said Jota peering over Ian's shoulder at the map.

"Tayos?" Dave stared at Jota for a moment and then went back to the map. "Where's that?"

"Is that a place?" said Ian.

"Si…it's a cave. Dave's right, there's nothing but jungle down there, so they must be going to Tayos."

"Cueva de los Tayos," said Dave finally finding it on the map. "That's it. That's where they're going alright." He grinned. "This is too easy, my friend."

Ian laughed. "You're right. I didn't expect it to be so easy."

Chapter 37

Ecuador 1968

Lana packed the last of her things into her backpack and strapped it closed. After days of rummaging it had become a bit of a mess. She reached into her pocket and felt the small crystal, rolling it between her fingers. She smiled.

"Are you ready, Di? We don't want to be late."

"Yeah…coming," came her reply from the bathroom.

She appeared a moment later, with her hair pulled back in a ponytail and her face looking flawless. Lana hadn't bothered with makeup. In the humidity, it just made her face feel sticky.

"Come on then," said Lana slinging her bag over her shoulder.

They left their room and knocked on Toby and Miguel's door. Toby opened it a moment later and grinned.

"I'm glad to see you two are on time." He stepped over the threshold. "Come on Miguel," he called over his shoulder.

Miguel appeared and closed the door behind him. He looked a little pale and Lana touched his shoulder as she peered at him.

"Are you alright?"

"I'm a little nervous."

"Don't be," she said as they started walking. "It's just a bus…I don't imagine it will be as frightening as flying."

"Nothing would be that frightening," said Miguel with a serious expression. "I'm glad I never have to do that again."

"Just remember, in a few days you'll be back in your own time among familiar things," said Toby.

"I hope so," said Miguel.

It was only a short walk down the street to the bus stop. The main thoroughfare was choked with traffic and half a dozen people were already waiting for the bus. Lana found a spot to stand in the shade while they waited. She understood Miguel's nervousness, she was feeling a bit anxious herself. She glanced up the road, but there was no sign of a bus coming yet.

"Are you okay?" said Toby coming to stand beside her. "You look a little worried."

"I am," she said with a frown.

He put his arm around her shoulders and squeezed. "It'll be alright, Lana."

"Are we going to get back here in time for our flights? This seems like this is a bit of a hair-brained idea."

"We'll be back in time," he said with a grin. "Anyway, what would you have us do? You're the one who wanted to help Miguel."

Miguel glanced at them and moved closer. "Is everything alright?"

"Lana's just a bit worried," said Toby releasing her. "But, it'll be fine. We'll get you back to Tayos and then we'll get back here in time."

"I am sorry," said Miguel with a frown.

"No, don't be," said Lana shaking her head, "I'm just being silly."

A few minutes later the bus arrived and everyone started to climb aboard. Toby got on first and dealt with the driver and the tickets. Lana followed Di halfway down the bus before they found two spare seats. Lana slipped off her backpack and shoved it half under the seat before plonking herself down beside Di.

"This is going to be so much fun," said Di giving Lana a nudge. "A whole weekend to relax. I hope they've got a nightclub in Cuenca."

Lana nodded. *A nightclub?* That was just so typical of Di. Only concerned with having fun and probably finding some guy to latch onto. It was the last thing on Lana's mind.

The bus started moving and Lana did her best to push her concerns aside and just enjoy the scenery. They travelled through the busy streets of Guayaquil until they finally reached the outskirts and the open countryside. Mountains loomed ahead of them and Lana couldn't wait to see the view from up there.

It was a slow trip up the mountain but the view back across the city and the bay was breathtaking. They passed through several townships, stopping at various places until they finally arrived in Cuenca at around one o'clock.

"I'm starving," said Lana as she stepped off the bus at the Central Plaza.

"Me too," said Di joining her on the footpath. "Let's get lunch and have a look around before we check in."

"Okay," said Toby glancing around at the food stalls set up in the plaza. "They look like emborrajados over there. I really want to try them."

"They sound interesting," said Di slinging her backpack over her shoulder. "Just one for me, I'm not sure I'll like them."

"They're banana pancakes," said Miguel with a grin. "You'll love them."

After munching their way through several emborrajados they wandered around the plaza and down the street, looking at the shops and stalls. Lana nudged Di as they walked past San Juan's nightclub and bar.

"That looks good," she said reading the signs plastered beside the main door. "Tomorrow night's salsa night."

"Ooh…they have tapas," said Di licking her lips. "Let's come back here for drinks and dinner tonight."

"Alright," said Toby with a shrug. "But first, we've got to get our accommodation sorted."

"Yeah, we do," said Lana with a frown. "What are we going to do about the Rio Paloma?"

"I'll call them and move our booking…hopefully," said Toby.

They found the two-story cream-coloured Hospedería del Seminario without any trouble, thanks to Toby and his collection of maps. It was barely a five-minute walk from the Central Plaza nestled among shops and cafes. The lobby was lined in dark timber and ghastly green carpet, which was threadbare in places, and didn't look like it had been cleaned in a while. Lana screwed up her face and hoped the rooms were better than this. Although that seemed unlikely.

They checked into their rooms. Di and Lana's room was dark and dingy with one double bed that looked like it was sagging in the middle. Lana looked around with distaste. At least it appeared to be sort of clean, but she wasn't looking forward to spending three nights here.

***

Ian was relieved to finally have reached Cuenca. The trip from Guayaquil had been hot and uncomfortable in Jota's delivery van. He couldn't wait to get out of it. They were driving up the main road towards the Central Plaza, where Ian had agreed to meet Dave.

"Go around the back or down a side street or something," said Ian pulling his hat down further over his eyes.

"Si," said Jota with a grin.

He turned down the next side street and parked the van. "Shall I go and find Dave?"

Ian glanced at his watch – it was one-thirty, and hopefully, Lana and her friends had already left the plaza. "Yes…I'll wait here."

Jota left to find Dave and Ian settled back in his seat, doing his best to find a comfortable spot, but not finding one. At least Jota was working out as a good go-between. In fact, he seemed to be very much enjoying being 'undercover' as he called it. A smile spread across Ian's face; in a matter of days, they would have their prize. There were still a lot of unknowns of course. He presumed this library would be hidden in the caves somewhere and they'd need to keep close to Lana to find it. How they were going to do that wasn't quite clear in Ian's mind. But, he was confident they'd find a way.

Jota returned about fifteen minutes later with Dave in tow.

"Hey," said Dave poking his head in Ian's open window. "Comfy trip?" He laughed before shoving a paper bag through the window. "I thought you might be hungry."

"Oh, yeah, comfy. Thanks," he said taking the bag and peering in. "So, I presume Lana and her friends have arrived?" He pulled out an empanada and started munching.

"Yes. I don't know where they're staying, and can only hope it's nowhere near us," said Dave before tossing his bag in the back of the van. "Move over."

Ian shuffled over to make room for Dave to climb into the van. He was now even more cramped and uncomfortable, but it wouldn't be for long. Jota jumped in the driver's seat and started the engine.

"Where to?" he said with raised eyebrows.

"Hotel Carvallo on Grand Colombia," said Ian shifting over slightly. "I booked one room for the three of us." He glanced at Dave. "I hope that's okay?"

"Sure." Dave looked nonplussed. "Honestly, I don't care."

They found their hotel and checked in and Ian and Dave spent the rest of the afternoon working out their final plan.

"Do you know anything about this cave, Jota?" asked Ian.

"Not really." Jota shrugged his shoulders. "It's big and deep, that's about all I know."

"Is there a road?" asked Dave.

Jota shrugged again. "I don't know. Probably not…it's in the jungle."

"Well, we'll probably have to walk from Yuquianza, or whatever the place is called," said Ian. "And, not be seen. I'm not sure how we're going to do that."

By the time they left their hotel to find somewhere to have dinner, they were no closer to working out how they would accomplish the final leg of their journey. They'd discarded so many ideas and had reached no final conclusion.

The three of them wandered down the street and around the corner. Ian glanced furtively in every direction. He wished Dave had been able to find out where Lana was staying and he could be sure to avoid her. It was still early, and so he hoped they'd have dinner and retreat back to their room, before young people like Lana and her friends ventured out.

"This looks good," said Dave stopping outside a bar. "They've got tapas…perfect with a beer."

The three of them went inside and found themselves a table in a corner beside some potted palms. A few people were drinking at the bar, and several groups were sprinkled around sitting at tables. Ian sat down and took in his surroundings. Music was playing through some speakers which reverberated nicely off the panelled walls.

"Beer and tapas?" said Dave.

"Of course," said Ian. "What about you Jota?"

"Si," he said sitting down beside Ian.

Dave went off to the bar and returned a few minutes later with three beers in hand. He put them on the table before easing himself into a chair.

"Cheers." He picked up a beer and took a big sip. "Here's to our successful venture."

Ian grinned. "We're almost there."

Ian sipped his beer and sat back in his chair with a satisfied sigh. He couldn't believe how easy it had been to track Lana to this point. He was anxious to get to their final destination and knew he'd need patience. He'd been thinking of nothing else except the metal library and the riches it held. He and Dave would be set for life and be on the world stage as the discoverers. Lana would of course be furious with him, but he consoled himself with the fact that she would forgive him - eventually.

"Shit…Ian, it's Lana," said an alarmed Dave.

Ian's heart leapt into his throat as his eyes lit on his daughter coming in the door with Toby, Di and Miguel. She was laughing and distracted by whatever Toby had said to her and it only took a moment for Ian to dive behind the nearest palm. He crouched down, feeling like a complete idiot. His heart was racing and he could feel the adrenaline coursing through him. He peered out from behind the fronds just as Lana and her friends approached the bar. They were standing with their backs to him. *Could he make a run for it?*

"Come on," said Dave getting to his feet. "Ian…we need to get out of here." His voice was low and full of urgency.

Ian sucked in a breath before scurrying out from behind the palm and racing to the door. He didn't look back and just prayed that with Dave and Jota behind him, no one would notice. He wrenched open the door and almost fell out onto the footpath. Gathering himself, he ran down the street and didn't stop until he was around the corner. He leaned up against the side of the building gasping for air. *Shit, that was close.*

Chapter 38

Cueva de los Tayos 1597

Alonso drew in a breath before walking towards the open doors and into the library of gold tablets. His eyes were still firmly fixed on the large orb. It was as black as night, except for the outer edge, which was clear and appeared to shimmer. Alonso crossed himself as he walked around it. He could feel Mintaka's eyes boring into him and he managed a weak smile.

"It is extraordinary," he said as he approached one of the shelves.

Every spare inch of space was taken up with the large gold tablets. There were hundreds of them and the enormity of his task was overwhelming. He would be here for much longer than he'd anticipated. The thought that he may never see Spain again crossed his mind and he felt desolate.

"Brother Miguel has already transcribed some of the tablets," said Mintaka joining him. "He has done this section, and you can see where he has taken the tablet that is in your workroom."

Alonso nodded. The clean line left in the dust showed clearly where a tablet had stood.

"Perhaps you should rest and start work in the morning?"

"Yes," said Alonso turning away from the shelf and drawing in a breath. "That's a good idea." He felt completely overwhelmed and all of a sudden, quite exhausted. "I shall go and rest."

"Good. I've set Wawae to work preparing our supper."

"Thank you."

***

Alonso awoke late the next morning. He noticed Mintaka and Wawae had already left their small dormitory. He rolled out of bed and stretched. Today he would start to transcribe the tablets, and he was actually looking forward to it. Writing was familiar and calming, and after the previous day, he yearned for the familiar. He dressed and made his way down the passage to his scriptorium.

He settled himself at the desk and lit a candle before reaching for his satchel. He pulled out his parchment and writing implements and arranged them on the desk. His unfinished letter to Padre fluttered to the floor and he reached down to retrieve it. *How would he describe all of this to Padre?* It would be difficult to convey the grandeur of the library. He prepared a quill and set to work on his letter.

Half an hour later he finished it and signed his name, knowing he hadn't done justice to the library. He'd omitted any mention of the orb; Padre didn't need a detailed account of that. He carefully folded the letter before preparing the seal. He held a small spoon with a lump of wax over the candle until it melted. Pouring it onto his letter he pressed his seal into it with a satisfied smile.

He set the letter aside and reached for the half-written parchment left by Miguel. He was surprised to see it was addressed to him.

> *Alonso,*
> *I wrote to Padre some time ago about the artefact I sent him. You know the one to which I refer. I have now come to believe that the missing piece of this apparatus is the small coloured crystal I sent you last year. Please, give the crystal to Padre and tell him that I believe this is needed for its operation. I wish I understood more about how this apparatus can be used to heal our*

people, and I will endeavour to uncover its secrets.
I will write to Padre directly on this

The letter ended abruptly and Alonso sat back in his seat and rubbed his hands down his face. *How could he do as Miguel asked?* Diego was the only one who could retrieve the crystal, and he dared not write to him. He folded the parchment and put it in his pocket. Perhaps it would be better if he just forgot about it. There was nothing he could do until he returned to Spain.

"Ah…I see you're out of bed, Brother Alonso," said Mintaka entering the room. "I trust you slept well?"

Alonso turned and smiled. "Yes. And you?"

"Very well," he replied with a grin. "Would you like some tea?"

"Not right now," said Alonso rising to his feet. "I've not yet said my morning prayers. Where did Brother Miguel pray?"

"Oh…come, Brother Alonso and I'll show you."

Alonso followed him down the hall past the dormitories. Mintaka stopped and gestured to a small alcove. A simple wooden cross was sitting on a ledge with a candle placed on either side of it. Mintaka lit the candles and smiled.

"This is Brother Miguel's chapel."

"Thank you, Mintaka," said Alonso noticing the Bible and folded blanket on the floor. "I'll pray here."

'I shall bring you tea when you're done."

Mintaka retreated, and Alonso knelt and bowed his head. He prayed he could find God in this place. He recited his prayers and crossed himself before rising to his feet. He wasn't at all sure that God had heard him. This place felt desolate of all things Godly.

He returned to his scriptorium and gazed around, his eyes drawn to the shelves. Walking over to the shelf he lifted down the gold tablet and stared at it. It wasn't as heavy as he'd imagined it to be and the carving was precise and beautiful. He put it on his desk, resting it against the stone wall. Reaching for a fresh parchment he began to transcribe the tablet. It was difficult and painstaking work and he wondered how Miguel had managed it.

Mintaka arrived a short time later with a mug of tea which he placed at Alonso's elbow. He quietly retreated and Alonso sighed as he took a sip of the hot liquid. He never imagined he'd find himself here with such a difficult job ahead of him. He yearned for Spain and the comforts of the monastery.

Chapter 39

Cuenca 1968

Lana teased her fringe, fluffed up her hair and admired herself in the mirror. Di and Lana had spent the afternoon browsing the local shops, and they'd both bought new dresses to wear salsa dancing tonight. Lana's was a pretty printed shift made of soft silky fabric that felt so good against her skin.

"Come on, Lana. You must be ready by now?" she heard Di yelling at her from the other room.

She smiled inwardly. How nice that Di had to wait for her for a change. "Coming," she called back.

She left the bathroom and joined Di. She was standing by the door, ready to go in her short dress that clung to her curvy figure with her creamy breasts swelling out from the low neckline. Lana felt like a little brown hen beside her. As usual, Di would be the centre of attention.

They collected Toby and Miguel, and the four of them walked down to San Juans.

The music was blaring out onto the footpath and Di grinned.

"This is going to be so rad," she said over her shoulder to Lana as she entered.

Lana followed her into the bar and glanced around. The place was packed with people, but there were a few spare bar stools. They wound their way through the milling crowd to the bar, and Lana grabbed a stool.

"Do you girls want tapas?" yelled Toby over the noise.

"No…I'm still full from tea," said Lana shaking her head. "I'll just have a gin squash."

"Me too," yelled Di as she sat down beside Lana.

It took a while for them to get the attention of the bartender, but Lana couldn't have cared less. She was loving the atmosphere and soaking in the salsa vibes. Through an open archway, she had a great view of the dance floor and she was keen to get out there.

They finally got served their drinks and Lana clinked her glass against Di's. "Here's to a great night of dancing."

"We're not going to get dance partners sitting here," yelled Di before leaning closer to Lana. "We need to lose Toby and Miguel."

Lana giggled as she sipped her drink. "Let's have a drink first."

Di rolled her eyes and smiled. “Yeah, alright.”

Lana was only halfway through her drink when a rather cute blonde guy approached Di. She wasn’t surprised – like moths to a flame.

“I’m going to dance,” Di yelled at her before jumping from her stool and walking off arm in arm with her first conquest.

Lana sighed and took another sip of her gin. Well, at least Di was having fun. She glanced around the bar, but none of the young guys made eye contact with her. She blew out her breath before sculling the rest of her drink.

She soon ordered another one and spent the next half hour brooding over it. She looked up and smiled when Toby nudged her.

“Do you want to dance?”

Neither of them knew how to salsa, but at least she’d be on the dance floor. “Yes.”

Toby took her hand as they wound their way through to the dance floor. The music was blaring and the dancers were a swirl of colour. Toby grabbed her around the waist and swung her around. She laughed as they did their best to copy the salsa dancers, not with much success, but she was having fun trying.

The song ended and Lana was panting, but threw herself into the next dance as soon as the music started again. Toby pulled her close, wrapping his arm tightly around her waist as he led her back and forth. She breathed in his masculine scent and hugged him close. Her heart was racing as she stared into his smiling eyes. *Why had she never noticed him before? Because he was her best friend's brother, that's why.* All of a sudden, he released her and grabbing her hands swung her around. Lana threw back her head and laughed as they spun around the floor.

The music stopped and Toby let her go. "That's enough for me."

"Yeah, me too," said Lana panting.

She followed him back to the bar and gulped down what was left of her gin squash. She looked at Toby sideways from under her lashes. He was rather cute and smart. She could do a lot worse. *Wake up to yourself Lana*, she scolded herself. *He's Toby*.

An hour later Toby nudged her again. "Miguel wants to go," he yelled at her. "It's too loud in here for him."

She glanced at Miguel who looked rather terrified. She nodded before getting down from her stool.

"I'll go grab Di," said Toby before racing off towards the dance floor.

"Come on," she said looping her arm in Miguel's. "We'll wait for them outside."

They made their way out of the bar and onto the footpath. The noise followed them but it was a lot less intense.

"Are you alright?" asked Lana peering at Miguel.

He shook his head. "I've never heard anything like it…I…I don't feel well."

He took two staggering steps before Lana grabbed him around the waist. "Have you been drinking, Miguel?"

"Yes." He gave her a sheepish smile. "Toby said I had to try the tequila."

"Tequila? No wonder you're not feeling well."

She propped him up against the window of the bar while she waited for Toby and Di. *What was Toby thinking?* He knew very well the strongest thing Miguel drank was beer. He'd probably never had anything like tequila.

Toby appeared a few minutes later, by himself. He looked at Miguel and then at Lana. "Is he alright?"

"No, he isn't," said Lana with a frown. "Where's Di?"

"Oh, she's not coming," said Toby wrapping his arm around Miguel's shoulder. "Let's get you home, my friend."

"Yes, before he's sick all over the footpath." Lana positioned herself on the other side of Miguel as the three began walking back to their hotel. "I gather Di's dancing the night away?"

"Yeah, something like that," said Toby with a grin. "John, the guy she's with said he'd see her home safe."

Lana smiled to herself. Toby might have swallowed that story but she didn't. Well, good on Di for having found herself a date and some fun for the night. Lana left Toby and Miguel at their door and went into her room. She changed into her nightie and climbed into bed, and immediately rolled into the middle. She giggled as she snuggled under the covers. Too bad if Di did come home tonight.

***

Lana woke up and glanced at the clock. She groaned as she hauled herself out of bed. It was nearly ten o'clock and there was no sign of Di. She was happy for her and knew Di would tell her all about it when she finally got back to the hotel. Lana showered and dressed before heading out and knocking on Toby and Miguel's door. Toby answered almost immediately. He was dressed in jeans and a t-shirt and his hair was damp and ruffled like he'd just stepped out of the shower. He looked so cute.

"Good morning," he said with a grin. "Want to grab some breakfast?"

"Yes, I'm starving," said Lana peering into the room. "How's Miguel?"

"Not well. He won't be joining us. Where's Di?"

"I have no idea. She didn't come home last night," she replied with a shrug.

"Shit," said Toby as he stepped out and closed the door behind him.

"I'm sure she'll be fine," said Lana as they began walking. "She's a big girl."

"Yeah, but she promised me." He drew in a breath. "She's in a strange town with some guy she's only just met."

"Are you jealous?"

"No," he replied emphatically.

They made their way down the street to a busy café and found themselves a table outside in a shady courtyard. Lana settled herself while Toby went off and ordered coffee and tortillas for them both. She smiled as she thought of poor Miguel. He'd probably never had a hangover in his life, and wouldn't forget this one. She sighed as she watched Toby return to their table. She hoped she was right and Di was fine. She was a little concerned about her, not that she was going to let Toby know that.

They enjoyed a leisurely breakfast and returned to their hotel at around midday. There was still no sign of Di and Lana was now getting quite worried about her. They had no idea where she was or where to even start looking for her. She kept glancing at the door as she packed her backpack ready for an early morning departure tomorrow. The last leg of their journey and they'd soon be at the library. She hadn't thought much about it in recent days, but she was sure Miguel was anxious to get there. *How incredible would it be?*

The door to her room opened and Di came tumbling in.

"Thank God you're back," said Lana grinning. "I was getting worried."

"Oh my God, Lana. He's so dreamy and I had the best time."

"John?"

"Yes. He's taking me out on a boat this afternoon. I think I'm in love, Lana."

Lana was tempted to say 'what, again?', but she kept her thoughts to herself. "So, tell me all about him."

"Well, he's totally gorgeous, and he's from New York," said Di with a dreamy look on her face. "Anyway, I've got to shower and change, he's picking me up in half an hour."

Di grabbed her jeans and a top from the pile sitting on the chair and disappeared into the bathroom. Lana stared after her and sighed.

Well, obviously she'd be spending the afternoon cooped up in her room alone.

***

Lana rolled out of bed early on Monday morning. Di hadn't returned from her afternoon excursion with John yesterday, and she presumed she'd spent the night with him, again. Lana stared around at the untidy mess of Di's clothes and groaned.

She showered and dressed and then tackled the mess Di had left behind. She collected Di's belongings and folded them neatly and packed Di's backpack. Slinging them both over her shoulder she gave the room one final glance. She headed out the door hoping to see Di hurrying up the path. There was no sign of her.

Toby and Miguel came out of their room just as she arrived.

"Where's Di?" said Toby with a look of concern.

"She didn't come home last night. I'm sorry, but I've got no idea where she is. She was going off on a boat with John yesterday and that's the last I've heard of her."

"Damn it. Wait 'til I get my hands on her," said Toby in frustration. "Well, we can't wait for her. I need breakfast and we have to get to the bus. She bloody knows that."

Lana nodded. *What else could she say?* Toby was right to be angry on this occasion and she just hoped Di would meet them at the Central Plaza on time.

"How are you this morning, Miguel?" she asked as they began walking. "Feeling better?"

"Much better, thank you," he said with a smile. "No more tequila for me."

She laughed. Poor Miguel. She could only imagine how he felt about being stranded in the twentieth century. She thought he'd handled it pretty well, all things considered.

They arrived at the Central Plaza after a quick breakfast and it was still only a quarter to ten. There were a handful of people waiting for the bus and they joined the throng, but there was no sign of Di.

"Listen, if she doesn't get here in time, I'll have to stay behind," said Toby with a groan. "I can't leave her."

"What? I can't go by myself," said Lana. The thought of being left all alone, once Miguel returned to his time, terrified her. "You have to come with me, Toby."

"I can't, Lana."

"Well, I'm not going either," she said with a note of finality. "We'll just have to make new arrangements once she shows up."

"What about Miguel? Lana, you have to go with him."

"No…we either all go or we wait."

A cab pulling up on the other side of the road caught Lana's attention, and she nearly squealed with delight when she saw Di climbing out of the back seat.

"Di," she yelled across the street.

Di waved before hurrying across the road towards them. "Sorry…but I'm not coming with you," she said reaching for her backpack. She slung it over her shoulder and grinned. "I'll see you when you get back."

"No, you bloody won't," said Toby scowling. "You're coming with us."

Di rolled her eyes and groaned. "I'll be fine, Toby."

"I'm not leaving you here. You either come with us or we don't go," said Toby in a determined voice.

"Don't be ridiculous," said Di slumping her shoulders.

"I mean it, Di. You either get on this bus with us or none of us are going."

The bus pulled into the plaza bus stop and came to a halt. Lana looped her arm in Di's.

"You have to come with us, Di. Please."

“Shit,” said Di with a groan. “Alright. But I’m not going to forgive you for this, Toby.”

“I don’t care,” said Toby gesturing towards the bus

. “Get on.”

With a stamp of her foot, Di climbed onto the bus, followed by Toby. Lana blew out her breath before getting on board. She wasn’t looking forward to the day ahead. Di would no doubt complain the whole way.

Chapter 40

Ecuador 1968

Ian stood with his bag between his feet as he waited for Jota. He was thankful for the shady trees out the front of his hotel. The day was already warm and he expected it to get much hotter. He wasn't looking forward to another day in Jota's uncomfortably hot van, but he was also excited for what lay ahead.

Tomorrow they would discover the library. He was confident Lana and her friends wouldn't delay; they only had a limited amount of time. He and Dave, on the other hand, could take all the time they wanted. The treasures they would discover had been haunting his dreams, and now he was so close, he could almost taste it.

Jota's van pulled up, and Ian grabbed his bag and walked to the rear door. Jota's grinning face appeared around the side of the van just as he got there. Jota wrenched open the doors and gestured.

"I've got everything packed," he said looking pleased. "Our food supplies and water…and…surprise…I bought us some empanadas for lunch on the road."

"Well done, Jota," said Ian tossing his bag in the back and surveying the van.

They'd brought blankets and pillows with them from Guayaquil and purchased enough food supplies to last them at least a week. A small one-burner stove was jammed into one corner. It looked well-used and battered, and Ian just hoped the damned thing would work. Otherwise, it would be cold canned sausages and vegetables. He shut the door and exhaled.

"Dave got on the bus alright?"

"Si, Mr Fuller," said Jota nodding vigorously.

"Good, come on let's get going then," said Ian before climbing into the cabin.

Jota joined him a moment later and revved the engine before driving down the road. Ian shifted as he tried to find a comfortable spot where the springs didn't jam into his backside. Jota was quiet as they wound their way through the streets of Cuenca until they reached the outskirts of town.

"Your daughter and her friends were arguing before they got on the bus," said Jota glancing sideways at him.

"Really?" That didn't sound like Lana. "What about?"

"I'm not sure," he replied with a shrug. "I don't think her friend wanted to go. Dave waited 'til they got on."

"That was a good idea," said Ian with a nod. "Was it her girlfriend she was arguing with?"

"Si."

Ian shook his head and hoped it wasn't anything to worry about. Lana and Di had been friends since starting school together, and he couldn't recall them ever arguing. Di was loud and opinionated, but Lana's calm and sensible nature had always been a good influence on Di. He hoped this wasn't going to impact their plans - they were relying on Di to be noisy.

They pulled over to the side of the road on the top of a steep hill for lunch. Mountains and jungle stretched in every direction and Ian could see the road ahead winding its way down. After a short break, they began the drive down the mountain. It was slow going on the narrow road with so many tight corners. Ian had to admire Jota's driving, although he was relieved when they reached the bottom and the road straightened out.

As the afternoon wore on, Ian became more anxious. Not only to be out of the damned van, his back was killing him, but to get to their final destination. He prayed Dave was going to be able to stay on Lana's tail. They both knew the last leg to the cave was going to be tricky.

Late in the afternoon they finally arrived in Yuquianza. Ian looked around in dismay - not exactly a thriving metropolis. He'd hoped there'd at least be a pub, but there was only the Entrada Rio Paloma. And that looked like little more than a shack with a few cabins surrounding it.

"Where to, Mr Fuller?" said Jota pulling over on the side of the road.

"Not here," said Ian looking alarmed. "See if we can find somewhere secluded, back down the road."

"Si."

Jota turned the van around and drove back down the road. Ian kept his eyes peeled for a likely spot where they could park for the next few days. Either side of the road was jungle, and they'd gone about half a mile before Ian spied a track going into the undergrowth.

"Down there, Jota," he said pointing.

The van came to a screeching halt and Jota backed it up several yards before turning down the track. A short distance along the track a clearing opened up on the left-hand side. Ian hoped it would be secluded enough.

"Here, Jota. This will do perfectly."

Jota pulled the van into the clearing and Ian got out as soon as it came to a stop. His back was aching and his right leg had gone numb. He stretched his back and stamped his feet as he tried to get the blood circulating. Thank God he wouldn't have to get back into the van for a while. How long they'd stay here, he wasn't sure. He and Dave hadn't made final plans, they were waiting to see the library before deciding how to retrieve it.

"Shall I gather some wood for a fire?" said Jota glancing around the clearing.

"I'll do that while you head back to the Paloma and find Dave."

"Si. Shall I bring him here?"

"Yes."

***

Lana grimaced as she followed Toby and Miguel into the Rio Paloma. It didn't look like much from the outside but she was pleasantly surprised by the interior. It had a cosy open fireplace with a large couch and a comfy chair set in front of it. The rest of the room was taken up with several tables and chairs and a rather rotund woman greeted them with a warm smile.

"La acogida," she said grinning.

Miguel smiled and spoke with the woman. Lana turned and smiled as she spied Di coming in the door. She'd complained for hours about Toby, and although Lana agreed with Toby, she'd commiserated with Di.

"What do you think?" said Lana.

"I should've stayed in Cuenca," replied Di with a scowl.

Lana smiled and hugged her friend. "I'm sure you'll catch up with John again."

"Yeah, I know." She finally removed her scowl and smiled. "You're a good friend, Lana."

"Alright, we're all organised," said Miguel handing Lana a key. "You're in cabin five and I've arranged dinner with our host, Ruth, for half past six."

"Oh, thank you," said Lana smiling as she took the key. "I was a bit worried about dinner."

"Okay, let's get settled and meet back here in half an hour," said Toby. "We need to discuss our plans for tomorrow. It's getting exciting."

Lana grinned as she followed Toby out the door and down a dirt path towards the cabins. It was getting exciting. Tomorrow Miguel would return to his time. She'd tried to imagine how that was going to happen and what it would be like, but it was impossible. It was like a part of her mind refused to accept it.

She slipped the key in the door and pushed it open. A stale musty smell assaulted her as soon as she entered and she screwed up her nose.

"Ew," said Di grimacing. "Leave the door open."

Apart from the stale odour, the cabin looked neat and clean. A small kitchenette with a table and chairs took up the entire room. Lana walked through to the other room, which consisted of four bunk beds.

"We've got bunks, Di," she called.

"Well, I'm not sleeping on the top." Di arrived a moment later and smiled. "Oh good. Why don't we both take the bottom ones?"

"Yeah," said Lana grinning as she dumped her backpack on one of the beds. "Have you seen the bathroom?"

"Not yet…but I'm about to," said Di dropping her backpack and opening it. "I feel so sticky…I need a shower before we meet Toby and Miguel." She rummaged in her bag and pulled out a clean top and undies.

"Alright, you do that. I'll shower later," said Lana sliding the window above her bunk open.

It was nearly an hour later before Lana and Di met with Miguel and Toby. They were both lounging on the couch, and Miguel jumped up when he saw them.

"About time," said Toby glancing at them.

Di plonked herself down on the couch beside Toby. "Well, you should've left me behind."

Toby scowled at his sister but didn't say anything further. Lana sighed as she sat down in the chair. Toby and Di's bickering was so tiresome at times. Miguel sat back down beside Toby and Lana thought he looked a bit worried.

"Is everything alright, Miguel?"

"Yes…I'm just a bit worried about Di. It will take us a few hours to get to the cave from here."

Di's eyes widened and she shot Miguel a withering look. "I've come this far…you don't have to worry about me."

"Miguel didn't mean that," said Toby blowing out his breath. "There's not much of a track and it's a couple of miles of hiking through the jungle to get to the cave. It won't be easy."

Di folded her arms across her chest and gave Toby the same withering stare. "I'll be fine. Anyway, you should've thought of that before you made me come."

Lana groaned inwardly – sometimes they were impossible. She leaned forward in her chair and smiled, hoping to change the subject and end the bickering. "So, what's the plan then?"

"Miguel and I have already discussed it," said Toby with a nod. "We leave straight after breakfast, which will be at seven-thirty. So, by eight o'clock you need to be ready to leave."

"We can do that, can't we Di?"

"Sure." Di shrugged her shoulders and slumped back on the couch.

"It will take us a couple of hours to get to the cave." Toby grinned. "And then the library."

"Keep your voice down," said Lana glancing around the room.

Toby had spoken quite loudly and she was sure he didn't want to be overheard. Ruth, their host, was flipping through a magazine over in the corner, and Lana didn't think she was paying them any attention. Thankfully, there was no one else. She'd noticed a middle-aged man had gotten off the bus with them, but she had no idea where he'd gone.

"Ah…sorry," said Toby looking sheepish.

Miguel leaned forward and nodded. "It's not far once we're in the cave," he said in a low voice. "Bring your torch…is that what it's called?"

"Yes…bring your torch. It'll be dark in there," said Toby.

***

By the time Lana and Di arrived for breakfast, Toby and Miguel had already started. Plates of food and a pot of coffee were spread out on the table. Lana was surprised to see the older man she'd seen yesterday sitting with them.

"Morning," said Toby waving his fork in the air. "Grab a plate and help yourselves."

"Good morning," said Lana as she eased herself into a chair.

"Oh, this is Dave. He's writing a book." Toby grinned before going back to his plate of eggs and potatoes.

"I think I've seen you before," said Di sitting down.

"Well, I was on the bus with you yesterday. I've been travelling around for the past week or so," said Dave looking unconcerned. "So, what are you all doing here?"

"We're going for a hike," said Toby slurping his coffee.

"Oh," said Dave grinning. "That's sounds adventurous."

"What about you?" said Di as she loaded her plate.

"There's a rather interesting cave not far from here. I thought I'd go and take some photos for my travel book."

"Hmm, we'll probably check that out too," said Toby.

Lana glanced at Toby, she was surprised he'd mentioned it.

"Well, I must be off." Dave wiped his mouth with the paper serviette and got to his feet. "Perhaps, I'll see you tonight."

"Yeah. Have a great day," said Toby with a smile.

Chapter 41

Ecuador 1968

Dave hurried from the Rio Paloma and walked down the road as fast as he could to where Ian and Jota were camped. He hoped he hadn't made a mistake by making himself known to Lana and her friends, but he'd had no choice. Toby had invited him to join them for breakfast, and it would've appeared odd for him to refuse.

When he arrived at their camp, the two were sitting around a small stove. He thought Ian looked rather dishevelled and he smiled inwardly. Poor Ian. It can't have been good sleeping in the back of the van last night.

"Morning," he said joining them.

"Morning," said Ian with a grunt. "So, what's happening?"

"Ah well, your daughter and her friends are just finishing breakfast. They'll be leaving for the cave soon. Are you ready?"

"Yes." He gulped down the last of whatever was in his mug and stood up. "Jota, head down to the Paloma. Dave and I will be right behind you. Check and make sure they've left. If they haven't wait 'til they do and then come and fetch us."

"Si, Mr Fuller."

Jota got to his feet and sprinted down the track. Ian grabbed his pack from the back of the van and slung it over his shoulder. He glanced at his jumper hanging over the back of the camp chair. He considered for a moment if he might need it.

"So, did you sleep well?" asked Dave as they began walking down the track.

Ian glared at him. "No, I bloody did not."

Dave chuckled. "It'll be worth it."

"It better be. My back is still killing me from the drive yesterday, and my shoulder feels like I've been sleeping on a bed of nails." He groaned as he stretched his right arm out.

"Think of what lies ahead, my friend."

They made their way down the road staying close to the undergrowth and keeping a watchful eye on the road ahead. They concealed themselves behind some bushes about a hundred yards from the Rio Paloma.

"I hope Jota's not being too damned obvious," said Dave as it dawned on him that he could give the game away.

"He won't," said Ian in a reassuring tone. "He loves all this secrecy."

Five minutes later they stepped out from behind the bushes as Jota came hurrying down the road towards them. He was panting when he reached them, but smiling.

"They've gone…about five…minutes ago," he said gasping for air.

"Good," said Ian grinning. "Wait for us at the camp. We'll return before nightfall."

"Si, Mr Fuller."

"Come on, Dave, we don't want to lose them."

Dave and Ian pushed on down the road. Not far beyond the cabins they came to the river and crossed to the other side. A wide track wound its way south through the jungle and they slowed their pace as they tried to pick up any sounds of Lana and her friends. Dave strained to listen for any signs of them, but the only thing he could hear was the sounds of the jungle.

"We need to pick up the pace," said Dave in a low voice.

Ian nodded as they quickened their stride and plunged further into the jungle. Twenty minutes later Dave came to an abrupt halt as a scream rent the air. He smiled inwardly.

"That'll be Di," whispered Ian with a grin. "I told you she'd be our guide."

They crept along the path, keeping as quiet as they could. They hadn't gone far when Ian put his hand on Dave's arm to stop him.

"Get it off me," they heard Di yell. "Oh, my God, I hate this place."

Dave stopped and crouched down. Lana and her friends weren't too far ahead of them, and obviously, Di had become acquainted with one of the many creepy crawlies that inhabited the jungle. Dave could hear several voices coming from the track up ahead. It sounded like they were just around the next corner from them, and he crouched lower, breathing slowly. Several minutes ticked by before the voices slowly faded.

"Come on," said Ian standing up.

A little further along, the track narrowed to no more than a faint path through the undergrowth. They trudged along in single file, all the while Dave was listening intently and his heart was racing. They needed to keep their distance, but at the same time not lose them.

Every now and then Dave heard voices faintly wafting to them. "We need to get closer," he whispered. "The cave can't be too far away now."

Ian nodded as they picked up the pace and hurried after Lana, keeping as quiet as they could. Half an hour later, the cave opening came into view and Dave's stomach dropped. *Where were they?* If they'd already entered the cave they might not be able to find them. He hurried up to the huge cavernous opening and peered in. It was dark and deep and there were no flashes of torchlight.

"Here," said Ian grabbing his arm in a hushed whisper. "Up ahead."

"What?" Dave hadn't expected them to keep going beyond the cave, but he looked up just in time to see a colourful backpack disappearing into the undergrowth.

Dave drew in a breath as they hurried after them. There was no discernible path and it looked like they were heading straight into the jungle. He was perplexed, but that soon turned to excitement when he spotted a smaller cave just ahead of them. He could hear voices, and the flickering of torchlight was all too apparent.

***

Lana reached into Di's backpack and pulled out two torches. She flicked hers on before handing the other one to Di. Toby turned around and grinned at them.

"Are you ready?"

"Yes," said Lana with a nod.

"I suppose so," said Di with a groan. "I'm not coming back here again tomorrow. I hate it."

"You don't have to," said Toby with a shrug.

"Be careful," said Miguel flashing his torch down the cave. "It gets steep just up ahead."

Lana nodded before following Miguel, Toby and Di deeper into the cave. She'd never been in a cave before and the darkness looming ahead of her made her more than a little scared. Not too far into the cave, the floor fell away into a steep descent and her boots began slipping on the dirt.

"Be careful," she heard Miguel say.

She stopped and steadied herself against the cave wall before taking another step. "Toby."

"Yes." He turned, his torchlight flashing against the cave wall.

"How are we going to find our way out of here?" Her voice sounded small and tremulous even to her ears.

"I have a map," said Toby with a laugh. "Miguel drew it for me…don't worry, Lana, we'll find our way out."

"Okay."

"Good," said Di sounding more than a little annoyed. "Because there's no way I'm getting stuck down here."

They continued down the steep descent until it finally levelled out. Lana let out a sigh. She hoped she'd be able to climb back up there. They continued, taking a right-hand turn down another passage, until they came to a halt, in what looked to Lana, like a dead end.

"The library is just through here," said Miguel as he approached a stretch of wall.

Lana couldn't see where she thought he said he was going to go. The walls of the cavern were all the same, with no discernible opening. Miguel, Toby and Di went ahead of her, and the three of them disappeared through the wall. She was amazed but soon realised there was an opening as she got closer to the wall. She stepped between the fold into a smooth narrow tunnel with steps leading down.

Lana's footsteps reverberated off the walls as she followed the others down the stairs, ever deeper into the cave. The passage widened out at the bottom and she breathed a sigh of relief. She didn't like tight spaces and she wasn't sure she liked being down here either.

Miguel struck a match and lit two wall torches that were positioned on either side of the tunnel. "So, you can easily find your way back here."

Toby grinned. "Good idea."

They walked down the tunnel, which soon widened into an even bigger passageway lined with huge statues. At the end of the hall were a pair of massive double doors. Miguel lit several more torches, and the light glinted eerily on the statues. Lana shivered.

"The library is through here," said Miguel stopping beside the doors. "It's time to give me the crystal, Lana."

"Of course." She reached into her pocket and pulled out the key with the small crystal attached to it. Light seemed to emanate from it, and she drew in a breath before handing it to Miguel. "I'm going to miss you."

Miguel stared at the small crystal in the palm of his hand and nodded before folding his fingers around it. "Thank you for everything." He smiled before he wrapped his arms around her. "I'll miss you too."

Lana kissed his cheek. "I do hope you get back safely."

Miguel nodded before turning his attention to Di. "I'm going to miss you too."

"Yeah, me too."

"Toby, I can never thank you enough," said Miguel with tears in his eyes.

The two embraced and Toby slapped him on the back when they parted. "Good luck, my friend."

Miguel approached the doors and as soon as he grabbed the handle, a loud booming voice echoed down the passage, 'Do not come here'. Lana let out a squeal of fright. The voice seemed to reverberate right to her very bones. Di looked terrified as she slowly backed away from the doors.

"It's alright," said Miguel holding up his hands. "It's just a warning. A warning I should've listened to the first time."

"Impressive," said Toby staring at the doors.

"Yes…the ancient's were very clever," said Miguel.

Once again, Miguel grabbed the door handle and pushed the heavy doors open wide. Gold glinted from every corner of the library, but it was the orb sitting on a pedestal in the middle of the room that Lana's eyes were glued to. It was pulsing and glowing and emitting a humming noise. Her heart was already hammering because of the voice, and now it felt like it was going to leap right out of her chest.

She turned, as the sound of footsteps echoing down the hall reached her ears. "Someone's coming."

The four of them turned, waiting to see who the footsteps belonged to. Lana was more than a bit alarmed. *Had someone followed them?* They'd gone to such lengths to keep this a secret. She was breathing heavily as she peered down the dimly lit tunnel, her heart beating loudly in her ears.

A moment later, a rather tall gangly man with close-shaven dark hair appeared out of the gloom.

"Tom, is that you?" said Miguel.

Two rather burly men were right behind him, and they appeared to have hold of two others. Lana couldn't see them clearly in the dim light.

"Miguel, my friend," said Tom in a friendly tone as he walked towards them.

Lana thought he sounded friendly enough, and Miguel knew the man, but his face was like a thundercloud.

The other two men dragged their captives forward into the light.

"Dad!"

"Dave?" said Toby looking from one to other with a puzzled expression.

Lana stared in disbelief at her father who had his hands tied behind his back and was being held by one of the burly men. *What?* Her mind went into freefall, with a dozen thoughts slipping and sliding over one another. *What was he doing here?* And then it dawned on her.

"You followed us!" Tears pricked her eyes as she stared at him. "How could you?"

"I'm sorry, Kitten."

"Quiet," said Tom in a voice that brooked no argument. "We found these two at the entrance, and you've just confirmed what I suspected."

"Tom, what's going on?" said Miguel frowning.

Tom smiled. "My name is Tomwata, and these are my friends, Moss and Patakis." He gestured to the two large men standing behind him. "When you went through the time portal, Miguel, you caused a ripple in time. We were sent to find you."

Miguel looked as confused as Lana felt. *Who were these people?* She pushed the thought aside as she continued to stare at her father. She couldn't believe he'd lied to her and followed her. She should've listened to her Nan and never told him about the box.

"I'm sorry…this is all my fault," said Lana in a small voice barely above a whisper.

"No…it's not your fault," said Tomwata shaking his head. "It's ours. We left the box of time crystals behind. I can assure you it was an oversight, and I'm sorry, Miguel."

Miguel shook his head. “Are you an ancient?”

“Yes, that is what you call us,” said Tomwata with a nod. “We soon realised that you knew about another time crystal, and you were the only one who could find it. So, we followed you and helped you. And now, it’s time for you to return to your own time, Miguel.” He approached Miguel and putting his hand under his elbow guided him towards the library and the orb. “Just touch the orb, my friend.”

“Wait,” said Miguel stiffening as he came to a halt. “The healing apparatus. Can you tell me how it works? It could change everything for Spain.”

“No…trust me when I tell you it cannot help you.” Tomwata once again urged Miguel forward. “Now go.”

Miguel nodded and turned. “Goodbye, my friends. Thank you.”

He took another step towards the orb and stood there staring at it for what seemed an eternity to Lana. And then, with a flash of white bright light that nearly blinded her and a loud crack, he was gone. Lana blinked unable to believe her eyes.

“Now,” said Tomwata turning his attention back to them. “I understand that you three will keep the location of our library a secret?"

"Yes," said Toby nodding. "We've all taken a vow and we'll keep it."

"Then please, explore our great monument and marvel at our treasures and we will leave you in peace."

"Thank you," said Toby.

"Come," he said gesturing to Moss and Patakis, who immediately walked towards the library, dragging Ian and Dave with them until they were standing beside the pulsating orb.

"What about my father?" said Lana frightened of what might happen next. "He'll promise too. Won't you Dad?"

"Yes…yes, we promise not to say a word," said Ian, his eyes wide in fright. "We didn't mean any harm."

"I'm sorry," said Tomwata.

Before Lana could say another word, there was another flash of bright light and they were gone.

"Dad!"

She raced towards the orb, putting both her hands on it, but nothing happened. The orb had turned to pitch black and ceased humming.

"Dad. Oh, my God…Dad." Tears welled in her eyes as she pressed her hands to the orb again, hoping that something would happen.

"He's gone, Lana," said Toby wrapping his arms around her shoulders.

She buried her face in his shoulder and let her tears go.

Chapter 42

Cueva de los Tayos 1597

Over the next two weeks, Alonso settled into his routine in the cave. He spent his mornings in the scriptorium and after his midday meal he left the cave for an hour to enjoy some fresh air and exercise. The days started blending together and he lost all track of time.

He'd been avoiding the library but after today he would have to venture in there himself. Wawae had refused to enter it under any circumstances. He strapped his satchel closed and pushed it towards Mintaka.

"There's a letter in there for Father Acevedo," he said with a nod. "There's also a letter for Padre and the rest is for Brother Pedro."

"Don't worry, Brother Alonso," said Mintaka tucking the satchel under his arm. "I will see it safely delivered to Father Acevedo."

"Are you sure you cannot wait a few more days?" Alonso had grown used to having Mintaka with him and he'd miss his calming presence.

"I have delayed as long as I can," he said with a serious expression. "I must inform Father Acevedo of your safe arrival, and that we have lost his ponies."

Alonso hoped Father wouldn't be too disappointed about the loss of his ponies. "When will you return?"

"It will be more than a month," he said with a smile. "But, Wawae will take care of you in my absence."

Alonso nodded. "If I cannot convince you to wait a little longer, then I wish you safe travels, my friend."

Mintaka shoulders slumped. "If it will ease your mind, I will delay until tomorrow, Brother Alonso. But, then I must go."

"Thank you," said Alonso grinning. "Would you fetch me another tablet?" With another tablet on the shelf, he may not have to go into the library before Mintaka returned."

"I'll get two."

With a nod Mintaka departed the scriptorium, leaving Alonso to return to his work. He bent over his desk and continued to transcribe the tablet sitting in front of him. In no time, he was fully absorbed by his work and didn't notice Mintaka returning with the tablets. It was only when a loud crack echoed through the passageways that he pulled himself away.

Leaping to his feet, he raced from the scriptorium and down the hall. “Wawae, Mintaka,” he called as he raced towards the library.

Wawae appeared from around the corner, his hair almost standing on end and his eyes wide with terror. “Come quick, Brother Alonso.” He turned and disappeared around the corner.

Alonso’s heart leapt into his throat at the sight of him. Drawing in a breath and slowing his pace he turned the corner and stared down the wide hall towards the library. The doors were wide open, and he could see someone standing beside the pedestal. It wasn’t Mintaka and he was dressed very strangely.

Wawae, who was standing beside the open doors, raced towards Alonso when he saw him. Without stopping, he ran past him. Alonso was about to call after him, to fetch Mintaka, but he arrived a moment later.

“What was that, Brother Alonso?” Mintaka looked from Alonso to the library and gasped. “Where did he come from?”

Alonso shook his head. “I don’t know.”

The man turned and when he saw them, he started laughing before slowly walking towards them. “I can’t believe it,” he said grinning. “Mintaka, Brother Alonso, it’s me.”

Alonso stared at him in disbelief as recognition dawned on him. "Brother Miguel?" He crossed himself and uttered a quick prayer of protection. It wasn't possible, Miguel was dead and this must be some sort of apparition. Alonso took a step back as he continued to stare and his mind tried to make some sense of what he was seeing.

"Please…do not fear me," said Miguel coming to a halt. "I promise you, it is me and I am alive." He laughed. "I can hardly believe it myself, but it's true. I did not expect to see you here, Brother Alonso."

"It's not possible…you're dead. I saw it happen in my dream." Alonso took another step back and shook his head.

Miguel nodded. "I understand that you think that, but I promise you, I am very much alive. I've been…" He groaned and ran his hands through his hair. "This is hard to explain, but this orb and the crystals created some sort of time distortion. I have been to another time and now I'm back. I have much to tell you."

Mintaka took a step towards Miguel and peered at him. "Is it truly you?"

"Yes, Mintaka." Miguel reached his hand out towards him and smiled. "Touch me and you will see that I'm real."

Alonso watched, unsure of what was about to happen as Mintaka reached out his hand and touched him.

"See," said Miguel grinning. "It's me."

"Brother Miguel, we thought you were dead." Mintaka embraced him, and the two hugged for what seemed like minutes to Alonso. "Brother Alonso, come and see for yourself, it is Brother Miguel, returned to us." Mintaka was smiling with tears in his eyes.

Pushing his fear and uncertainty aside, Alonso approached Miguel and tentatively reached out and touched his arm. His flesh was warm and alive beneath his fingers and although his mind was still denying the fact, his hand wasn't lying.

"Brother Miguel," he whispered as he looked into his familiar face. "I don't understand how you have come back to us, but I thank God for your safe return."

"Thank you, Brother Alonso." Miguel had tears in his eyes as he embraced his Brother. "We have much to discuss."

"Come, Brother Miguel," said Mintaka grabbing him by the arm. "Wawae will prepare us a meal and you can tell us everything."

Miguel smiled. "Not everything is for your ears, my friend."

***

Half an hour later, Miguel and Alonso settled themselves on the bench in the kitchen. Wawae had prepared fried fish and potatoes, and then he and Mintaka had retreated, leaving the two Brothers alone.

Miguel relayed his travels and how he thought the orb and crystals worked together to create a time portal. Alonso wasn't sure he believed him. It was all too fantastical and yet here he was sitting before him.

"Now, Brother Alonso, you must tell me about the box. Who has it and where is it?" asked Miguel looking intently into Alonso's eyes.

"Brother Diego made the box and his sister, Maria is keeping it safe," he replied. "I plan on retrieving it when I return to Spain, which will be sooner than I'd thought." He grinned. "I'm so very glad you're back and I can return."

"You cannot retrieve it. If you do, then I won't be able to get back here." Miguel looked anguished. "I know that doesn't make sense, because here I am," he said shaking his head. "But, it must find its way to England somehow, and that can't happen if you retrieve it."

Alonso leaned his elbows on the table. Miguel was right, that didn't make sense, and yet it did. "Alright…I'll leave it in Maria's care. But…how will we continue to unravel the secrets of the ancients without your vocabulary? Spain has much to gain if we can understand how they healed their people."

"I will write you another so that you may continue," said Miguel. He blew out his breath and sighed. "I asked him, Tomwata, about the healing apparatus, but he wouldn't tell me. He said it couldn't help us…but I know it can."

"Then we must discover it for ourselves." Alonso reached into his pocket and pulled out the half-written letter Miguel had left him. "Do you still think the crystal is the missing piece of the apparatus?" He slid it across the table towards Miguel.

Miguel glanced at the letter before picking it up and crumpling it in his hand. "No…I don't think so. Tomwata referred to the crystal as a time crystal…I don't think it has anything to do with the healing apparatus. There must be something else."

"Well, I hope we can uncover its secret before too long," said Alonso sitting back. "Now, I think Mintaka and I should take our leave in a few days. I will return to Spain with the good news that you are alive and well. I can only pray that Padre will set Brother Pedro aside and give me the job of transcribing your pages."

"I will wait to hear that you have been restored to your previous job before I send anything that might fall into the wrong hands," said Miguel. "We cannot risk Brother Pedro discovering our purpose."

Alonso nodded. No, it would be them that would unravel the use of the mysterious apparatus, not Brother Pedro.

Chapter 43

The Secret Library 1968

Toby's mind was in a spin as he hiked through the jungle towards the cave. He was anxious to explore the library and tunnels. This was a once in a lifetime opportunity and he wanted to make the most of it. Dulling the excitement of what he'd find in the library, was guilt. It gnawed at the edge of his thoughts and Lana's distress was foremost.

She'd refused to return to the cave and he understood that. If his father had disappeared into a time portal never to return – well, he wasn't sure how he'd feel. He flicked on his torch at the cave entrance and pulled the roughly drawn map from his backpack. The sounds of the jungle receded as he went deeper into the cave until all he could hear were his own footsteps.

He paused at the bottom of the cave and drew in a breath. His heart was racing as he stepped through the fold in the rock and began walking down the steps. He was surprised by the nervous feeling coursing through his veins. *Or was that excitement?* It was, but it was tinged with just a little bit of fear at being down here alone. It was unnervingly quiet and his heavy breathing filled the air as he approached the hall of statues. Their eyes glinted in the torchlight and a shiver went down his spine.

He shone his torch towards the library and the dark orb sitting atop the pedestal. There was no glow or humming sound coming from the orb, but still, he approached it with caution. He paused and stared into its blackness. It was like looking up at a starless night sky that was dark and endless.

Toby placed his torch on one of the shelves so that it illuminated the cavern. The shelves were stacked with gold tablets; there must've been hundreds of them. He lifted one of them from the shelf, weighing it in his hands. It was beautifully crafted with strange writing carved into the surface. If only he could read them. What they would tell of Tomwata and his people was almost unimaginable. He put it back on the shelf and retrieved his notebook and pencil from his backpack. He spent the next hour drawing a rough sketch of the library and did his best to copy some of the writing.

Gathering his torch and slinging his backpack over his shoulder, he walked back down the hall of statues. Here, two tunnels went off to the left and right. He placed his torch on the ground and pulled Di's torch from his backpack. He flicked it on and proceeded down the hallway to the right.

Not far along the hall, he came to an open doorway. He flashed his torch into the small room. Apart from some debris on the floor, it was empty. He walked on, past several closed doors to the end of the tunnel where it branched off in two directions.

He glanced back down the hall where he could see his torch glowing. Grabbing his water bottle from his pack he placed it on the ground and then turned left. He hadn't gone far when the tunnel widened and two large arched openings appeared. A large disc was carved into the floor with lines radiating out from it. He flashed his torch through one of the openings and then walked through it into a cavernous room. Two large monoliths stood on either side of a smooth stone table and the walls were covered in carved images of animals.

The images reminded him of the zodiac and the night sky, although he wasn't sure why. The animals weren't the same as the zodiac, but they seemed familiar. He walked closer to the huge vertical stones and noticed they were also carved with animals and celestial bodies. Yes, this room definitely had something to do with astronomy. It was an awe-inspiring sight.

Toby took out his notebook and made a rough sketch of the room and its carvings. He sighed as he put it back in his bag. He wished Lana had come with him to explore the caverns. He was sure she would've loved it, but since her father's disappearance, her usual sunny disposition had been replaced with despondency. *What had happened to Ian? Would he return?* He had no idea what they would do to him – they might even kill him. He shuddered at the thought and quickly pushed it aside as he left the cavern and went to explore the other arched room.

He stared in wonder at the large cavern full of tall columns. There were at least a dozen of them and they appeared to have been carved out of the bedrock. He approached one, shining his torch up the length of it. He gasped and took a step back as the light hit on a face with bared teeth carved into the column. He shone his torch on the other columns, all of which were carved from head to foot with frightening images. *Gods perhaps?*

He retrieved his sketchbook and did his best to draw the columns, making a rough sketch of some of the carvings. Toby wished he had someone to share his discoveries with. Lana would eventually come around and be interested but he wished she was here with him.

He knew Di couldn't care less. She was more concerned with her love life than anything else.

He put his notebook back in his pack and wandered out of the cavern and back down the hallway to where he'd left his water bottle. The tunnel continued straight on, and he flashed his torch ahead as he walked. He passed more openings and doorways and at the end of the hall, there were steps leading down. *How big was this place?*

He went down the winding stairs which opened into a large cavern at the bottom. Large statues, similar to the ones outside the library lined the walls and he could see the passage went on into the gloom. He flashed his torch onto his watch – it was already two o'clock and his stomach grumbled. He would leave this level for tomorrow. Going back up the steps he settled himself on the ground and pulled his packed lunch from his pack.

While he munched, he sketched a rough map of the tunnels and rooms he'd already explored. It was much bigger than he'd first imagined it would be, and he couldn't help but wonder why. If the ancients had simply wanted to hide their library down here, there was no need for all the rooms and two levels. Maybe there were even more levels. He wouldn't have enough time to explore the whole thing if that was the case.

He finished his lunch and packed his notebook back in his pack before wandering back the way he'd come. He stopped at the first door he came to and pushed it open. He stared in amazement at the artefacts crammed into the small room. There were shelves of painted pottery jars and small statues. In the middle of the room was a carved table – it looked like a leopard, with striped legs and cat-like paws for feet. The leopard's head was large and flat with eyes painted into the top of it. It was beautiful.

He dropped his pack before approaching the shelves. He lifted one of the small statues down and turned it over in his hand. It was just like the one Miguel had shown him. And there was a name on the back of it, not that he had any idea what it said. It was intricately carved and painted in subtle colours. He carefully put it back on the shelf before reaching for a jar. He gasped as he nearly dropped it and quickly put it back. It had been heavier than he was expecting and peering at it he saw there was a stopper in it. He had no intention of finding out what was inside it.

He spent the next hour sketching the shelves and the table. He wished he could bring his camera down and take photos of it all. He screwed up his face as he closed his book. He couldn't do that. *What if the film developer were to ask questions?* Slinging his pack over his shoulder, he left the room and headed back towards his water bottle. He opened the next door and flashed his torch into the room. It was just like the other one; jam-packed with pottery and wooden boxes. He didn't have time to explore anymore today, but promised himself he'd get a much earlier start tomorrow.

He retrieved his water bottle and his torch before climbing the stairs to the cave. His mind was awash with the wonder of the library and the other rooms. He would remember this place for the rest of his life. It truly was a once in a lifetime discovery.

When he got back to the cabin it was nearly dark. He dropped his pack inside and went to find Di and Lana. They were lounging in their cabin and in no better moods than they had been this morning. Thank goodness he could escape back down to the library tomorrow.

Chapter 44

Ecuador 1968

Lana and Di spent the next few days moping around the cabin, while Toby explored the library. Lana couldn't bear to go back there. She was angry with her father for lying to her, but her concern for him had pushed those feelings aside. *Where was he? Was he dead*? These thoughts kept rolling around in her mind until she thought she'd go mad.

Di was of little comfort. She was getting angrier with Toby by the day and kept going on about how she should've stayed in Cuenca. Lana thought she'd scream if she had to listen to her for another minute. Didn't she realise she'd lost her father and that her new boyfriend was nothing in comparison?

"I'm going for a walk," said Lana over her shoulder as she went out the door.

She sucked in a large lungful of air as she wandered down the path and around the shack that was the main building. It was a lovely morning. The sun was out but it wasn't too hot, and the road was shaded by the trees that grew right up to the edge of it. She increased her pace as she tried to push thoughts of her father aside. The road wound its way north from the cabins and after walking for about half a mile Lana felt the tension beginning to leave her. This was just what she needed.

A little further along the road, she noticed a dirt track leading off into the undergrowth. She stopped and stared at it for a moment before heading down there. It was quiet and secluded and the tears she'd been holding back for days finally let go. She continued walking as the tears ran down her face and she gulped in air. She didn't care, there was no one to see her or hear her wailing.

All of a sudden, she came to a clearing. There was a van parked and a small campsite, and a young man was staring at her from the rear of the van. She swallowed and did her best to wipe her tears aside.

"Good morning," she said in a strangled voice.

The young man said nothing but his eyes darted from her to the camp like he didn't know whether to run or hide.

"Sorry to intrude," said Lana.

She didn't want his company any more than he wanted her in his camp. She smiled and turned to leave when she noticed a jumper hanging over one of the chairs. It was knitted in one of those Fair Isle patterns that had been all the rage a few years ago. Her father had one just like it.

She walked over to it and ran her fingers over the soft wool. Picking it up she held it to her face and breathed in the lingering scent of old spice aftershave. Her eyes widened and she stared at the man.

"This is my father's jumper."

Several emotions flashed across his face and then he nodded. "Si."

Fresh tears sprang into Lana's eyes and she pressed her lips together. "You're waiting for him?"

He nodded again.

"Well, you can go home, he's gone."

"Gone? Mr Fuller's gone?"

"Yes."

Lana hugged the jumper to herself as she hurried back down the track. Tears streamed down her face and right at this point in time, she thought her heart would break in two.

***

Over supper, Toby was full of talk of the wondrous things he'd seen at the library. Lana pushed the food around on her plate with her fork and Di scowled at him from across the table. They were leaving in the morning and Lana was anxious to get home. The only good thing that had come out of their trip was that Miguel had returned to his own time. As for her father, she had no idea what to do or even what to think.

The bus trip back to Guayaquil took two days and Di spent most of that time arguing with her brother. Lana let their arguing wash over her. She felt numb and detached from them and Di's concern for herself.

Two days later they landed in New York and after passing through customs Di made a beeline for the public telephones.

Toby groaned as he sat beside Lana. "I can't stop her…I've tried."

Lana sighed. "Let her be, Toby."

He glanced sideways at her and shook his head. "How do I explain to Mum and Dad that I left her in New York?"

"You don't. She's a grown woman Toby and can make her own decisions."

"I'm her brother."

"Exactly." Lana turned to face him and saw the concern etched on his face. She smiled and reached out and took his hand. "She's in love."

His eyes met hers and he squeezed her hand. Lana was surprised by the flutter in her stomach and quickly withdrew her hand.

A moment later Di came bouncing up to them grinning like a mad woman. "John's coming. He's going to meet me at the hotel in an hour. Let's get going."

Lana found Di's obvious excitement contagious. Her mood lifted as they left the airport and walked across the road and down a few blocks. She was happy that John was meeting Di. She'd been unbearable since leaving Cuenca and Lana hoped that John would live up to Di's expectations. Although, Di generally didn't make good choices where men were concerned.

Di and Lana settled into their room at the Holiday Inn and Di immediately headed for the bathroom. She emerged half an hour later with her hair pulled up in a bun and impeccable makeup. She looked gorgeous.

She grabbed Lana in a warm hug. "I'm sorry about your Dad."

It was the first time she'd mentioned him and Lana blinked back the tears that threatened. "Thanks. I hope you have a good time with John."

Di let her go and grinned. "He's the one, Lana." She grabbed her backpack and slung it over her shoulder. "I'll call you. I've not yet told him that I plan to stay for a few days…I just hope he agrees."

Lana smiled. *How could he resist?* "Have fun."

"Thanks," she called over her shoulder as she went out the door.

Lana and Toby had dinner together in a cosy café. Neither of them spoke much, and Lana was glad when they returned to the hotel and she could be alone. Di called her around eight o'clock. She wouldn't be coming back tonight and she'd be staying until the following week. Lana was happy for her but she knew Toby wouldn't be. She groaned as she hung up the phone. She'd have to tell him.

With a feeling of dread, she left her room, crossed the hall and knocked on Toby's door. He opened it almost immediately.

"Lana…come in."

"Thanks."

Toby closed the door behind her and let out a long breath. "She's not coming back tonight, is she?"

Lana shook her head. "No." She put her hand on his arm and smiled. "Don't be mad, but she's staying until next week."

Toby brushed her aside and ran his hands through his hair. "I knew it."

"He seems like a nice guy and Di knows what she's doing."

"Yeah…I know."

He surprised her by grabbing her in a tight hug. "You're a good friend, Lana."

She stiffened and then melted against him, wrapping her arms around his shoulders. "So are you."

Chapter 45

Monastery of Santa Maria de Huerta
Spain 1597

Alonso thanked Brother Pablo for answering his urgent knocking and opening the heavy doors to the monastery for him. He knelt on the cold entry stones and pressed his lips to them. He'd been gone for nearly six months, and after the long trip back from Ecuador, he was relieved and thankful to be home. He never wanted to leave again.

"Padre will want to see you," said Brother Pablo in a quiet voice. "We weren't expecting you."

Alonso smiled as he rose to his feet. "I also wish to see Padre…I have much news."

"I will advise him of your arrival, Brother Alonso."

"Thank you."

Alonso watched him retreat down the wide hall before gathering his satchel under his arm and slinging his bag over his shoulder. He was anxious to pray in the chapel and then rest, but he resigned himself to the necessity of speaking with Padre first.

He slowly made his way down the hall, drinking in the familiar sights and smells. The stone walls welcomed him and he felt a sense of ease and comfort seeping into his bones. Brother Pablo was waiting for him outside Padre's office, and he smiled.

"Padre is waiting for you."

Alonso nodded before knocking softly and entering Padre's office. The surprise must've been evident on his face when he saw Brother Benito seated at Padre's desk.

"Brother Benito?"

"I thought Brother Pablo was mistaken, but I see he wasn't," said Benito staring at him. "What are you doing here, Brother Alonso?"

Alonso hadn't expected to see Benito sitting here and his mind was whirring with questions and confusion.

"Please sit down, Brother Alonso. I am Padre now."

"What?" He sat down hard on the nearest chair. "What happened to Padre?"

Benito shook his head. "I have written but my letter must've missed you. He took ill several weeks ago and Brother Pablo did all he could, but he couldn't save him. The order elected me the new Abbot."

"I will pray for him." Alonso clutched his satchel close to him and he drew in a breath.

"Now, Brother Alonso, what are doing back here?"

"Ah…a miracle has occurred, Broth…Padre," he stammered. "Brother Miguel is alive and well and has returned to us."

"He's not dead? A miracle indeed," said Benito.

"Yes," said Alonso nodding. "I'm sure he can explain better than I can." He unstrapped his satchel and pulled out two letters which he placed on the desk. "I have letters from Father Acevedo and Brother Miguel for you."

"Thank you." Benito reached for the letters and smiled before opening the drawer of his desk. "It is good that you're back, Brother Alonso." He pulled a set of keys from his drawer and placed them on his desk in front of Alonso. "The keys to your scriptorium."

Alonso frowned as he looked at them. "Thank you, I was hoping to return to my work, but what about Brother Pedro?"

"Ah, unfortunately, Brother Pedro is no longer with us. There was an incident before I became Padre," he said shaking his head. "He took his own life."

Alonso gasped and stared at Benito. "I will pray for him."

"That is most kind of you, Brother Alonso. Now, I'm sure you're tired after your long journey. Rest, and we will speak more tomorrow."

"Yes, of course," Alonso got his feet and scooped the keys from the desk and slipped them into his pocket. "Thank you, Padre."

Alonso's mind was in a spin as he left Benito's office and made his way to his scriptorium. *Both Padre and Brother Pedro dead? And Brother Bentio the new Padre?* He couldn't have imagined a worse choice and knew in his heart that somehow Benito had a hand in all of it.

He locked his satchel safely in the drawer before dropping his bag off in his dormitory. At least, he hoped that was still his room. Gathering his thoughts, he left his small cell and made his way out of the monastery. His thoughts were on Diego as he walked down the covered walkway to the carpenter's workshop.

Several Brothers looked up in surprise when he entered.

"Brother Alonso, how good it is to see you," said Brother Jose with a wide grin on his face.

"Thank you…I have only just returned."

Diego looked up from his work and with a look of joy and surprise he raced towards him.

"Brother Alonso." He grabbed him in a tight hug. "Padre didn't tell us you were coming back."

"It was unexpected," said Alonso with a wide smile. "I have much to tell you." He lowered his voice. "Will you meet me tonight, in the scriptorium?"

"Yes…yes, of course. I can hardly wait."

Alonso grinned and slapped him on the shoulder. "It's so good to see you…until then."

Alonso went back inside the monastery and headed for the chapel. He had much to thank God for and to pray for the souls of his dearly departed Brothers. He was feeling at ease as he left the chapel and went to rest. He only hoped Diego would be able to answer some of the questions that were going around in his mind.

At supper, Padre announced Alonso's return and told the order that Brother Miguel was alive and well. Alonso saw the surprise on Diego's face. He glanced at Alonso with his eyes full of questions. Alonso was sure he and Diego would talk long into the night.

After prayers, when his Brothers had settled for the night and the halls were quiet,

Alonso cautiously walked to his scriptorium. Staying in the shadows and listening for anyone who might still be up and about. He saw no one and sighed with relief as he closed the scriptorium door behind him. Lighting his candle, he sat and waited.

He didn't have to wait long. Barely five minutes later there was a soft knock on his door and Diego entered a moment later, closing the door behind him.

"Before we discuss anything else, you must tell me about Brother Miguel," he said settling himself in the other chair. "You saw him…in your dream."

"I did, but what I thought was him being killed was…this will sound unbelievable," said Alonso rubbing his hands down his face. "But, trust me, I saw it with my own eyes."

Alonso did his best to explain what had happened to Brother Miguel. He could see by the look on Diego's face that he was having trouble believing him. He didn't blame him. Had he not seen Miguel appear out of nowhere in the library, he wouldn't believe it either.

"So, he went to another time? Truly?" said Diego with a look of astonishment.

"Yes, I swear it's true. He met with the ancients and asked for their help, but they refused to tell him about the healing apparatus." Alonso leaned forward on his elbows. "It's up to us to discover its use for ourselves."

"Then we continue our work," said Diego with a grin. "I shall write to Maria and recover your box."

"No." Alonso shook his head. "Brother Miguel has written another vocabulary for us. I've brought it back with me. But, the box must stay with Maria. It's complicated…but the time crystal must find its way to England somehow so that Brother Miguel can recover it…later."

Diego gaped at him. "Maria is no longer in the village. After what happened with Brother Pedro, I was afraid Brother Benito would search for her. She's gone to Barcelona and plans to go to her brother-in-law in London." He paused and ran his fingers through his hair. "It seems this has been preordained."

Alonso nodded. He hadn't expected that piece of news, but knowing what he knew, it made perfect sense. *Did God have a hand in this?* He had thought there was nothing Godly about the library and the ancients, but perhaps he was wrong.

"What happened with Brother Pedro?"

"Ah…I am ashamed for my part."

Diego spent the next little while relaying the events that led to Brother Pedro taking his own life. Alonso could see it was painful for Diego to admit he'd betrayed Pedro, but Alonso could also see that he'd had little choice.

"I'm sorry, and thankful that you blamed Brother Pedro," said Alonso reaching out and touching Diego's arm. "It was either him or us, my friend."

"I know." Diego drew in a breath and slowly let it out. "But, I feel so guilty that he poisoned himself…it's all my fault."

Alonso had no words of comfort to give his friend. He withdrew his hand and grimaced. "What about Padre? What happened?"

"I truly don't know," said Diego with a shrug. "He fell ill…it wasn't a fever, but something that sapped his strength and in a matter of weeks he was gone."

"And Brother Benito took full advantage."

Diego nodded. "As you know, many of the Brothers fear him, and he was the Prior. He gathered a lot of support before the vote. He approached me as well and I feared he may know about my sister, but he didn't say. I do not trust him, Alonso."

"How could he know, Diego?"

"The note…I fear Brother Pedro may have shown it to him."

“Well, if he did, your sister is now well out of Brother Benito’s reach,” said Alonso. “And we will need to be vigilant. I don’t trust him either.”

They sat in silence for a time before Diego spoke again. “If we are to help Spain, you will have to share what you learn with Brother Benito. He, no doubt, has the healing apparatus that Brother Miguel sent to our Padre.”

“I know.” Alonso nodded and drew in a breath. There was no point wishing that Benito wasn’t the new Padre, he was.

Chapter 46

Manchester 1968

A week back at work and Lana couldn't wait until knock-off time. The weekend loomed ahead with nothing planned. She was happy about that. Several letters from her Nan's solicitor had arrived while she was away, and she'd been ignoring them all week. She'd have to face whatever was in them, but without her father, she had no idea what to do.

The clock ticked five and Lana sighed with relief. She covered her typewriter and tucked her chair under her desk before slinging her bag over her shoulder. Work had at least enabled her to push her concerns aside, that was something. She left the office and as she waited for the bus, her thoughts turned to Di. She was back in England, staying with her parents in London until Monday. Lana couldn't wait to see her.

After a short bus ride home, she walked up the path to the front door. She slipped the key in the door and went inside. Toby greeted her from the kitchen at the end of the hall.

"Hey…I've got beers and I've ordered pizza."

"Great."

She went upstairs, dumped her bag on the dressing table and kicked off her shoes. Perhaps a few beers was just what she needed to forget her troubles. She changed into a pair of jeans and jumper before going back downstairs to join Toby.

"Are we celebrating?" she asked as she entered the kitchen.

Toby grinned at her. "Well, I know you've been down, and I don't blame you. But, yeah…let's celebrate." He handed her a beer. "To great friends and an amazing holiday."

Lana felt her mood lift as she clinked her glass against Toby's. "To great friends." She took a big gulp and grinned. "And, to the amazing library. I hope you enjoyed yourself."

"I did." Toby put his glass down and smiled ruefully. "I can't imagine how you're feeling about your Dad, but just know that I'm here for you."

"I appreciate that," she said putting her glass down beside his. "I just don't know what to do."

He wrapped his arms around her and squeezed her close. She let herself melt against him and draw from his strength. *What was she going to do?* She had no idea. He pushed her from him and stared down at her. His eyes were full of care and she tilted her face up to his, losing herself in his gaze. His eyes held her and he lowered his face to hers, their lips nearly touching. She could feel his arms around her and his breath on her face. Her heart was racing. *Was he going to kiss her?* She leaned into him and then wrenched herself away as the phone started ringing. She was breathing heavily as she grabbed the receiver.

"Hello, it's Lana."

"Hey, Kitten."

"Dad? Is that you?"

"Who else would it be?" he said with a laugh.

Joy thrummed through her veins and tears pricked her eyes. "You're back. Oh, Dad, it's so good to hear your voice."

"Are you okay, Kitten?" said Ian in a puzzled voice. "You're the one that's been away. Did you have a good time?"

"Yeah…it was great." A hundred different thoughts were slipping over one another all at once. He was back, but he didn't sound quite right. "How are you?"

"A bit tired…I've been busy as hell," said Ian with a groan. "What are you up to?"

"Nothing much. Toby's ordered pizza and we're just hanging out." She paused and glanced at Toby. "Do you want to join us?"

"I'd love to. See you in twenty?"

"Great."

She hung up the phone and stood staring at it for a moment. Toby touched her on the arm and she swung around to face him. "That was Dad. He's coming over."

A wide smile spread across Toby's face and he grabbed her in a hug. "Thank God he's back. Are you okay?"

"Yeah…I don't think he remembers."

Toby smiled and stared down at her. "It doesn't matter…you've got your Dad back."

Lana blinked back her tears and smiled. "Yeah."

The End

Author Notes

Thank you so much for reading The Secret Library of Tayos. I'm an Australian indie author. As such, I maintain complete control of my work and self publish. That also means I have to market and promote my work, which I'm not very good at. I find it hard to self promote.

So, I'm taking this opportunity to not only thank you for taking the time to read my book, but if you liked it, would you mind leaving a rating or review on Amazon. It's the best way to show any author that you appreciate their hard work. It also helps other potential readers to decide if they should invest their time and money.

If you enjoyed this book, please consider reading one of my other titles.

Thank you

My Very Occasional Newsletter

I love to connect with my readers and share updates with them. I don't send emails too often – but you'll be the first to know about promotions and upcoming releases.

Subscribe on my website.

www.cjbessell.godaddysites.com

Get a free E-book when you subscribe.

Follow me on Facebook

I post regularly on my Facebook page, and it's a great place to connect and stay up to date with all things in my author world.

I'd love to connect with you.

https://www.facebook.com/CJBessell/

Printed in Dunstable, United Kingdom

70280585R00262